DRAGON GEMS

SPRING 2023

Published by Water Dragon Publishing
waterdragonpublishing.com

Cover design copyright © 2023 by Niki Lenhart
nikilen-designs.com

ISBN 978-1-959804-58-1 (Trade Paperback)

10 9 8 7 6 5 4 3 2 1

FIRST EDITION

FOREWORD

Y OU'RE ABOUT TO EXPERIENCE something amazing. Months ago — maybe even years ago — someone had an inkling and began to write. Lonely and alone, they struggled and persisted. They wrote. They agonized over the details. They revised. They sweated over the language. They considered each sentence, each word. And, finally, they gathered up all of their courage and sent their little creation off to battle in the submission arena.

Oh, there were many fierce battles! There were many, many competitors and many bouts. After every round, they patched their little champion up and sent them in again. And, in the end, they emerged victorious. They received the happy announcement: their champion was a winner! Their story had been accepted for publication!

You, the reader, get to reap the results. You're about to enjoy the delights of a dozen amazing stories. They may look ordinary, but don't be fooled! They fought tooth and nail to be here for you, among these Dragon Gems. Savor their victory. And yours!

Steven D. Brewer
Author of the "Revin's Heart" series

CONTENTS

Mike Morgan was born in London, but not in any of the interesting parts. He moved to Japan at the age of 30 and lived there for many years. Nowadays, he's based in Iowa, and enjoys family life with his wife and two young children.

·   ·   ·

I think many parents will understand the inspiration for this story: the mind-worm of a thought that one day you'll forget your child is in your car and leave them locked inside, only to find them dead when you return. When my kids were very little we lived in Texas, so we'd hear often about animals and children suffering terribly from being locked in cars, even for short times. I suppose it's not such a surprise that concern was never far from my thoughts. Mine is the sort of brain that then thinks "What if you add aliens to the mix?" and — hey presto — there you have it: the most inconvenient timing imaginable for an alien invasion.

FIFTEEN MINUTES

MIKE MORGAN

P ORSCHE AND CLEMENTINE were arguing in the rear of the car. They were so loud their father, Colin Hamble, kept checking for cracks in the rear window.

Colin tried distracting them with a handheld games console he kept in the glove box for just this sort of emergency, waving it at them with one hand while negotiating the roundabout near their house. His efforts met with miserable failure. It seemed the toffee-flavored lollipop they were battling over was far more interesting than a retro arcade game.

The ride home had, so far, been a headache-inducing experience. For Colin, at least. For the kids, it was another normal twenty-five-minute trip back from school.

Being five and seven years old, respectively, it didn't occur to them that Daddy didn't enjoy full-throated screams coming from the back seats of the vehicle. At least they were nearly home.

Home, yes. Where he expected he'd have to listen to yet another telephone message from his ex-wife, Olga. The second-generation descendant of Russian steel workers had a way of talking that left Colin a nervous wreck.

Her current demand was that Colin ship her last few possessions to her new address. Since these possessions were an extensive collection of commemorative plates featuring various members of the royal family, and her new address was in South America, he was not looking forward to hours of wrapping each piece of china in bubble wrap, let alone paying the postage.

"Have you considered not being foul to each other?" asked Colin as he pulled up the handbrake handle and swung open his door.

The caterwauling from the back seats did not diminish one iota. Colin took a deep breath, shut the driver's door, and stepped up onto the pavement in front of his semi-detached house. Tomorrow was the fourth anniversary of his ex-wife's abrupt decision to run away to Uruguay and take up bricklaying.

Olga took pains during the irregular video calls Colin organized to slide in comments about what a lousy job he was doing as a father. Finding fault was a talent of hers. That and bricklaying, obviously.

He was reaching out to Porsche's child-locked handle, wondering whether the prospect of a chocolate hobnob from the biscuit barrel hidden on top of the fridge might defuse his daughters' interminable squabbling, when the aliens' teleport beam caught him.

The next thing Colin knew, he was standing in a close-packed crowd of naked men and women. Inside a flickering blue force field. With no clothes on. In a room that did not appear to be of Earthly design. And he was nude.

"Clem? Porsche?" There was no sign of his children.

He was God knew where, and the kids were locked in the car.

•　　•　　•

Colin estimated there were a hundred people in the shimmering pen, crammed into an area way too small for comfort. It was standing room only, and for once that wasn't an exaggeration.

The shocked mass of humanity wasn't enjoying the complete absence of attire. Many of the jostling men and women were attempting to cover up using their bare hands. Colin wasn't a fan of going *au naturel* either, but decided to get over his awkwardness. Enforced nudity was the least of their problems. Besides, he was English. Being embarrassed was his default state.

He tried to piece together what must have happened. One second, he'd been reaching for the car door handle, the next — *pow!* — here he was, body still tingling with the aftereffects of some sort of physical dislocation. It felt as if his body had been ripped from one place and dumped in another. What had caused it? A teleportation device, like in *Star Trek*?

What did that mean? He, and everyone else here, had been abducted by aliens? They were on board something that certainly gave the impression of being a spaceship, which meant that most likely they were no longer on Earth. What was happening down on their fragile blue-and-green world? Was Shropshire now a smoking ruin?

Colin looked around, his heart beating wildly. No matter how hard he searched, there was no sign of his young children.

So, teleportation, then. But not for everyone. And the ones who'd been scooped up were corralled like livestock. Priorities began to coalesce in Colin's mind.

The aliens had either not bothered to bring their prisoners' clothes along for the ride or they'd vaporized them during transit. Either way, it struck Colin as a deliberate attempt to intimidate their victims. Or a means of stripping the crowd of anything that could be used as a weapon.

His position near the edge of the throng gave Colin a clear view of a lady with voluminous hair, stepping backward. She was trying to avoid being pushed by the unpredictable motion of the crowd. Before he could call out a warning, the woman had blundered into the force field.

There was a bright flash and a yelp from the woman.

"Bugger! That stung!" she exclaimed, more cross than injured.

Colin didn't have the luxury to ponder this turn of events. A guttural voice cut through the hubbub of annoyed captives. The voice of their new alien overlords, Colin assumed.

The aliens were giving a speech. It was in English, so that was a relief.

•   •   •

"We are Torgoth," began the voice, struggling more than a little with the nuances of the unfamiliar language. "We rule your world now. We bring all useful humans here. You are slaves, you belong to Torgoth. Soon, you all be sold to great empires of this galaxy, on many other worlds."

Wait, they were a species capable of interstellar travel, and they were kidnapping humans for slave labor? That made zero sense to Colin. Any species sophisticated enough to build spacecraft that powerful wouldn't need slaves.

He poked his head around the taller prisoners blocking his view and glimpsed the creature giving the speech.

It was large and blubbery, standing on four limbs that sprouted from a torso wrapped in tatty furs. Its body sported two other appendages, presumably the equivalents of arms, as well as a long, rectangular head. The toothy maw from which the voice was emanating was positioned at the top of the smooth face.

4

"Furs?" breathed Colin. What, no artificial fibers? The Torgoth didn't run to nylon?

Colin was the first to admit he was no expert in extra-terrestrial life, but this fellow didn't give the impression of being a representative of a technologically advanced species.

"First we take the humans of the major population center you call Shrewsbury. Next, we capture Telford and part of Much Wenlock."

From this pronouncement, it was clear the aliens were abducting the people of Shropshire town by town. Colin could hardly imagine where it would all end. Was even Herefordshire safe?

Colin craned his head, looking left and right. Sure enough, there were other groups of unclad people in similar pens to either side. So, the alien's claim of mass kidnappings was true. Shrewsbury was home to more than thirty thousand.

Tens of thousands of point-to-point teleportations? The construction of a vast starship? Those accomplishments required extraordinary technology.

Colin pursed his lips. *They didn't build this vessel. They've half-inched it,* he decided.

He didn't bother listening to the rest of the speech; it was predictable and depressing. Do as we say, or we'll kill you, blah blah. The Torgoth were interested purely in their human chattels staying quiet during transit.

Having delivered its spiel, the quadrupedal slave-master moved on, no doubt to stand outside an adjacent pen and repeat its instructions.

How much time had passed since his kidnapping? Colin's mind raced. At least three minutes, maybe four. Too much time.

He had to do something. He had to do something *right away*.

"I know how to get out of here," said Colin to the people pressed against him, at first with a stutter and then with growing confidence. "I know how to beat these creatures. Do as I say, and we'll be out of here in no time."

Heads began to turn in his direction. Colin wasn't used to people listening to him. They usually talked over the top of him the second he attempted to offer an opinion.

"Honestly," he went on, "I'm in engineering. I know about machines. Those guys didn't make any of this. I bet they stole this ship. If the best they can do with the technology is to abduct salves, my guess is they don't even know how to work half of it. We can exploit that weakness, turn the tables on them."

Colin could hardly credit it, but the crowd was nodding, looking interested. For a few seconds, Colin allowed himself to think his speech might work.

Then a full-framed man with hairy shoulders decided to stick his nose in.

"We can't just stop a bunch of alien slavers," objected the hairy-shouldered man. "We're trapped inside a force field. We've got no weapons. We haven't even got clothes! Be reasonable."

Colin could sense he was losing the confidence of the group. He had to say something stirring. He had to keep them on-side, and he had to do it sharpish.

Word tumbling upon word in an unplanned heap, Colin gabbled, "My last name is Hamble. Do you know what it means? In Middle English, I mean. It's a name from Middle English."

He was rewarded with a sea of blank looks. He couldn't blame his audience — he wasn't entirely certain where he was going with this, either.

"Since we don't have phones to Google it on, I'll just tell you. It means 'to hamstring or mutilate.'"

Colin smiled, what he was going to say next coming to him in a revelatory flash. "I'm going to live up to my family's name. I'm going to make these things rue the day they thought they could come to our planet and muck humankind about. We're not only going to stop this invasion, we're going to set a record for the fastest defeat of an alien threat in galactic history. We're going to show these chancers exactly what humans are capable of! We'll send them packing in fifteen minutes flat!"

Arms crossed, the hirsute heckler asked, "What's the great big hurry? Why do we need to beat them in the next quarter of an hour? You trying to be all Warhol — getting in your fifteen minutes of fame?"

"Because I left my kids in my car and that's how long they've got before they overheat and die." Colin took a deep breath. "So, I promise you this. We're going to stomp these git-faced poseurs, take over their ship, reverse their teleportation device, and get home. And we're doing it fast enough for our children to still be safe when we get back."

He let that sink in. "There's no way I'm the only parent here. I'm speaking to the mothers, the fathers, the grandparents now. Look around you. Do you see your children, your grandkids? Well, do you? No, the Torgoth left them behind. Children, babies, infants, they're all unproductive units that've been left to die. The clock is ticking, and we need to save them."

A woman shrieked in horror. "My Natalie is napping in her crib! I left the potatoes boiling on the hob. The house could burn down!"

He pointed at her. "She gets it. Every second counts. Anyone who wants to argue, sod off out our way. The rest of you, let's take this ship."

An older gent with a pronounced limp pushed through the crowd to Colin, clapped him on the shoulder, and roared, "You heard the man! We're hamstringing the lot of 'em!"

He inclined his head and whispered in Colin's ear, "Please, God, tell me you have a plan."

•   •   •

"You want us to run at the force field," repeated the silver-haired gent. He'd introduced himself as Gerald. Now, he seemed to be regretting his earlier show of support.

"It won't hurt us," Colin assured the dubious throng. "You saw what happened earlier. It gave that lady with the big hair a bit of a shock, but it was non-lethal."

"You think the Torgoth have imprisoned us in a cell that won't kill us if we try to get out?" scoffed hairy-shoulders.

"I think the Torgoth have hot-wired a ship constructed by a civilized species. And a civilized species is going to make a glorified electric fence that's purely a deterrent. It's enough to shock but not permanently injure."

"You willing to bet on that?"

"You willing to be the one who rolls over when we could've escaped?"

Hairy-shoulders shut up.

Gerald coughed politely. "We run at it. Then what?"

"We run at it in waves. We pile up our bodies and refuse to move out of the shock range. That triggers the safety cut-out. Then the next lot of us make a dash for the hatch over there. We find the crew, overwhelm them by force of numbers and take their weapons. Next, we find and take over the ship's control area. Once we have control of the ship, we restrain the Torgoth and persuade them to hit 'undo' on the teleporters."

"Undo?" Colin could hear the air quotes in Gerald's voice.

"Control-zed cannot be a concept so original the people who built this ship didn't think of it."

"Fair enough," allowed the older man.

"Everyone goes home. A few of us stay behind to contact the ship's original owners to come get their stolen property, avoiding any risk of retaliation for keeping what doesn't belong to us. We can even see if there's compensation available from whatever passes as the galactic police, since it sounds like the galaxy is teeming with organized life, and at this point nothing would surprise me."

"I see." Gerald nodded. "You make it all sound so straightforward."

"Yes. Now, if you all don't mind, could we make a start, please? Kind of in a hurry."

The woman with the huge frizz of hair called out, "Who exactly is running into the electric fence thing? Because I'd like to volunteer to not do that part."

Damn, he'd expected this type of objection. He hadn't thought of a way of answering it yet, but he'd definitely seen it coming. For a moment, Colin thought he heard Olga's no-nonsense tones, remarking how unutterably useless he was.

To Colin's surprise, instead of responding to the outburst Gerald motioned to hairy-shoulders. "My dear chap, and all you gentlemen standing next to him, can I impose on you a little?"

"You're not asking us to go first, are you?"

"Good God, no. I'm suggesting you give the people in front of you a push. Make them go first. Yes, that's the ticket. Just like that. Yes, keep going. Pick up some steam there. We need a fair bit of momentum. Yes, that's right."

There was a considerable amount of noise and anguish from the people being shoved. Then there was a pronounced sizzling sound. Then there were screams. And shrieks. And a number of full-throated howls that quite surprised Colin because he hadn't known human vocal cords could produce sounds like that.

"Used to be in the army," Gerald confided to Colin. "Quite miss it."

The screams continued.

Gerald smiled politely. "Hate to be a bore. Feel I have to ask, though. Shouldn't the force field contraptions have turned off by now?"

"Um," said Colin. "Possibly." He winced at a particularly high-pitched screech.

The ex-army officer nodded. "I see. This plan of yours. Bit of a work in progress, is it?"

"The thing about engineering is," replied Colin, "is that really well designed plans often don't work, and we have to try something else."

"Leaving to one side how your first idea was completely wrong, am I correct in thinking you have a 'something else' up your sleeve?"

No, reflected Colin, he really didn't. Maybe Olga was right. Maybe he was good for nothing. He looked upward. It was a reflexive gesture, the sort of thing he always did when seeking inspiration or not wanting to answer an awkward question.

He saw it.

The field emitter. The device that produced the force field. It was overhead. Twenty feet, maybe twenty-five, directly above them.

The silver globe glowed with the same blue energy as the pen's walls. It had to be the source of the force fields. There was an opening at its base. Colin could glimpse fragile circuitry within.

"Bit of a personal question, sorry. Do you, by any chance, happen to have false teeth?"

"Beg your pardon?"

"A long shot, I know. The aliens took our clothes, but I'm hoping they left us with artificial body parts. I need something to throw. Something conductive, with metal in it. Like the cobalt-chromium alloy that you find in the wires and plates that hold false teeth together."

Wordlessly, Gerald took out his bottom teeth. "I want those back," he said with a stern expression.

The pens didn't have safety cut-outs. Okay, that had been a miscalculation. But the corrals came with the ship, Colin was sure. The Torgoth hadn't built them. That meant they had an original purpose. Not for transporting slaves, no, but for moving something else. Dangerous organisms, maybe? Things that weren't intelligent? Things that wouldn't know a force field emitter when they saw it, he hoped. Because if that was true, the emitters wouldn't be shielded.

Colin ignored the sliminess of the half-denture and squinted at the target. He drew in a breath, held it, and with memories of every cricket match he'd ever bowled at running through his mind, he hurled the u-shaped object up at the silver machine.

The teeth missed by a good four feet.

"Yeah," breathed Colin. "Always was hopeless at bowling. Got thrown off my last pub team."

He did catch the teeth as they fell. He was a much better fielder.

Gerald coughed. "Give them here. I'll do it."

He scored a direct hit on the first go. The teeth sailed through the opening without touching the edges.

There was a loud pop and the field emitter cut out.

•   •   •

Colin blinked, rather taken aback, as an ecstatic hairy-shoulders jumped over twitching heaps of stunned human flesh, yelling at the top of his lungs. Others sprang into action as well, following his lead.

"Ah," observed Gerald. "Our friend has noticed the barrier is down. From his happy demeanor, I'd say he's found his calling in life. Do excuse me. I'll be pootling off myself to bag a Torgoth. I have the suspicion they don't like it up them."

Gerald started hobbling after the much younger, and hairier, man, but paused for a second. "You can leave the rest to us."

Colin glanced at his wrist before remembering he didn't have his watch on anymore. "Try to be quick," he begged. "We're almost out of time."

Gerald nodded, a dark gleam in his eyes. "Yes, of course. I do understand. I have a grandchild, barely six weeks old. The urgency is not lost on me. We would murder the world for our children." He snorted. "A few Torgoth are trivial by comparison."

The old soldier set off across the wide deck of the starship.

In the distance, Colin saw a Torgoth being rugby tackled. Not knowing how to play any Earthly sport, let alone one so

11

violent, it went down with a squeal. Seconds later, the triumphant human wrestled free what looked like a remote control and the walls of every other pen snapped out of existence.

With hundreds of reinforcements, Colin was half tempted to join in with the hand-to-hand combat. But, really, these things were best left to people with the right temperaments, and to even get to a Torgoth now he'd have to push his way through crowds of people, and he didn't want to be rude.

•   •   •

"I'm back!" screamed Colin, every worry and fear ever suffered by a frantic parent running through his mind. "Daddy's back!"

He nearly overbalanced as the teleport field faded. Clothes and possessions that had been stored in the matter transmitter's memory were reintegrated about his body.

Please don't be dead, shrieked his inner voice.

Nerves jangling, fingers trembling violently, he lurched toward the car. The street was completely silent. Sunlight gleamed on the hatchback's windows, making it impossible to see inside. One hand fumbled for the key fob in his pocket, pressing the button to release the lock. The other clutched at the handle.

Child locks, he remembered. There was no way his daughters could've got out, even before the doors re-locked themselves after the pre-set period of inactivity. Clem and Porsche could be dead, baked in the lingering heat of early evening. They could be collapsed in their booster seats, swollen tongues lolling from foam-specked mouths.

Oh God, oh Jesus ....

His palms were sweating so much he almost lost his grip on the handle. Somehow, he yanked the closest door open.

Clem looked up from the small, battery-powered games console. Leaning over from her own booster seat, watching every move her sister made on the tiny screen, was Porsche. She frowned in annoyance at the interruption.

"Dad!" complained Clementine, just as unhappy. "We were nearly up to level six! Can you go away and come back later?"

They hadn't even noticed he'd been gone.

Half of him thought, *what did you expect?* The other half considered throttling the pair of them.

It may not have occurred to them to undo their seat belts, but they hadn't wasted any time leaning forward to grab the old-fashioned game from where he'd tossed it minutes earlier, so long ago.

Colin steadied himself and tried to hide the residual panic in his voice.

"No, I can't go away. Not in my nature, my sweethearts. Daddy is never going away, and nothing can make him."

"I'm hot," realized Porsche in a wondering tone. "May I have some water?"

"Of course you can, love," answered Colin. He straightened up. "Now, if you don't mind, can you both unbuckle and get out of the car? I know I'm being ridiculous, but I'd really like you out of there."

As for Olga, he was going to put her ghastly plates in storage, and she could ruddy well fetch them herself.

Sam Muller loves dogs and books and spends much time trying to save one from the other. Her first novel, *I will Paint the Night*, a YA fantasy-murder mystery, will be published by Fractured Mirror Publishing in July. *I will Paint the Night* is the story of how Allii, a fugitive princess, and Spooky, an opinionated daemon-dog, joined forces to unmask the killer of Allii's beloved stepmother.

·   ·   ·

Zom-Zom was a port-cat, living the good life — dead fish, living rats, long afternoon snoozes, the occasional night out on the roofs — until his unwanted encounter with Allii and Spooky, a human-daemon-dog investigative duo. Now Zom-Zom is chasing a murderous hunter on the high seas. A salt-watery grave is not the future he wants. But opting out is impossible. He doesn't want to prove Spooky right about cats; he wants Allii's promised payment; most of all, Zom-Zom, the master of indolence, is beginning to enjoy the risky business of unmasking killers.

WHY THE SEA DOESN'T SMELL OF FISH

SAM MULLER

I LOVED THE PORT. Good pickings there; dead fish, living rats. Once I was quite the cat-about-town. *Dashing Paws*, they called me as I cavorted under the three moons. The bright lights palled after Mum vanished. I abandoned the rooftops and retired to the Port. That was Mum's home. That's where she'd return to, if ever she does.

I was enjoying my customary afternoon snooze in an old shed when a hand grabbed me by the scruff of my neck. I tried to scratch my way to freedom and failed. My assailant knew the art of grabbing a cat.

If cornered, think before you do something dog-stupid, Mum used to say. I ceased struggling and took stock.

My assailant was a thin young woman, skin and cropped hair the color of copper. A scar ran from the corner of a gray eye to a squarish chin. A black and white dog stood near her, reddish eyes glinting nastily.

"Please pardon me for grabbing you. You are Zom-Zom, son of Kittin, aren't you?"

By the scale of a whale! Cat-grabber knew not only my name but also Mum's! And she talked to me, as if she expected an answer.

Only witches understood animal lingo. Witches were stately creatures, rather like us cats. Cat-grabber looked like a downbeat human, shabby and careworn.

"How do you understand animals?" I asked.

Cat-grabber smiled. Not a bad smile. "I've witch blood in me. Zom-Zom, I must talk to you. If I put you down, will you promise not to run?"

I assumed what I hoped was a solemn expression. "I promise. Cat's honor."

The dog guffawed. "Cats have no honor, Allii. He's gulling you."

I was planning to scat. Not now, since that would prove this canine monstrosity's vile prejudices. "I'll stay and listen, lady. Listen only. Nothing more."

Cat-grabber put me down. Under the shed's only window was a sailcloth as gray as my fur. I sat on it.

Cat-grabber settled comfortably on the dirt floor. "I'm Allii, and this is Spooky. He is a daemon-dog."

A shape-shifter. Dogs I could deal with. But a dog who could turn into a wolf was another matter.

Cat-grabber was watching me, as if she could glean my thoughts. I decided to go on the offensive. "So, tell your story, lady."

The gray eyes twinkled before turning somber. "What do you know about silver-caracals?"

Silver-caracals? Some kind of a fish, perhaps? "This and that," I said. When in ignorance, pretend.

The dog chortled. My hackles rose.

Cat-grabber intervened hurriedly. "Silver-caracals are a wild-cat species, probably the rarest in planet Pegala. Fast runners and good climbers with a silvery coat, found only in Angel Mountains. To see a silver-caracal in that snowy landscape is an unforgettable experience." Her eyes turned luminous. Then the light died. "Sadly, they are close to extinction due to hunting. There's a popular human belief that powdered silver-caracal teeth slows down aging and wards off death."

"Humans!" I muttered. They thought they were the tops, but couldn't grasp simple facts of life, like old age and death.

Cat-grabber nodded. "Angel Mountains are located in the Leaban Republic. Five years ago, Leeban Republic banned silver-caracal hunting. Since then, many more lands have passed similar laws. Illegal hunting almost stopped. But this year, there was a sudden spike. I presume you've heard of the Kikilonian Empire?"

"Who hasn't?" A bad place for animals. We got killed for meat, fur, fun, and to appease that four-headed god of theirs.

"The Emperor is old. He is using all his power and wealth to prolong his life, including offering massive rewards for silver-caracal teeth. Four hunters responded. All had been caught, but one, the best. His name is Vede and he is a master at disguises."

I affected a yawn.

"Spooky and I are investigators. Leeban Republic hired us to nab Vede. According to our information, he's planning to board a ship here, disembark from Port Sheebatiya, and travel overland to Kikilonia. Trafficking in silver-caracal teeth is illegal in the city-state of Sheebatiya. If Vede can be caught disembarking with his haul, he'll spend the rest of his life in jail. I plan to make that happen."

I stood, stretching myself. "Good work, lady. I wish you every success. Now I must see a mouse about a ..."

"I'm not done, Zom-Zom. You promised to listen. Cat's honor, remember?"

Eel of a woman. I stopped.

"The ship Vede plans to board will sail in two days. Its name is *Little Judi*."

Finally, the sprat dropped. *Little Judi* was owned and captained by Mollina, the young woman who rescued Mum when she was an abandoned kitten.

"You're friends with Captain Mollina, Zom-Zom. You voyage on *Little Judi* occasionally. The crew knows you. No one will suspect a cat anyway. There'll be five human passengers on board, excluding me. Any of them could be Vede. All I ask from you is that you keep an eye on them and report anything suspicious."

I arched my back. "I've kept my word, lady. I listened. I considered. My answer is no."

"If you help me find Vede, I'll find your mother, or at least what happened to her." Cat-grabber's smile turned steely, rather witch-like. "It's a deal."

•   •   •

Mollina was on the wharf supervising some loading. She picked me up and cradled me, as if I was still a kitten. "Coming for the ride, Zom-Zom?"

I said, "Yes," though all she would have heard was a purr.

She laughed and put me down. "That, I think, was a yes. Now, let's get you some cream."

Cream!

We were headed to the kitchens when a shriek intervened.

"Oh what an adorable pusskin!" The voice soared above Port's hubbub. Then I was grabbed by someone who knew nothing of the art of grabbing a cat.

My assailant was a woman proportioned like a whale and dressed like a peacock. I could have clawed my way to freedom but didn't. If I developed the reputation of a cat-out-of-hell, my chances of snooping in passenger cabins would be nil. Controlling my bitter instincts, I gave Moll a heart-rending look.

"Zom-Zom owns herself, Lady Booteflika," Moll said, as she saved me from being suffocated by a sea of satin.

18

"I sooo love pusskins," Lady Booteflika trilled.

A bark rang out. "Puss-king, is it?" The daemon-dog bounded up the gangway grinning from one oversized ear to the other. Allii followed, helping a gaunt man with a wispy white beard and misty blue eyes.

"Mistress Allii and Doctor Gerb, welcome aboard." Moll smiled. "A physician, of course, is doubly welcome."

"Sadly, I'm more patient than physician, Captain." The old man's voice was hoarse. "My colleagues have failed to cure my throat cancer. I'm hoping the witches in Sheebatiya might do better ..."

A flurry of footsteps drowned his frail voice. A silver-haired young man careened to a stop near us. His green eyes darted around, fell on Allii, and stayed there.

"Welcome aboard, Master Mizsha." Molly did a round of introductions, ending with, "Now we can begin."

Lady B fluttered her eyelashes. "Only four passengers, dear captain?"

"Five, actually," Moll replied. "Master Gauntan is in his cabin. He's prostrated with seasickness."

• • •

Having polished off two dishes of sprats-in-cream, I was heading to Allii's cabin to discuss strategy, when a querulous voice emerged from a half open door.

"... complain. I can feel that soup causing me indigestion. My health is delicate."

This had to be Master Gaunten, the seasick passenger. I slipped in.

A tubby man in a furry robe sat on the berth. "The fish was raw, RAW."

His victim, Rokko the kitchen porter, made ineffectual noises.

Master Gaunten seemed thoroughly enamored of his bodily ills, real or imagined. I decided to use his distraction and explore the room.

A shriek stopped me in my tracks. "A cat. What is a cat doing here? I'm allergic to cats."

Rokko said, hurriedly, "It's the captain's cat, Master. He must be after mice."

"This is an outrage. Outrage ..."

I looked from the man's florid face to the empty dishes on the portable table. Seasick, my whiskers.

•   •   •

"All hail Puss-king," sniggered the dog as I entered Allii's cabin.

I ignored him and turned to Allii. "Sorry about the delay. I paid a call on Master Gaunten. High color, excellent appetite. If he is seasick, I'm a dog. He must be Vede."

Allii frowned. "Definitely a possibility. But people pretend to be what they are not for many reasons. We have to investigate other passengers as well." She beamed. "Great work, Zom-Zom."

I bit back a purr. "These silver-caracal teeth, what do they look like?"

Allii took a small box from a bag and opened it. On a piece of black velvet, something gleamed; a molar, about twice the size of a cat molar. It looked like it was made of silver-glass. As I stared at the tooth and tried to imagine its dead owner, anger seized me. I too wanted Vede to be locked up until the end of his days.

•   •   •

The meeting over, I was heading to Mizsha's cabin for a spot of snooping when an unforgettable voice stopped me.

Lady B stood holding Doctor Gerb by his arm. "Dear Doctor, you must call me when you next need to stretch your legs. I'll accompany you. What if you fall and break your silly neck?"

Doctor Gerb muttered something. The words weren't intelligible, but the strain in the voice was clear. He preferred a broken neck to Lady B's company. Who'd blame him?

Another door stood ajar. I peeped. Innumerable boxes were piled up in two corners. This had to be Lady B's cabin. I slipped in and began snooping amongst the bags.

The trilling voice bidding goodnight to Doctor Gerb made me stop and hide in a corner. I didn't want to be called Pusskin and smothered in pink silk.

Lady B closed the door, drew the bolt and discarded her night robe. A lacy shift was next, followed by layer after layer of clothing until, with the last one, she turned into a man in leggings and a vest.

Shock petrified me. Gradually, life returned, bringing a dilemma along. *How do I escape?*

The creature was at the wash stand wiping off layers of war-paint. I shrank into the shadows feeling like a mouse ... a mouse.

I padded out and dived noisily into the other luggage mountain.

Lady B jumped back then sighed. "Zom-Zom! Chasing mice I suppose." She watched me as I tried to burrow under a box. "Fortunately you are a cat, or I'd have had to wring your neck."

After a decent amount of pretence, I sauntered to the door. The creature opened it a sliver. I slithered out resisting the urge to flee.

Was this how mice felt when I had them cornered?

•   •   •

The next morning, I sat on the promenade deck surveying the scene before me.

Allii was talking with Mizsha. Lady B, arrayed in a purple robe, was trilling to Mollina. Doctor Gerb was asleep on a deckchair, a bag on his lap large enough to hold those teeth.

Keeping clear of Lady B, I padded up to Doctor Gerb and jumped onto his lap. He awoke startled, his milky blue eyes confused. Then he smiled and scratched under my chin. It felt good. I didn't even mind his heavy ring scratching me occasionally.

Lady B had collared Allii. Moll walked over to us. "Zom-Zom likes you," she told Doctor Gerb.

"I don't call him Pusskin," he murmured. "Does he always voyage with you?"

"When he feels like it. He is very independent."

"Cats are. It's such a shame when they are treated degradingly."

I purred some more and jumped down.

Doctor Gerb's bag contained no teeth. When I sat on it, it crinkled, the way paper does.

•   •   •

That night, we had our second war-council. Though raring to reveal my findings, I exercised restraint. Let that dog think I spent the day eating and sleeping.

Revenge is best as a nightcap.

Allii said, "Zom-Zom, will you go first?"

I affected a yawn. They shouldn't suspect I was finding this investigating business interesting. "After you."

"Too much sprats-in-cream, Puss-king?"

Allii said hurriedly, "Spooky stop."

I twitched my tail. "Let him have his fun, Allii."

The dog didn't like it. Before he could respond, Allii intervened, opening a notebook. "I'll start then. Mizsha says he is an herbalist traveling to Sheebatiya to work in a healing house. He is lying. I asked him several test questions. He failed all but one."

"A fraud, then?" I felt a bit crestfallen.

"Yes. We need to investigate him further." She made a note. "Doctor Gerb always carries a bag."

"I sat on the bag," I said. "It didn't feel as if it contained teeth."

The dog gave me an unloving look and turned to Allii. "I managed to get a sniff at it. I got a strong smell of herbs."

Allii sighed. "Must be his medicine bag."

The dog scratched an ear. "Still, my nose tells me there's something not quite right in him."

I grinned nastily. "Nose the investigator?"

Allii intervened again. "Any discoveries, Zom-Zom?"

Ah, revenge time. "Lady Booteflicka is a man."

The reaction was most satisfying. Allii's mouth fell open. The dog's head whipped up and his hackles rose.

Once my tale was told, Allii groaned. "Looks like we can't rule anyone out. Zom-Zom, can you watch Lady Booteflika? And Master Gauntan too, if possible. Spooky, keep your nose on Doctor Gerb. I'll handle Mizsha."

•   •   •

After the meeting, I headed to seasick-Gaunten's, cabin wondering how to find a way in. I took a corner and stopped, my heart racing inside my still body.

A human shadow slithered from one patch of darkness into the next, and climbed up to the promenade deck.

I followed. The door was ajar. I padded out. My quarry was nowhere, as if it had been a figment of my investigative imagination —

I was grabbed. I was flying through the air. I was in the sea. A wave lifted me. I screamed in terror. *Can I swim? Do cats swim?*

I was grabbed again. By a set of teeth.

The fish had come for me.

Fish … why doesn't the sea smell of fish?

•   •   •

The world was warm and soft. The world was Mollina, tears coursing down her cheeks.

I blinked. "Why doesn't the sea smell of fish?"

"Oh, Zom-Zom." Molly's voice was hoarse. I tried to lay a paw on her. And failed. I was cocooned in a blanket.

"I think he's fine, Captain," said Allii's voice. I turned. She smiled, eyes sparkling like stars. "Fortunately Spooky and I saw you on the railing, Zom-Zom. When you fell, he jumped in and grabbed you."

I owed my life to a *dog*? To *that* dog?

Allii touched Moll's arm. "Captain, why not see to the steam-vat problem the first mate was worrying about? I'll stay with Zom-Zom."

Molly stood, wiping her face. "This is the problem with steamships. Last month, we were grounded for two days with a steam-vat issue. Didn't I wish for good old sails!" Her voice dropped to a near-whisper. "I don't know how to thank you and Spooky. You've saved my dearest friend."

My heart leaped. Hearing that was worth a dunking in the sea.

Once Molly was gone, Allii said, "What happened, Zom-Zom?"

Until that moment, I hadn't felt any fear. But remembering my near-death brought the terror back. Still, I managed to tell my tale, though in a shaky voice.

"That was Vede. He lured you out and tried to kill you." Allii said when I was done.

"I thought it was a fishy grave for me," I said, and stopped as anger banished fear. I wanted to dig my teeth into Vede's neck until he dropped dead. How dare he try to kill me? Silver-caracals were bad enough. But *me*?

"Allii," came a bark. Allii opened the door and the dog walked in.

"Thank you for saving my life," I said. Sooner rather than later, that was my way, from sprats to rats.

The expected wisecrack didn't come. "I was afraid, I'd be too late," the dog said, sounding as if he meant it.

I gawped beyond words.

He looked me in the eye. "Why don't we call it a truce, Zom-Zom? Having spats is stupid right now."

"Having sprats is never stupid," I said and felt beyond stupid when Allii and Spooky stared. "Joke. Yeah, let's be colleagues and catch the monster."

Allii laughed. "That's better. Zom-Zom, can you remember anything more about the incident?"

Something was hovering at the edge of my memory. But every time I reached for it, it slipped away. I shook my head.

She sighed. "Pity." Her face turned solemn. "Zom-Zom, I owe you an apology. When I made you work on this job, I never thought it would bring you into danger. I release you from your promise. You've helped enough. Once Vede is caught, I'll look for your mother."

I sat up, blanket and all. "My word is my word. Plus, this is personal. No one's going to try to kill me and get away with it."

"But ..."

"Allii, quit worrying. Cat o' nine lives, that's me."

Allii frowned. "I thought it was cat o' nine tails."

I grinned. "I'm my own linguist."

•   •   •

Shadowy killers stalked my sleep. Next morning, I made my lethargic way to the promenade desk. Allii was talking with Mizsha. Lady B had cornered Doctor Gerb. If anyone was surprised to see me alive, there was no sign of it.

Lady B pounced on me, trilling Pusskins. I allowed her to pick me up, even though squalls of terror made my innards lurch.

Underneath the war-paint, Lady B's face was haggard.

What kept her awake? Was she busy feeding cats to fish? Was I being cuddled by my would-be-murderer?

•   •   •

That evening we were having our third war-council in Allii's cabin when someone banged on the door. Molly stood outside her face bloodless. "You said you are an investigator, Mistress Allii." She drew a shuddering breath. "I need your help. Master Gaunten has been murdered."

•   •   •

Gaunten lay on his back, brains bashed into pulp. Allii first inspected the body, then the room, checking bags and rifling through drawers. Eventually she returned to the corpse began looking through its clothes.

I looked at Spooky, who rolled his eyes. Before either of us could say anything, Allii whistled.

Moll, who had been staring out of the porthole, turned around. "What's it?"

Allii held out a piece of paper. "A letter. Listen." She started reading out. "What a delightful surprise! Naturally, I'll help you. How can you doubt that, given our long association? I'll see you after dinner to discuss this matter in detail."

I was beginning to see a glimmer of light, but Moll's brow furrowed even more. "Who wrote that letter?"

"Vede, the hunter. He is heading to Kikilonia with a haul of silver-caracal teeth. From this letter, it seems Gaunten recognized Vede, tried to blackmail him, and got killed as a result."

Moll's brows were drawn together and her mouth was in a tight line. "Mistress Allii, would you mind telling me why you are on my ship? The truth, please."

Allii bowed her head.

A few minutes later, we were seated in Moll's cabin, Allii relating the story of the investigation. Moll listened, her face unreadable even to me.

When the tale was over, she picked me up. "Zom-Zom, why didn't you tell me you were looking for Kittin? Of course; you had no way." She turned to Allii. "I have something to tell him. Will he understand if I just, you know, say it?"

"Yes."

Moll hold tightened. "Kittin is dead, Zom-Zom. She had a growth in her stomach. I realized she needed help, so took her to Sheebatiya and showed her to the witches. They tried, but it was too late. Still they were able to alleviate the pain, and ease her passing." Her voice was a whisper. "I thought you knew. I'm sorry, Zom-Zom. I'm sorry."

•   •   •

I sat in a corner of the promenade desk staring at moon-lapped sea. The cord of grief and guilt tightened its grip round my neck. I gasped for breath. For how long had Mum been sick? Why didn't she tell me? Why didn't I notice?

The door leading down opened and Spooky came through. "Everyone has been asked to stay in their cabins until they are questioned. Allii wants to start with young Mizsha because he seems to be in a fit state to murder somebody. Will you come?"

My limbs were like deadwood. It took me a while to get up.

Spooky gave me a sidelong glance, as if he was weighting something in his mind. "My sister vanished when we were both young." His voice was hesitant. "I think she's dead, but I'll never know for certain."

"I'm sorry." What a sorry response. But what else could I say?

"The loss never leaves. But you learn to live with it, Zom-Zom." He hesitated. "And friends help."

"They do," I said. "Thank you."

Moll and Allii were waiting below. Once we joined them, Moll opened Mizsha's door, after a perfunctory knock.

Mizsha was standing near the porthole. He whipped around. "What is the meaning of this?" he snarled. "Why am I being confined here?" His face was all crunched up.

Moll responded, at her captain-best, polite, firm. "Master Mizsha, a passenger has been murdered. I'll be talking to all of the passengers, and examining their cabins. Mistress Allii is a professional investigator and she has agreed to help me."

Mizsha laughed a little hysterically. "I know who she is. Recognized her from the scar." He turned to Allii. "I know you are after me."

I gawped. *Mizsha is the hunter?*

Allii raised an eyebrow. "Why should I be after you, Mizsha?" Her voice was soft.

"Because you were hired by my parents."

I blinked, feeling lost.

"I've never met your parents, Mizsha," Allii said in that same soft voice. "I don't even know who they are. All I know is that you are no herbalist." She laid a hand on his arm. "We are looking for a murderer. I don't think you are him. But to clear you, we must know the truth about you."

He stared, looking a bit like a cornered mouse. Then his shoulders sagged. "I'm Prince Mizsha of the Kingdom of Bulo."

Allii frowned. "The Archipelago of Sky Islands?"

He nodded. "I'm a younger son. My parents wanted me to marry the daughter of the kingdom's wealthiest man. I didn't want to, but they wouldn't listen. They wanted the money, I suppose. So I ran away. There was no other escape." He looked at us defiantly, as if challenging us to contradict him.

Mizsha was a runaway prince. Did they even exist?

Allii smiled. "Very sensible."

He searched her face as if suspecting her of sarcasm, then sighed. "There's someone I love. I'm to meet him in Sheebatiya."

The rest was bit of an anti-climax. Mizsha's cabin and possessions were searched, but yielded nothing of relevance.

Our next stop was Doctor Gerb's. After the hysterics of Miszha, the old physician's calm demeanor was a relief. Once again, a quick but thorough search was made, and nothing incriminating was found.

Lady B was atwitter when we entered her cabin. She swooped on me, then demanded to know why the murdered man was murdered, wanted a guarantee she was safe.

Moll said that she needed to search the room. Lady B let out a howl, followed by a lot of words: affront, intrusion, thieves ...

Allii moved towards a pile of bags.

Lady B dropped me, jumped at Allii, and would have socked her on the jaw had Spooky not brought her down with a graceful leap.

The next moment, Moll was down by her, holding her in a grip faster than manacles. All Lady B could do was kick at air, drum her heels, and scream ... which she did unstintingly.

Allii started looking inside the bags methodically. Lady B's screams increased in volume and vitriol.

From a valise, Allii extracted a razor and a small pouch. The screams stopped. A silence fell. Allii opened the pouch, and held out the contents, as if they were an offering.

Two silver-caracal teeth.

My anger boiled over. I wanted to claw at the painted face until it turned red. My only comfort was that this evil killer would rot in jail for life.

•   •   •

We reached the Port of Sheebatiya next morning.

Lady B was held in the cabin, under guard. A thorough search of the cabin and the ship had yielded no more teeth. An effort to search Lady B's person had to be abandoned due to non-cooperation.

"Why don't you knock that creature on the head, and search her?" I asked Allii.

"We don't have the authority to forcibly search anyone." She gave me a reassuring smile. "Once we are in Sheebatiya, the Prefects will attend to the matter. They have the authority. Don't worry, Zom-Zom, everything's under control."

But to me, nothing felt under control.

The moment the ship docked, several members of Sheebatiya police force boarded, led by a stout woman who seemed to know Allii well. I left them to it, and sat in a corner, watching the scene below, a busy morning in a busy port.

I was thinking not of silver-caracals or murderers, but of Mum.

Why didn't she tell me about her illness? But that wouldn't have been Mum. She never complained.

The sound of footsteps brought me out of my reverie. Mizsha and Doctor Gerb were heading out.

I walked up to them. Doctor Gerb, bending with some difficulty, scratched the top of my head. "Goodbye, Zom-Zom. You are a very special cat. Take care of yourself."

I meowed a goodbye.

The two men went down the gangway, Mizsha helping the old man. I watched them.

The sea should smell of fish, but it doesn't.

Memory dawned, like a streak of lightning, that elusive something I'd been searching for.

I ran, jumped, and landed on the bent back of Doctor Gerb, screaming, "He's Vede! Get him!"

Even the most dexterous man would find it difficult to extract a cat from his back. He tried though, with surprising strength and agility. But fury had turned my claws into steel hooks. I dug them through the cloth, into the flesh, howling a song of rage and revenge ...

• • •

It took the combined efforts of several sailors and prefects to secure Doctor Gerb, alias Vede the hunter. And to get me off him.

Finally, he was taken away to Sheebatiya's secure jail. Mizsha too was gone. Lady B followed, waiting only to give me a final hug.

"I must hurry, Pusskin," she trilled, "or my quarry will escape."

Lady B was the investigator hired by Mizsha's parents.

We sat in Mollina's room once the excitement was over. Every face was turned to me. I was the star of the show. I should have been preening. Yet, empty was all I felt.

"What made you recognize Vede, Zom-Zom?" Allii asked.

"The night I was almost murdered, I felt there was a missing piece of memory, but it remained elusive. Doctor Gerb tickled my head while saying goodbye and the memory came. His ring; the person who grabbed me that night was wearing a ring. I know it wasn't much of proof, but call it cat's intuition." I looked at Spooky. "Dog's too. You said he smelled wrong."

Allii rendered my words to Moll.

Moll smiled. "Clever Zom-Zom."

I felt even emptier.

Allii said, "Gerb had the pouch lined with cloth and filled with medicinal leaves. The teeth were in there, wrapped in cotton wool. He saw through Lady B's disguise and planted two silver-caracal teeth amongst her belongings. I blame myself for being misled by Gerb's eyes. It turns out he was wearing extremely thin lenses, which gave that milky look to his eyes. My failure cost Gaunten's life."

"Gaunten died because he was too greedy," I objected.

Allii sighed. "And it is no thanks to me you are still alive, Zom-Zom."

"We all made mistakes, Allii. We did get things right in the end."

Allii smiled. "You did Zom-Zom. Without you, Vede would have walked away."

This was my moment. I should have been overjoyed. But I felt lost.

Moll had promised to take me to see where Mum was buried. And then what?

Moll ran her fingers along my spine. "I'm so proud of you Zom-Zom. When I think of how many more of those magnificent animals would have been killed ..."

The lost feeling vanished, and I knew what I wanted to do. I turned to Allii. "I have a favor to ask. No obligations. During our first encounter, you said that seeing a silver-caracal in the snowy landscape is an unforgettable experience. I'd like to have that experience."

Allii laughed. "What do you say to a trip to Angel Mountains, Spooky?"

Michael D. Burnside earned a master's degree in political science at Ohio University but earns a living as a computer systems analyst. His fiction writing includes steampunk, science fiction, fantasy, and horror. His stories have been featured in multiple anthologies including *Fossil Lake: An Anthology of the Aberrant*, *Fossil Lake II: The Refossiling*, *Beautiful Lies, Painful Truths Vol. II*, and *Ink Stains Vol. 8*. His short stories have also been featured in magazines such as *Devolution Z*, *Outposts of Beyond*, and *Gathering Storm Magazine*. His story, "The Message" can be heard on episode 240 of the *StarshipSofa* podcast. Michael lives in Dayton, Ohio with his wife, two giant dogs, and lots of cats.

•   •   •

I wrote this story after wondering what happens to the adventurers in a thrilling fantasy after they retire. Would there really be a happy ending after they finally get some monster's great hoard? The greed that propelled the story's plot forward would likely linger. The thorny personality conflicts that made for entertaining quips between the party members might grow sharp enough to become deadly.

THE DEVIL OF GREYSTERN CASTLE

MICHAEL D. BURNSIDE

A KNIGHT MARSHAL is a member of the highest order of gentry. We are warriors for the king and law enforcement for the populace.

As a youth, I believed being a knight marshal would mean a life filled with prestige, romance, bravery, and grand adventures. I can confirm that my position does garner me renown. However, I remain single as I creep toward the age of thirty years, so the romance part has turned out to be a fable.

Bravery always came naturally to me — that is, until I acquired a squire, and now the fear of failing him hounds my every thought. As for grand adventures ... well, this tale begins after I spent two weeks camping in a swamp.

The road grew firmer the farther we travelled from the marshes. The increased vigor of my horse's gait told me he was happy to be away from the bogs. My squire, Allen, rode beside me. The hood of his mud-splattered cloak hid his straw-colored hair and blue eyes. I knew he was cold and exhausted. So was I, but we were back in Skarvon now, where the air was warm and dry. The chill of the wetlands would soon leave our bones.

Our trip had been fruitful. We'd tied large bundles of Tormentil to the backs of our horses. The cheerful yellow flowers had been easy to spot in the dreary, gray swamp. With luck, the scholars at Calum University would find a way to grow the flowers a bit closer to home.

As the sun rose, we came to a fork in the road. I led us onto the path to Greystern Castle. The road not taken would have led us into a small town with the promise of a comfortable inn, but my status as a knight marshal meant we'd find free lodging at the castle. In truth, I find castles to be drafty and filled with more politics than I care to engage in, but if we're being truthful, then I must admit I'm annoyingly frugal.

I'd never visited Greystern Castle. Built only three years prior, I considered it a vanity project constructed by men with more gold than sense. The castle served no strategic purpose that I could tell, but if a castle offered no purpose other than to give me a free bed, who was I to question its existence?

The sun had begun its descent when I heard a horse behind us. I looked over my shoulder and saw a lone rider approaching. Likely, the rider sought company on the road, but I made sure the hilt of my sword was in easy reach.

As the rider drew closer, I noted he was a powerfully built man. His stiff posture was a telltale sign he wore a breastplate beneath his black cloak. Given the amount of coin I'd had to part with for my own, this meant the rider was a man of some means.

The rider's dark skin marked him as a refugee from the central plateau. The plateau's steady collapse had sent many of its people into the southern realm, where their culture of hard work and martial training had greatly benefitted the kingdom.

I raised my off-hand in greeting as the rider drew alongside us. The rider nodded in return. "Greeting, travelers," he said. "It's been a while since I've seen strangers on the road to the castle."

"I'm Sir Morvyn and this is my squire, Allen," I replied. "We seek only a night's rest before we continue on our way."

The rider raised his eyebrows in recognition of my name and bowed slightly in his saddle. "Your reputation precedes you, knight marshal. I am Captain Donall, head of the guard at Greystern Castle. It will be an honor to have you stay with us." Some distressful thought must have crossed the captain's mind then, for he frowned slightly.

I tried to allay his possible concerns. "I assure you, we'll be no trouble. No need for a banquet or any ceremony. A quiet night in front of a warm fire with whatever food and ale you can spare is all we ask."

Captain Donall flashed an apologetic smile. "I have no such concerns. You will be no burden at all. What troubles me is that you may not find the castle very comfortable."

"How so?"

The captain hesitated before speaking. "I hope you don't think me a mad man for saying this, but the castle is cursed. A devil resides within its walls. Items are thrown from shelves. A specter stalks the halls. Screams wake the residents every night."

Allen shifted in his saddle.

I held out a reassuring hand. "Fear not, my squire. You handled the hobgoblins that crept into our camp with ease. How much trouble can a few ghosts be?"

Allen shook his head. "Hobgoblins are real. Scary, ugly, thin things with mouths full of pointed teeth, but physical. They die when you poke a sword into them. But a sword is no use against a phantom."

"Has this devil or these ghosts caused any deaths?" I asked the captain.

"No," replied Donall. "Just discomfort and unease."

35

I smiled. "We've just come from the marshes. We're accustomed to discomfort and unease. I doubt we'd sleep well without it. The castle will suit us just fine."

I urged my horse forward and my two companions fell in alongside me.

Donall glanced at the bundle of plants fastened behind my saddle. "You journeyed to the marshes and faced off against hobgoblins to collect flowers?"

"Tormentil," I replied. "It staunches the flow of blood from wounds. It's my hope we can grow it within the kingdom."

Donall nodded. "That sounds quite useful."

"Hopefully not tonight," muttered my squire.

•   •   •

We arrived as the sun vanished and unleashed a painted sky of pink and orange hues. The castle stood in shadow; an immense structure of stone blocks lit only by the occasional torch posted along its outer wall. Square towers capped each corner and an additional four towers made up the gatehouse.

As we approached, I could just make out the color of the castle walls in the flickering torchlight, a light grey that looked like ash. The blocks were crudely carved and ill-fitted, providing too many handholds for an agile raiding party.

The gate house featured double portcullises, the first of which dropped from stones carved to resemble teeth.

I leaned back in my saddle as I took it all in. "Well, it is grey." I squinted at the castle's maw. "And I suppose it looks stern."

Captain Donall suppressed a chuckle. "Lord Roken is quite concerned with being taken seriously. He worries the manner in which he earned his wealth is looked down upon by some."

"Certainly not me," I replied. "The life of an adventurer is often exciting and short. Given that Lord Roken excelled at it, I know he's not a man to be trifled with." It was a small castle, but easily capable of housing several hundred people. "Did the rest of his party invest in the castle as well?" I asked.

Donall shook his head. "Magus Belthar built a tower to the north. Father Cleary joined the clergy at Calum Cathedral. Sir Lachlan did spend time here, but he and Roken had a falling out a year ago, and Lachlan departed in the middle of the night. I haven't seen him since."

"So, none of Roken's old adventuring companions want anything to do with him anymore?"

Donall sighed. "Lord Roken is not an easy man to get along with."

When we reached the gatehouse, Captain Donall shouted a password to a guard atop one of the towers. A moment later, the portcullis clanked up into the castle's upper jaw. As we rode into the gatehouse, the second iron gate rose as well. I glanced up and noted the murder holes in the ceiling. Any intruder unfortunate enough to be trapped in the gatehouse would be filled with crossbow bolts. The castle had flaws in its construction; it could be taken … but there would be a price to pay.

In the courtyard, Captain Donall led Allen and me to the stables, where we made our horses comfortable for the night. We then walked toward the main keep, an imposing structure that featured barred windows and arrow slits. Although recently built, the keep had an ancient weight to it, as if centuries pressed down on its stones instead of only a few years. Wind whistled along the walls, and a chill returned to my bones.

"You know," I said to Donall as we walked toward the keep's doors, "most castles have the decency not to be cursed for the first hundred years or so."

"The evening will go smoother if there's no mention of curses, spirits, or devils," said Donall with a dour tone.

"Does Roken not know about the rumors?" I asked.

"He knows," replied Donall. "But it is an unwelcome subject."

•   •   •

A valet, a distinguished looking elder gentleman with a well-trimmed silver mustache, showed us to our room on the second floor. It was a modest space that featured a single bed, a desk, a chair, and a couch.

As the valet lit the candles in the room, I asked, "May I have an additional room for my squire?"

"I'm afraid not, sir," replied the valet. "Dinner is available whenever you are ready." He departed with a slight bow and hastily shut the door behind him.

Allen frowned. "The hallways were deserted. There must be a dozen empty rooms on this floor. Why can't they spare an additional room?"

"Perhaps the servants don't like to make the beds," I mused.

The room was cold and smelled of mildew. A single sheepskin rug lay upon the wooden floor. A small, dark fireplace was built into one wall. An empty wood bin stood beside it.

I walked over to the desk. Dust covered its surface. Several books with unmarked leather covers were stacked along the back edge. I opened one of the books and found it contained nothing but blank pages.

I began to regret my frugal ways.

"I shall sleep on the couch, sir," said Allen.

I nodded. "Very good. It's those kinds of sacrifices that may eventually remind me to recommend you for knighthood."

"Perhaps you could mention the fight with the hobgoblins in the recommendation rather than 'slept on the couch'?" suggested Allen.

I shrugged in an effort to pretend indifference but couldn't quite hide my smile.

I was fond of the boy, too fond for his own good. I feared my affection would lead to a lapse in his training. What if I offered him too much praise or comfort, and it resulted in a lack of self-discipline that led to his death? How could I live with such a thing? I could not, and so I was sparing in my praise and unyielding in my demands of him. I was a bad master, but that was acceptable if my squire lived long enough to resent his time with me.

Dinner had already begun by the time Allen and I entered the great hall of the keep. The hall had a high ceiling with large wooden rafters. An archway in the western wall led off to a kitchen area. A table, large enough to accommodate twenty, took up the center of the room. Only five people were seated.

I nodded at Captain Donall, who returned my greeting. Lord Roken sat at the head of the table. He was a large brute of a man. The chair he sat in would have been oversized for a normal person, but it barely accommodated him. A ragged brown beard grew from his chin and cheeks. The hair atop his head was thinning and unkempt. He had a great bulbous red nose that betrayed his love of alcohol.

The remaining three people at the table were the typical sycophants you find in any wealthy household. Hangers-on and leeches, hopeful that if they praise the object of their attention enough, they'll be welcomed to share in that person's good fortune. They wore fine silk robes, styled wigs, and plenty of shiny rings on their fingers. I took deliberate care not to learn their names.

Seven hydra heads were mounted on the walls. Each enormous serpentine trophy had been posed with a wide-open mouth revealing long curved fangs. The largest of the heads was mounted above Roken's chair. It stared down at me with its lips pulled back in a frozen growl, its emerald eyes filled with unblinking hate, and yet I still found it more welcoming than the glare Roken threw at me.

"Welcome to Castle Greystern," said Lord Roken, in a tone which told me I was most certainly not.

"Thank you for your hospitality," I replied. "I'm Sir Morvyn and this is my squire, Allen."

"You won't be staying long?" asked Roken.

I shook my head as Allen and I sat down next to Captain Donall.

The valet who had shown us to our room suddenly appeared with a tray of cold poultry. Next came a pair of wooden goblets filled with dubious smelling ale.

"Donall says you went into the marshes to pick flowers," said Roken as he picked up a slab of meat up from his plate. He tore off a chunk of chicken with his teeth.

"Yes," I said. "Tormentil. A plant with remarkable medicinal qualities."

Roken snorted. "When I went out into the wilds, it was to bring back real treasure."

"The right medicine at the right time can be more valuable than gold," I replied.

Roken rolled his eyes and bit deep into a drumstick.

I took a sip of ale. It was vile. I momentarily hoped it was poisoned so I'd never risk drinking it again. Unfortunately, I lived, and got to experience an aftertaste that reminded me of rotten cabbage.

Allen reached for his cup. I tried to dissuade him with a subtle shake of my head. He failed to notice in time and took a drink. I was forced to continue to converse with Roken to cover my squire's involuntary, but rude, reaction.

"These hydra heads are remarkable. Are they from a beast you slew?"

My flattering question earned me a grin from Roken and distracted him from Allen, who was spitting the ale back into his cup.

"The beast only had three heads when we started," chortled Roken. "Two new heads sprouted every time I cleaved one off. Cleary pleaded for me to stop my attack, but the beast kept coming. Fortunately, Belthar started throwing fire bolts to seal the wounds I made. That stopped the hydra from regenerating. She always was clever." The mirth suddenly fled from Roken's face. "Lachlan was useless as always."

Perhaps I like to live dangerously, because I pressed him on his point. "But Sir Lachlan was knighted. He must have some martial prowess?"

"Political connections," replied Roken with a sneer. "Lachlan could hold his own against a goblin or two, but he'd cower in the shadows whenever a dragon flew near."

I gave a small smile. "Hiding from a dragon seems like a reasonable decision to me. I've only ever seen one, and, I must confess, I viewed it from beneath a stone bridge as it winged its way overhead."

"Discretion is one thing; sniveling about it another. Lachlan knew the lands we were venturing into held danger, but he never ceased to complain about it." Roken poked at the remains of the chicken on his plate and frowned. "I don't wish to speak of him anymore."

Before an uncomfortable silence could embrace us all, I blurted, "I hear Magus Belthar built a tower to the north."

Roken glumly nodded. "Yes."

"Have you ever visited it?" I asked.

"Once. It's a fine wizard tower. Magus Evelyn Belthar is a powerful caster. I always admired her. She and I worked well together. Wished there could have been more between us, but there wasn't." Crimson crept into Roken's cheeks. "I don't wish to speak of her anymore either. Let's just eat."

Captain Donall had looked increasingly uncomfortable during the conversation. His eyes pleaded with me to stop talking, so I just nodded.

Roken took another bite of chicken and chewed it on one side of his mouth. He looked at me and said, "Last thing. This castle, like all castles, makes some noise at night. You hear anything, you ignore it. Don't go wandering about investigating. Captain Donall has everything under control, so just stay in your damn room."

I nodded again while internally vowing to never again visit a castle just for a free room.

•   •   •

"That was awful," whispered Allen to me as we made our way back to our room. "The ale was undrinkable. I may die of thirst."

"All castles have a well somewhere. I'll ask the valet to bring us up a pitcher," I replied.

"Ugh. Well water," he moaned.

That was precisely the sort of entitlement I needed to clamp down on. I fixed my squire with a disapproving look. "I could ask for more of that fine ale instead."

"What I meant was, well water will be just fine," said Allen with a false smile.

I nodded.

We were a hallway down from our room when we came across an open door, through which came the sound of some commotion. I couldn't help but peek in as we grew near.

The door led to a small storage room lined with shelves, but everything the shelves had held lay on the floor. A dented pitcher, a silver teapot, and a dozen metal plates lay scattered about. The valet was picking the items up when I caught his eye.

"Is everything okay?" I asked.

"A bit of a regular ritual I'm afraid," answered the valet. "Objects slide off these shelves every night. I've asked to stop using them, but Lord Roken insists I do. He refuses to acknowledge there's a problem. I've taken to only keeping metal things in here. They can survive the fall better than pottery."

I stepped closer for a better view. "Are the shelves uneven?" I asked.

"No, my lord," replied the valet.

"Is this a part of the curse?"

The valet frowned. "We're not supposed to talk about such things, my lord."

I nodded. "Of course not, my apologies."

The shelves appeared serviceable. The only odd thing about the storage space was that the mortar on the back wall appeared newer than elsewhere, but the storage room likely shared a common wall with another chamber which may have been built at a different time.

"Could you bring a pitcher of water to our room when you have the chance?" I asked.

"Yes, my lord," replied the valet.

I nodded my thanks and then Allen and I continued toward our room, though our path wasn't the quickest. We'd taken a different route down to the great hall. On our way back, we'd missed a turn somewhere. It hardly mattered. The keep was a great square building with all straight corridors. It was just a matter of walking in a grid pattern until we happened down the right hallway.

We found the right hallway, but not before we found a massive clock right around the corner from our room. The clock was encased in an eight-foot-tall wooden cabinet. The brass mechanisms of the clock could be seen through the glass panes of the cabinet. Cylinders as big as my head pulled down on the clock, causing its gears to spin. Steel hour and minute hands ticked the time away. At the bottom of the clock sat a golden bell as large as a dinner plate. A small hammer hung near the bell, cocked back and ready to strike.

"You don't suppose this thing is going to chime all night, do you?" asked Allen.

I sighed. "Oh, I suppose very much so."

•   •   •

Cold crept into our room and, with no wood for the fireplace, there was nothing we could do to warm the chamber up. I donated one of the blankets on the bed to Allen, so he'd have something to cover himself with on the couch. We both removed our armor and wrapped ourselves in our cloaks. I buried myself under the remaining blanket and managed to sleep through the first few chimes of the clock down the hall.

The clock's midnight serenade was one clang too many. I awoke as the last of its gongs echoed through the room. I then lay in the dark with my eyes wide open. Try as I might, I could not get back to sleep.

Across the room, Allen snored softly, a low snorting rumble that rose and fell.

Something, somewhere in the castle, dripped with a steady rhythm. I stared toward the ceiling, though it was too dark for me to make out its cracked plaster. My imagination conjured all sorts of apparitions in the shadows. They were mostly free forming shapes, abstractions that meant nothing, but faces formed too — haggard visages with hollow eyes and wide-open mouths that silently screamed at me.

My mind had worked itself into a terrible state when there came a sudden clatter. A cascade of clangs erupted from the hall. I leapt up with my hands wrapped around the scabbard of my sword.

Allen sprang up and blurted, "What was that?"

I crept toward the bedroom door. "I'm going to find out. Stay here and guard the room."

"Guard it from what?" asked Allen.

"That's what I'm going to find out." I unsheathed my sword.

"Didn't Lord Roken say to stay in the room?"

"Yes," I answered. "But I'm a knight marshal and not actually obliged to heed him." I grabbed the door handle. "Also, I don't like him."

I cracked open the door wide enough for me to slip out and then shut it behind me. The clattering noise had ceased, replaced by a deep moaning sound that reverberated down the hallway. I headed toward the clock. My bare feet were ice cold but silent on the rough wooden floor.

Sadly, the clock remained intact. A low groan emanated from the direction we had come during our return from dinner. I snuck toward the sound, edging along the wall with my sword held high. When I reached the end of the corridor, I peeked around the corner.

The door to the storage room had been flung open Something inside the small chamber wailed.

Fearing someone needed my aid, I rushed toward the room. Just as I reached it, a spirit stepped out.

The ghost had the characteristics of fog — white, translucent, with indefinable edges. It held the shape of a large man holding a great sword. The air around the phantom turned cold and clammy.

I halted. The thing turned and faced me. Black pools of darkness filled its eyes. Its mouth held no teeth. The gaping maw stretched and moaned. The other features of its face faded in and out of reality.

The ghost raised its sword and attacked me.

I stepped back and attempted to parry the blow, but my blade passed clean through the phantom's weapon. The foggy claymore cleaved through my body. Tendrils of cold followed the path of the sword as it went through me.

Stunned, I patted myself down where I'd been struck, but found no wounds.

The ghost screamed and charged, but its hollow eyes didn't track my movement. I stepped out of the way. The spirit ran past me, howled, and collapsed onto the floor. Its shape shifted into a blob of white that sank into the floor and vanished.

Footsteps approached from behind me. I spun around with my sword at the ready.

Lord Roken, dressed in leather hide and breastplate, stood before me holding an axe in each hand. "I told you to stay in your room," he growled.

"The ghost isn't sentient, is it?" I asked. "It's not independent. It would've done the exact same thing if I hadn't been here."

"It always appears after midnight. Sometimes I come up to watch it, see if I can find a way to kill it," replied Roken.

"But you can't, can you? Because it's a memory, an echo of something that already happened."

Roken pointed one of his axes at me. "None of this is your business, Morvyn."

"But it is," I replied. "I'm a marshal, responsible for investigating any crime that happens in the kingdom." I took a step back and moved into a defensive stance. I suspected his reaction to what I was about to say would be violent. "Sir Lachlan never left, did he? You killed him and buried him behind the wall of that store room. Captain Donall told me there was a devil in this castle. He was right. And that devil is you!"

Roken came at me with a roar and swung each axe at me in turn. I parried both blows but the attacks drove me back.

"Lachlan thought he deserved an equal share!" howled Roken. "But I carried the group! I slew the beasts!"

He swung both axes at me again. I ducked, dodged, and then lunged with a thrust aimed at his throat. Roken leaned back, causing my sword to skip off his breastplate. I tried to follow up with a slashing attack to his legs, but my swing smacked into a wall.

Accusing Roken had been a terrible mistake. Not because I was wrong, but because he held all the advantages here. My sword had reach, but his hand axes needed less room to swing in the corridor. He wore a breastplate and leather. I wore a cloth cloak and was barefoot.

I decided to keep him talking and hope he would grow distracted enough to make a mistake.

"Did Lachlan discover a secret stash of treasure and threaten to tell the others? Is that why you attacked him?"

Roken scowled at me. "You're a good marshal. You piece together what happened so easily. But you're a damn fool of a knight for challenging me here." He unleashed a flurry of attacks. I frantically parried the blows and retreated down the hallway.

One of his axes caught my blade and forced it down. I had nothing with which to stop his other axe. I watched the blow come at my head, shocked that my life had come to an end.

Roken suddenly screamed in agony. His attack faltered. My sword slipped free.

Captain Donall had come up behind Roken and delivered a savage strike to the back of Roken's head. Roken turned, exposing a cut on his scalp that went down to the bone. Blood ran from his head and flowed down his back.

"Traitor!" hissed Roken.

"I heard everything," replied Donall. "I should've listened to my suspicions." Donall closed in with his sword at the ready.

Roken pivoted sideways and held out his axes.

Some believe a pair of weapons means you can deal with a pair of opponents, but in truth, dealing with two trained fighters while flanked is all but impossible.

Donall and I attacked at the same time. Roken deflected Donall's swing, but had to glance toward Donall to do so, which resulted in my lunge getting through. I stabbed Roken in the armpit, down into his ribcage, and through his heart. Roken collapsed and died in seconds.

Donall lowered his sword and looked at me. "How'd you know? How'd you figure all of that out?"

I leaned against the wall and tried to catch my breath. "Honestly," I gasped. "I was just guessing." I looked down at Roken's body. "But with murder, fights over money are always a likely cause."

•   •   •

We buried Roken in a simple grave. The sycophants, upon learning their meal ticket had passed and finding their flattery did not work on me, departed hastily.

Donall met with us in the courtyard as we prepared to continue our own journey. He held the reins of my horse as I secured the saddle. His face betrayed no emotion but I knew he was ill at ease. "I owe you my life," I told him.

"I did my duty as best I could" he replied. "Though I served Roken, I owe my fealty to the kingdom. I have no regrets." He glanced back at the castle. "Though with Roken gone, I have lost my employment."

I swung up into the saddle and smiled down at him. "Though strategically questionable, the king isn't going to abandon a free castle. When I reach the capital, I'll make sure you're named captain of the guard of Greystern. You and your men will work directly for the crown from now on. I expect the pay will be better."

Donall's face broke into a grin. "Thank you, sir."

I eased back in the saddle. "No, thank you. I would be neglectful in my duty to not draft such an honorable man into service." I shifted my gaze to the grey rocks of the castle. They didn't appear so drab in the dawn's light. "With Roken gone, perhaps the spirit will fade. Hopefully, your new duties will be accompanied by restful nights,"

"And better ale," muttered Allen.

I threw a disapproving look at my squire, but Donall let loose a chuckle.

I gave Donall a nod and said, "We'll be on our way. It has been a pleasure to make your acquaintance."

"The same to you, Sir Morvyn," replied Donall.

I gave him a wave. Allen and I turned our horses and rode out the gate.

Allen glanced back at the fortress. "Do you really think the ghost will simply fade away?"

I shrugged. "I hope so, but Captain Donall is brave enough to handle a temperamental ghost."

Allen nodded and then gave me a nervous grin. "But for us ..."

I knew where his thoughts were going, and readily agreed. "For us, no more castles."

Jay Caselberg is an Australian author and poet whose work has appeared in numerous places such as *Interzone, Aurealis, The Third Alternative, Fangoria,* and various anthologies among others. He has a number of novels including the Jack Stein series first published by Roc Books. His stories, novels and poetry have been shortlisted for awards such as The Australasian Shadows Award, The Aurealis Award, and the British Fantasy Award.

·   ·   ·

"Fields of Ice" came from thoughts about expectations, about how our preconceptions not only shape how we see things, but also, in the end, what we see. Our protagonist misses things that are right in front of him. But in the end, he understands. Whether that understanding comes too late is another question.

FIELDS OF ICE

JAY CASELBERG

MARSIUS PULLED HIS COAT TIGHT against the wind. The snow blew in flurries swirling about his face and his fur boots sank deep. The sharp, dirt-ice smell crept under his hood, edged and filthy like the season.

He looked up at the sheer stone Academy walls, their tops lost in darkness. Somewhere above, the remaining college members were heading off to dinner, or the library, or bed, secure and warm. There was no point dwelling on it; the prison awaited. He pulled his coat around him more tightly and lowered his head into the icy wind.

It took him half an hour to trudge to the broad prison gates, battling through the narrow streets. The high buildings funneled the wind and whipped it around him. Twin torches sat on either side of the gate, guttering and flaring, sending the acrid scent of burning swirling about with the wind. He lifted a leather-gloved fist to bang on the iron-shod door. At his third attempt, someone heard; a small door recessed in the main portal swung inward and a head poked out. There was annoyance on the face it presented.

"I'm here for the children," said Marsius. "I'm Lector Filindal."

The guard gestured him impatiently through the door and into the central courtyard. Marsius looked around at the forbidding stone walls and the narrow cobbled space. Charming. The guard disappeared to a side room and reappeared a few moments later with a board. He checked through the roster, looked up at Marsius, then nodded.

"Right. This way, sir," said the guard. His breath fogged in the air.

Marsius wished the guard had asked him inside to perform the checks instead of leaving him to stamp and huddle in the courtyard. There was clearly a small fire inside the guardroom. He supposed common courtesy would have been too much to ask. This was a prison, after all.

The guard led him across the courtyard and to a rickety wooden platform that stood against one wall. He gestured with an open hand, and Marsius frowned his lack of understanding.

"If you'll just climb aboard, Lector Filindal."

"Oh, I see." Marsius finally noticed the ropes leading up into the blackness. He readjusted his pack, climbed aboard, and gripped the railing. The guard disappeared off to one side and started the winch. As the platform crept up the wall, Marsius looked up at the leaden darkness, hesitating to cast his glance downward. Heights had never been a strong point.

The platform creaked and strained beneath him. Even the ropes creaked, strung taut with his weight. He could just picture them giving way and his body being dashed upon the cobbled courtyard below. With each turn of the winch, the platform crawled higher and his fear grew. Finally, with relief, Marsius saw an opening in the wall far above him.

Another guard met him at the entrance. A deep tunnel lit by torches trailed away ahead.

"Lector Filindal. Here for the children," said Marsius, throwing back his hood and fumbling with the front of his coat.

"Oh, lucky you," said the guard. "I'll show you where they are, and then we can see to your chambers. You in for the duration?"

Marsius nodded.

"Hmm," said the guard. He tilted his head to one side, stuck a finger in his ear and worked it around and around, then grimaced. "You're a bit young, aren't you?"

Marsius frowned. So what if he was young? He knew what he was doing.

"This way," the guard said, gesturing down the corridor when he'd finished inspecting the results of his ministrations.

At least there was a hint of warmth inside. Marsius stripped off his gloves and tucked them under his arm as he followed along behind, feeling the gloom and the stone walls pressing down on him. The place smelled old, of dust, and old piles of rubbish left in forgotten corners.

He hadn't known what to expect of the children. Of course, he had seen images rendered of the royal family, but he'd never paid them much attention. His mind was normally on other things. So, when the guard finally led him up a passageway and directed him inside the small cell, Marsius stopped in the doorway, to observe. The boy was the image of his father, but the girl ...

The guard cleared his throat and Marsius shook himself.

"I'll come back for you in a while. Give you time to get acquainted," said the guard behind him.

"Very well," said Marsius over his shoulder, then turned and stepped inside. The door locked behind him with a loud clunk.

The two children watched as he stood there, returning his gaze. The boy was dark, with the same prominent nose and thick brow of his father. The girl — Antalya was her name, he thought — was as pale as the ice fields. Liquid blue eyes watched him impassively.

"Prince Sten, Princess Antalya —" He rolled the sound of her name over his tongue. "— I am Lector Filindal. I have been assigned to you for the duration of your internment, or until ..."

"Until they kill us," said the prince.

"I don't think that's —"

The prince waved his hand. "They did it to our father," he said. "Why not us? Why should we be any different? The mark of his blood is within us."

The boy showed all the dispassionate curtness his father had been known for. The girl sat where she was, saying nothing, simply watching. Marsius could feel her eyes upon him, even though he now faced the boy.

"I just don't believe that's likely, Prince Sten."

"Well, no matter what you say, we're here, and you have a job to perform. So, let us make use of the time," said the boy. He spoke as a man much older, clearly used to authority. Marsius wondered whether it was the child's upbringing that shaped his speech, or whether it was something else, something within. It could not be good for a child.

"No matter what the circumstance," said Marsius, turning to address the next to the girl, "I am here to do the best for you in the time we have ... however long that may be."

The princess looked at him. Slowly, her gaze traveled down to his toes and back up to his face. She looked away. Marsius swallowed.

"The guard will be back soon. I suggest we hold the start of our lessons until the morrow, as I need to become acquainted with my quarters and settle in before preparing. Perhaps as soon as we have broken our fast ..."

"Yes," said the boy. "That is acceptable to us, Filindal." He turned away and faced the wall, his hands clasped behind his back.

Marsius ignored the discourtesy shown by the omission of his title. It may have been deliberate. It may have just been the trappings of familiar power. Marsius waited in silence, watching them until the guard called from behind the door.

It was clear he had been dismissed, for there was no sign from either of the children that he even existed.

The key turned in the lock, and with as much dignity as he could muster, Marsius retreated.

"I'm Corum," said the guard as he escorted him down the corridor.

"Well, I am called Marsius."

"Aye, much better than Lector Filindal. We'll be seeing quite a bit of each other. What do you make of them, the royal brats? Strange birds, aren't they?"

"The boy … well the boy was much as I expected. But the girl …"

"Gives me the shivers, she does," said Corum. "But what would you expect from the Tyrant's daughter?"

"I know not, Corum. I know not."

•   •   •

Marsius sat up, looked around the room and grimaced. It had a high ceiling, a fireplace, and the thick stone walls were dressed with shelves in which to keep his things. The narrow cot was firm. It was not so different from the Academy, really, but he couldn't help knowing it was enfolded within a prison, high above the ground. He supposed he would get used to it in time. He had slept well enough, considering. He rose from the cot and reached for his pack.

He scattered the contents across the cot and started searching through his books. Where to start? Magic was a funny thing. He wished he had the power within himself to use it, but all he could do was teach. A person either had the talent or they didn't, and he had not been so blessed. He had enough within him to perform simple conjuration, and to practice adequately with the greater arts, but to show true power …

He had to be careful with the children. There was nothing to gauge how much latency they possessed. Their father, the Tyrant, had certainly had strength. It had taken four High Practitioners to subdue him, and even then, it was a struggle.

If the blood ran true, then they were likely to have more than a full share. If such power was released into the world again, then he hesitated to think ...

He could show them spells of Divination and Making first, he supposed. They could do little harm there. After that, the field was open, as long as he avoided Compulsion and Concealment. He must show them nothing that would aid any escape. Even part-trained, they were too dangerous to let loose into the world. The Tyrant's brats running free with power was not a pretty thought.

Marsius sighed and rubbed the back of his neck. He stared blankly at the wall. That it should come to this. For so long, he had spoken out against the Tyrant and his ways. Others had been more complacent, and Marsius had quickly become unpopular because of his outspokenness. Some had said it was the enthusiasm of youth, but others were not so forgiving. Here, now, he had the means to prevent the rise of the Tyrant's children, to educate them in the ways of real humanity. At least he could do that much. His natural urge was to have them done away with, but how could he even think it? He was pedagogue, not executioner.

He chose a book at random and headed down the corridor. The children were sitting waiting for him when he arrived.

"Good morning, Prince Sten, Princess Antalya," he said from the door. "I trust you slept well."

"Well enough, Lector," said the boy. "What's your name again?"

"Lector Filindal," said Marsius.

"Marsius," said the girl at exactly the same moment.

Marsius looked at her and frowned. She quickly looked away. She must have overheard him tell the guard as they walked up the corridor. That must have been it.

"Yes, well," said Marsius and cleared his throat. "We have work to do. I have brought a text with me to start the first of our lessons. Have either of you had any training to this point?"

"Oh, some," said Sten. "But not very interesting. The Lector assigned to us was old and he wasn't very enthusiastic. We touched on Making, but all he ever cared about was theory. We never got to do anything."

Marsius cast his mind back and tried to remember who had been assigned to the Tyrant's household, but it wouldn't come.

"So, you should be familiar with the principles of the elements," he said.

"Yes, yes," said Sten. "We've heard all that a thousand times before. Are you going to show us anything interesting?"

The boy's attitude was beginning to grate. Marsius felt a premonition of dread as he left the doorway and walked into the room to take his place at the table set aside for the lessons. The boy had all the makings of a dictator: his attitude, the tone; but perhaps there was something yet he could do. Marsius motioned the children to join him and they took up places opposite. He placed the text gently on the table and rested one hand on top.

"Here I have one of the texts dealing with craft, and yes, I hope I'm going to show you something interesting. In these pages, there are rituals that can lead you to mastery of certain spells. But you must be prepared to devote your energy to your studies, or mastery will elude you. To start with, I will have to test your knowledge of theory before we have any hope of progressing."

The boy groaned. The princess looked at him blankly.

"Yes, I know," said Marsius. "But without those principles, the spells will be beyond your reach, regardless of how much power or talent you might have. Did the Lector assigned to you test you at all?"

"Some," said Sten. "But he never told us anything. He kept it all to himself. He just did more tests."

Marsius nodded. "All right then. We can avoid the theory for a while in that case. Instead, I want to go through some exercises and see how much talent you possess."

Marsius opened the text to the section on Making and looked up the flame spell. The boy was smiling when he looked up again. The girl was still watching without expression.

"Now, Prince Sten, if you would repeat these words after me. At the same time, concentrate and form the picture of a small burning flame in the palm of your hand. Hold your hand out like so and concentrate on the place where you would have it appear. This may take a few times to get right. Don't be upset if nothing happens at first."

The prince did as he was told without complaint. As Marsius had expected, it took a few attempts to get it right. On about the fourth try, a small bluish guttering flame appeared on Sten's hand, then immediately winked out of existence. The boy chuckled his delight, then became serious.

"Again, another," he said.

"No, not just yet, Prince Sten," said Marsius. "I want to see how your sister performs." The boy glanced at his sister and bit his lip. "Well, Princess Antalya, would you join me?" said Marsius.

The girl looked at him and shook her head. Marsius frowned.

"And why not? I'm here to teach you. Do you not want to be taught?"

She looked at him for a long time before answering. "I don't want to," she said.

Marsius returned her gaze, then turned back to the boy. If that was the way she wanted it, what could he do? He couldn't teach someone against their will, child or not. Nor could he teach anyone without the talent. Perhaps she was ashamed of showing it. Or she might just be shy. Either way, he would have days and weeks to draw her out. With being a girl child, and showing such reticence, she could hardly be expected to perform. Marsius flicked to another exercise and proceeded with the boy.

He ran through several more with Prince Sten, taking up the rest of the morning, and more still in the afternoon. Each showed the boy to have a moderate amount of talent, but nothing superior, nothing out of the ordinary. He certainly had none of his father's. If this was the limit, and the girl was lacking, then he really needn't have worried about the morality of what he was doing.

The boy seemed pleased with himself, so at least that much was progress, but Marsius felt relieved when he finally heard the clank of keys outside the door. He could see himself condemned to day after dreary day tutoring a boy of moderate talent and a girl who may yet have none.

Marsius stood, bowed his head to the prince and the princess in turn, and then walked to the door, his book tucked under his arm.

"Until the morrow," he said to them and quickly stepped out into the corridor.

"Well," said Corum as they walked down the passage together. "How did you get on?"

"Not badly," said Marsius. "I appear to be making headway with the boy, but the girl ... I don't know."

"Aye, I said she was a strange one, didn't I?"

"That you did, Corum. That you did. If only there was some way of reaching her, of getting inside her head so I could find out what's there."

"Not that I'd know anything about teaching, mind," said Corum. "But they've been here nigh on two months now. The boy's all right once you get through those airs and graces, but the girl, she barely says a word."

"Hmm," said Marsius.

"This is where I leave you," said Corum. "If you feel like something to do later, wander down and we can share a mug or two."

"Why, thank you," said Marsius. "But I fear I'll be working this night. I have to put together a detailed training regime for the children and think on ways I might break through that wall."

"Aye, well, it's your choice. The offer is there."

"And I thank you for it, Corum. I thank you."

Marsius watched as the guard made his way down an adjoining corridor, his keys jangling with each step. He stood thinking about the princess for several moments before pursing his lips and turning for his own chambers. Perhaps he should have accepted the guard's offer after all. Corum seemed like a nice enough sort. He shook his head and wandered down to his room.

He closed the door and pulled out his books, then arrayed them neatly on the desk. Trying to ignore the wind shrieking outside the tower walls, he pulled the first book from the stack and started reading through the spells. Spell after spell he scanned, seeking the ones he could use and those he could not. He reached the end of the first volume, laid it to one side and pulled down the next.

When he had at last decided a rough course for the following days, he leaned back, entwined his fingers behind his neck and stared up at the ceiling. If he only had enough power himself, he could use Compulsion to draw the girl to him and test her. He wouldn't be completely content until he knew how much of the Tyrant ran through her veins. There was too much at stake. Unlikely though it was, if she did have some latent talent, it was better that he knew.

Right now, Corum's invitation was sorely tempting. Marsius sighed, scratched his neck, and reached for the third volume in his series. He turned to the chapter that dealt with Compulsion.

•   •   •

Once again, he was seated across the table from the boy. For three weeks now, he had been trying to reach the girl and test her, but at every turn, she had refused him. He had tried Compulsion, but his power had not been strong enough. Each night he searched for more esoteric spells, seeking something to break through that barrier. Whatever the cause, she sat wordlessly, watching, and listening, seeming to pierce him with her gaze on the rare occasions that she looked at him. Marsius had almost given up hope — almost.

The lessons with the boy had been progressing as well as could be expected. Marsius saw himself as a good teacher, but there was only so much one could do. He had been trying to sprinkle the lessons with talk of moral responsibility and the concepts of right and wrong. He tried to instill in the boy a sense of obligation and duty, but the ideas seemed completely beyond the boy's capacity. All he wanted to do was play with the power. It was like a game. For that much, Marsius was grateful. He was starting to believe that the boy would never have the strength of mind to do any real damage. Still, at least some acknowledgment of the drift of morality would have given him some better comfort.

"Prince Sten, will you concentrate please?" he said, as the boy once more got involved in his weaving. They were working on the Makings of Air, the last of the primary spells, and the boy kept getting carried away with his patterns. "It is as important to know when to limit your power as it is to know how to use it."

"I don't understand," said the boy.

"Clearly, Prince Sten," he said, barely disguising his impatience. "Let me put it another way. What if, sometime when you have progressed to the more advanced Makings, you are performing a vast web of Air? Now, what if when you've started the weaving, you did not know how to stop it? What then? You could crush the room and the tower and everyone within it, including yourself. You must know when to stop."

"Oh, I see," he said. He frowned, screwed up his face, and brought the spell back under control.

"Yes, that's it," said Marsius. "It's just as important to control yourself as it is to control the spell. You must know when it is right to stop."

He glanced at the girl, and saw she was looking thoughtful. A slight frown creased her brow. She always looked so serious, lost in her own thoughts. Marsius shook his head and turned back to the boy.

"Sten, I've heard enough," said the princess. "You can stop now." Her brother turned to her and frowned.

"But Antalya, I'm enjoying this," he said.

"No, Sten," she said. "As Marsius has just told you, we must know when it is right to stop. You must know when you have done enough."

Prince Sten bit off his reply and nodded his head.

Marsius frowned. These were the first words she had spoken in days. Why was her brother deferring to her?

"Prince Sten, you must concentrate. We have to continue with your lessons."

The Prince shook his head and turned back to his sister. Marsius frowned and stood. The boy had never refused to cooperate before. He glanced over at the girl.

Princess Antalya's pale face and liquid eyes turned to him. Slowly she spoke.

"No, the time for these games is past, Filindal. You will sit and be quiet."

Marsius felt himself dropping back, his limbs gone slack. Suddenly, he was seated against the stone floor, his head resting against the wall. He could feel the cold through the back of his head.

"And you will not move," she said. He could feel the power in her voice. She was Compelling him!

She got up from the table, walked across to him and held out her hand. Without even a blink, a brightly glowing flame appeared above her palm. It sparked with light and power. She waved her hand and it disappeared. She hadn't even uttered a word of invocation. Her brother moved around the table to join her. They stood there side by side, looking down at him. Marsius realized then that he had been right after all. There had been little to fear from the boy. Very little. How wrong he had been. He felt the cold growing inside, deep in his gut.

He lay back against the wall, trying to rise, but his body refused to obey. He looked up at her small face staring down at him, and the chill of her gaze washed through him.

What have I done?

"You could not have known, Marsius," she said. "As you sat here trying to teach us your petty spells, I walked through your mind. I followed you as you left us each night and watched you in your room. I saw the words you read and the rituals you kept from us. I saw everything there was to see. Although you tried so hard, you gave me everything I needed." She smiled. "And for that, I thank you. We, both of us, thank you."

Marsius tried to move his fingers, but they wouldn't respond. He tried to say something, but his mouth wouldn't work. He was stuck, and by the time the spell wore off it would be too late.

"Yes, much too late," she said. "You were right, Lector Filindal. Perhaps it would have been better to have the both of us done away with."

She turned and took her brother's hand.

"Come, Sten," she said. "We have to go now. We must find a place where we can stay until we're ready. It won't be long now."

The boy nodded, chewing at his lower lip as he glanced down at Marsius.

Marsius watched them leave hand in hand. He was powerless to move, powerless to utter a word, powerless to stop them leaving. And then, they were gone.

He knew with chill certainty that a new Tyrant had been born, but so much stronger than the last. If she had plundered his knowledge, then he was to blame. But, if, as she had said, she had wandered freely through his mind, then she might have seen other things. She might have seen the horrors caused by her father, the death and the suffering, the truth of what was right.

She might have seen.

He heard the icy wind buffeting the walls outside, swirling against the prison's sides.

She might have seen ...

In fifth grade, Tom Howard wrote a story where popular monsters were super-heroes, and he hasn't put the pencil down since. After careers in the Air Force and Corporate America, Tom retired from international banking software to spend time writing science fiction and fantasy short stories. Tom lives in Little Rock, Arkansas, and his four children and grandson give him lots of great story ideas.

•   •   •

Traveling around the world helping banks gave me lots of opportunities for sightseeing and story inspiration. One evening while working in New Orleans, Louisiana, I walked past Plaza D'Italia and an incredible wall mural. As I studied it, I wondered how many people took the time to stop and look at it and what had happened to the people who had.

DEPTH OF FIELD

TOM HOWARD

T HE MURAL SURPRISED NOEL with its beauty and strange perspective. Hidden among deserted warehouses, the wall glowed in the setting sun. The depiction of a twisted Parthenon, although painted on a flat surface, appeared three dimensional. Several stories tall, the building seemed condemned, but the painting of columns and upside-down stairways that would have inspired Escher looked fresh.

Black squares and rectangles dotted the colorful mural, and as Noel stared at one, someone peered down at him. Thinking the artist had integrated the building's existing windows into the artwork, Noel moved closer, but the black patch revealed only paint. The building had no windows. Weird.

Noel took more photographs as the sun sank behind the neighboring buildings. He walked across the patch of overgrown grass separating the building from the sidewalk.

Using his phone, he queried online for information about the mural and downloaded what little he found. A door-sized black rectangle had been painted at ground level, and Noel took a picture before he pressed his hand against it.

And fell through.

The sun's warmth disappeared as Noel picked himself up in the shadows. Grass lay outside the doorway he'd fallen through, but when he tried walking out, he encountered an invisible wall.

"What the hell?" he asked. Had he fallen and hit his head? Was he dreaming?

He stood in a shadowy hallway. The walls, ceiling, and floor appeared matte black. When he touched the walls, his fingertips felt smooth coolness.

Light came from the door and windows set high on the wall, windows Noel had seen as black squares from the outside. Confused, he walked down the corridor, hoping to find another exit. His shoes made no sound as he walked.

"Hello!" he shouted. "Is anybody here?"

A figure appeared in the corridor ahead of him. "Stay calm, dude. It's going to be all right," she said.

She had long curly hair, and wore a paisley shirt and low-riding bell bottoms with a macramé belt. If Noel had hit his head, his dream world could be populated by worse things than hippies. The woman needed a headband and a joint to make the ensemble complete. Maybe circular sunglasses.

"Who are you?" Noel asked. Had he fallen through a time tunnel of some kind and ended up in a commune? Why was it so dark and colorless?

"Reggie, man." She gave Noel the peace sign. "Folks call me Reg. I know this place is confusing, but you're going to be okay." She gestured at the corridors and stairways, all black like the rest of the building's interior. The high windows let in light from outside. "It's easier if you only meet one person when you arrive. Crossing over can be confusing."

"I don't understand," Noel said. "Did something happen? Am I dead?"

"No. Would you like something to eat or drink?" Reg asked. "Maybe a siesta?"

Noel considered it, but he felt fine. "No, I'm okay."

"Inside the Shadowlands, you lose the need for food or rest. I do miss a Tab." Reg led him to a flight of stairs.

Noel followed her. "A Tab? Do they still make those?"

"Well, they did when I arrived, in the sixties. What year are you from?"

"Twenty-twenty-two." Noel pulled out his cellphone to show Reg the date and time.

Her eyes widened in surprise. "Wow. That's a fancy gadget. I bet a lot has happened in sixty years. We'll enjoy hearing how things have changed outside."

"Sixty years?" Noel asked. "Is this a gag? Where are the cameras?"

"Nobody here laughs for very long." She stopped to let Noel enter a large room before her.

Tables and chairs, all black, held people in various styles of clothing. Like all the rooms they'd passed, there were no doors, and the ceilings were so high and dark they seemed invisible. People watched Noel with dull eyes.

Reg pointed to an old man in animal skins sitting in the corner. "Mr. Smith over there has been here the longest. He doesn't talk much."

Noel figured he must be experiencing the most lucid nightmare of his life. People stared, some smiling, some with expressions of sadness. All appeared to have just woken from a nap. Black, white, and every shade of complexion in between, Noel counted several dozen people. At least thirty. Some in suits, several in rags. Even a couple of kids.

"Everyone, this is our newest arrival," Reg said. "Sorry, I didn't catch your name, dude."

"Noel. Noel Jenkins. I'm a security consultant."

"A security consultant?" an old man asked. "What is that? A policeman?"

"That's Professor Barlow," Reg said. "Nineteen forty-three. Noel here is from twenty-twenty-two."

"You're kidding, right?" Noel asked.

Reg shrugged. "Time doesn't pass here in the Shadowlands. All we have to occupy our time is talking to one another. We don't eat, sleep, or drink, but we can teach and learn. Mrs. Nyberg taught us all French. Without a new face once in a while with news of the outside world, we'd go crazy."

"I suspect I already am." Noel must have fallen and hit his head. "Professor, a security consultant is someone who ensures your computer systems are safe."

"Computers?" a young man asked. "Isn't that one of those big machines? Can't be too many of those here in town."

"Almost every home has one now." Even unconscious, Noel felt the need to explain things to figments of his imagination. He held out his cell. "This telephone is a computer." Maybe he should turn it off. There was no telling how long the charge would last in dreamtime.

Several people stepped forward to look at the small screen.

"That's a computer?" someone asked. "It's so small."

"If it's a telephone," someone else asked, "where's the cord?"

"Not needed. Not only is it a telephone, but it stores photographs and connects me with other computers." He tried to find the internet but detected no signal. He turned his cell off to preserve power.

"That's amazing," Professor Barlow said. "With instant communication between people, I guess there's no more war."

Noel wished that was so. "Unfortunately, there are plenty of wars."

He took a seat, feeling like the black walls would topple onto him at any moment. "So, what have you done so far to escape Shadowland?" He might as well play along with his delusion.

"How do you know we have tried?" a teenage girl asked.

"I'm a problem-solver by occupation." Noel smiled at her. "You're a human trapped in a cage. What have you done so far?"

"Miss Carter is being contrary," Reg said. "It's one of her endearing qualities." Her tone said she didn't appreciate Miss Carter's attitude as much as her words implied. "In a world that never ends, we value the art of debate."

"I see," Noel said. "And information is shared? You work together?" If he'd been trapped inside a maze, he'd use all available resources to find a way out. If he wasn't dreaming and had to spend centuries in this place, he'd go mad.

Reg nodded. "We've hiked thousands of miles, bruised our fists against the windows, and even killed ourselves, but nothing worked. The worst part is when it's night outside, and there's no light coming through the windows. We just sit here. I worry about the elders, like Mr. Smith. He moves and speaks less every year."

"We're all breathing, so air can get in." Noel placed his hand on his chest to feel it move up and down. "Maybe we're not really trapped here, but asleep and dreaming somewhere else."

"Possible," the professor said. "This place seems more magic than science."

"Wait," Noel said. "I pulled up material on the painting outside before I came through. Maybe there is some information on this place." Awake or asleep, he couldn't help analyzing problems.

Noel turned on his phone and read the download aloud to the others. "The Tantalus Wall. Artist unknown. First recorded in 1615." He could have let the phone read it to them, but if these people had been stuck here for hundreds of years, a talking box might seem Satan's work.

"There couldn't have been a painting here that early," a woman said. "No town or building existed."

"Painted on a rock wall originally," Noel said. "Attributed to Native Americans, but obviously Greco-Roman. You're right, Professor. This is magic."

"A curse of some kind," Reg said. "Anything else from your little box?"

"No. Several proposals to tear the wall down, but it's always remained. Why would it trap us?"

No one replied, but even Mr. Smith listened.

Noel turned off his phone. "I know better than to ask this, but has every nook and cranny of Shadowlands been checked?"

Reg nodded. "Regularly. It gives us something to do."

"Why is it called Tantalus?" Noel asked. "I remember a Roman legend about him, but I don't recall the details."

"Miss Nyberg?" Reg asked.

A little white-haired lady in a French bun stood. "Greek, not Roman. Tantalus was a wicked king who killed his son and served him at a feast to the gods, to see if they were really omniscient. Zeus' punishment deemed he'd go thirsty and hungry in Hades, despite standing in a pool of water and being just out of reach of a fruit tree."

That didn't help. "Maybe Reg is right, and it's some kind of curse," Noel said. "Like the king, we see the outside world, but we can't reach it. Are we in hell?"

"I don't know," Miss Nyberg said. "Tantalus' followers formed a cult that believed in cannibalism and filicide. Perhaps they built this as a safe place for their outlawed cult."

"It's a long way from Athens," Reg said.

"Zeus would never have allowed them to meet there," Miss Nyberg said. "Perhaps, rather than destroying it, he moved their meeting place to the new world."

"Not realizing it would be populated one day," the professor said.

A shout tore through the air, and everyone jumped.

"What is that?" Noel asked.

"Shadowland's uncivilized folk," Reg said. "They show up when someone new arrives."

Noel stood as a group of people rushed into the room. Like the citizens he'd met, the intruders consisted of many shapes and sizes, and wore clothing from different time periods. They also all wore headbands torn from their own clothing.

A short man with dark hair and a red silk tie wrapped around his head pointed at Noel. "How much?"

Reg sighed. "Not for sale, Abraham. He's from twenty-twenty-two and will entertain us for years."

"I'll trade you a professional storyteller and a movie critic for him."

Reg shook her head. "Not for sale."

"We will have him." Abraham held up his fists, and his fellows followed suit.

"What is going on?" Noel asked. "Who are these people?"

"Believers in the Great Shadow," Reg said. "They think this place is heaven. They use people like currency, leaving them wrung dry and wandering the corridors until we take them in. The Believers don't want to find a way out."

"Destroy the unbelievers!" Abraham screamed and jumped atop a table. His people rushed into the room and pummeled everyone within reach. "Capture the newcomer."

Reg sighed, removed her macramé belt, and waded into the mob.

To Noel, it felt like a rehearsed play, with people scuffling until everyone lay unconscious or exhausted on the floor. He stood back, unsure of what to do. Surely, these people had more constructive things to occupy their time than fisticuffs. Maybe not.

Two Believers, a man and a woman, grabbed Noel and pulled him toward the doorway. He struggled to free himself. He had no desire to be questioned for decades by kidnappers.

"Help Noel!" Reg cried. She pushed Abraham out of the way and punched the man who held Noel. Several of the others left their opponents and yanked him free.

Noel jumped on a table. "We've had a black president!"

Everyone froze. Several people of color looked shocked, then pleased.

"Marijuana is now legal in twenty-three states, Reg."

"You're kidding," Reg said. "Next thing you'll tell me the Vietnam War is over."

"We lost," Noel said.

"Twenty-three states? No way." Reg unwrapped her macramé belt from a big guy's neck. He gasped and sat up.

"Yes," Noel said. "And it looks as if the others will follow. Some of them allow medicinal marijuana only, but you look a little run down, Reggie."

She laughed. "All the time, dude."

"What else?" Abraham asked. "Have aliens destroyed the White House? Do we have a hundred states?"

Noel resisted lying. "No. Sorry. We almost had a female president, and Europe is now one union."

"What about the USSR?" one of the Believers asked.

"That's enough free information." Reg held up her hands. "If you want to learn more, sit down. We're not going anywhere. Otherwise, go back to your floor."

Abraham and the others grumbled but leaned against the walls.

"First," Noel said, "let's find out what time periods we represent. Everyone, sit by your date of arrival in Shadowland, starting with Mr. Smith." Maybe if Noel saw the big picture, he could come up with some suggestions. That's why he was good at his job.

The Believers grumbled, but exchanged places with the others. When asked, Mr. Smith thought he'd entered in the late 1700s. Next to him sat a couple who had arrived together in the 1840s. As the town grew in population, more people became trapped. The professor lived in the 40s, Miss Nyberg, the 50s. An influx of people arrived in the 60s through the 80s, but Noel couldn't believe only one person had come through after that, a young Believer from 2005. As the neighborhood ran down, less foot traffic passed. More likely, people became too busy to stop and study a mural.

"We know your next question," Reg said. "It's the one we all ask. Why capture some of us, when hundreds, maybe thousands, of people have stopped to look at the painting outside?"

"It's a good question," Noel said. "Did you have an answer?"

"It's obvious," Miss Carter said. "We've each eaten a human or killed a child."

It must be hell to have decades of experience in a young person's body.

"No," Reg said. "We're not Tantalus cultists, Miss Contrary. We think it's because we studied the painting. There's a primary path that allows you entry."

"Makes sense," Noel said. "But if the cultists used the painting to enter, what did they use to leave?"

"We don't know," Reg said.

"There isn't a way to leave," Abraham said. "We should be here. We're immortal. Nothing hurts us. Finding a way out is blasphemy."

"Yet you crave news from recent arrivals," Noel said. "That doesn't seem very heavenly to me."

"Okay, savior," Abraham said, "show us how to get out of here."

Noel held up his hands. "I'm trapped like the rest of you. If you've been looking for answers for centuries, I can't hope to find the key on my first day."

"If it's still your first day," Reg said. "If we don't look out the windows occasionally, we can't tell what season it is. What next, Noel?"

He hadn't intended to take over as project manager and hoped he hadn't insulted anyone. They'd tried to solve this puzzle for decades. But he didn't want to end up drooling in the corner with Mr. Smith in a couple centuries.

"Ideas!" Noel shouted to get their attention. "I want to hear your thoughts on how to get out of here. No suggestion is too extreme. Everyone has input."

"How about we make a sign and ask for help from outside?" Miss Carter asked.

"That's a stupid idea unless you brought poster board and a marker with you," Abraham said.

Noel shook his head. "No idea is off the table. We have cloth and someone had to bring something to write with. It's doable."

"Kill Abraham and thrust him out the door," someone suggested, and several people mumbled agreement.

Miss Nyberg held up her hand. "If Zeus banished this place from Greece thousands of years ago, maybe we can summon him to do it again."

Interesting. "How would we do that?" Noel asked.

"It would involve a sacrifice," she said, "to get his attention. It has to be a pleasing sacrifice for him to grant a boon."

"But you said no one dies here," Noel said.

"True," Reg said. "We lay around for a while but soon are back on our feet." She looked to a passageway above. "I've jumped from there dozens of times. I remember leaping, but I never recall the landing."

"Blood?" Noel asked. Might be necessary for a sacrifice.

Reg shook her head.

"I'll do it," Mr. Smith said. "I'm ready to go. Kill me and put me on an altar before I come back."

"What else do we need, Miss Nyberg?" Noel asked.

"I'm no expert," she said, "but a fire, priests, and maybe chanting?"

Reg shook her head. "No fire here. No smoke. It's hell."

"It's unlikely Zeus is waiting around for us to call," Noel said. "So, let's find out how the cultists came and went. They entered by studying the mural and finding the primary path, but how did they leave?" Their theory about cultists might be completely wrong, but it had both groups working together and alert.

"We won't help you," Abraham said. "We'll return to our area."

"You don't want to hear about how the Washington Nationals won the World Series?" Noel asked. "Or who Elizabeth

Taylor's last husband was?" He smiled at Reg when Abraham stopped. Knowledge was power.

The Believers' leader sat. "Okay. What's your plan?"

Noel couldn't come up with a suggestion they hadn't already considered a hundred times, but he had to try. "If they studied a painting to get in, maybe there's a painting to get out."

"There's nothing near the door," Reg said. "We've checked a thousand times."

"Perhaps the light is too weak," Noel said. "My phone has a flashlight. It might show us something you couldn't see in the darkness."

He led the group to the doorway where he'd entered Shadowlands. The crowd stood back as he ran the light over the walls, the floor, and the distant ceiling.

Nothing.

He stared at his phone. There had to be something in the magic box to help. Why have all this wonderful technology if it couldn't provide them with a way out? All he'd done so far was use valuable battery power. It read below 50%.

He flipped through the other features on his phone, pausing at the photos he'd taken. He stared at them. It couldn't be that simple.

"What if the cultists brought a picture with them when they entered?" he asked Reg. "And used it to leave."

"They didn't have magic boxes like yours," she said.

"They wouldn't need one. All they'd require is a piece of parchment with the pattern drawn on it." He pulled up a photo he'd taken of the mural from outside. "Here, Reg. Follow the black line in this picture from bottom to top. The dark path is the longest one."

"Wait," Abraham said. "If we leave, will we become the age we should be? Will time fall on us? Mr. Smith and others would crumble to dust."

Mr. Smith stepped forward. "I'd trade an eternity of darkness for one moment of fresh air. Open the door, Noel."

"Reg," Noel said, "you go first. Even if you age after sixty years, you might still be alive and can help the others when they come through. I don't know if we can get everyone out before my battery dies. If you make it through, the next person should try without looking at the picture."

"Anyone who wants to go, get in line," Reg said.

Everyone formed up, including Abraham and his followers. They'd removed their headbands.

"Here we go." Noel showed Reg the image and waited for her to follow the mural's primary path with her eyes.

She immediately moved to the door but fell back when she tried to go through.

"Follow the black line from top to bottom this time," he said.

Reg stared at the screen, took a deep breath, and stepped through the door. They could see her clearly as she danced and shouted outside. They couldn't hear her. She did not grow any older as they watched.

Miss Carter rushed through the door but bounced back.

"One at a time then." Noel held the image up for the young woman to study before she ran through the opening to join Reg.

Power down to 45%. With over fifty people to get through the door, they'd never make it.

"Next," he said. "Let's try two at a time."

It didn't work. The doorway had rules.

"Next." He couldn't leave anyone behind. "Miss Nyberg, a word."

The woman approached as Noel sent the 1880 couple through one at a time. "Bring the children to the front and think of a way to draw the pattern on the wall. My phone's battery won't last long enough to send everyone through."

She nodded and moved back up the line, pulling out the children and sending them to the front. When she reached the end, she disappeared into the shadows.

Noel shoved them through as fast as he could, but some of them, especially the children, had difficulty tracing the convoluted path on the little screen after so long being inside. At 40% power, the children clustered around Reg and Miss Carter outside.

Miss Nyberg reappeared, and Noel multi-tasked, showing Abraham the screen while the professor stepped through.

"Noel," Miss Nyberg said, "will this work?"

She held up a stick of lipstick.

"Miss Nyberg," he said. "I could kiss you."

She blushed.

Noel didn't wonder how she knew of its existence. After a few decades, everyone probably knew everything people had brought with them.

Miss Nyberg turned to the wall. "Show me the miniature."

He hated stopping the line, but 2005 looked over his shoulder and exited. Others followed suit. 25%.

"Just draw the dark line," he said, and Miss Nyberg drew the primary path in a series of loops and lines on the wall.

Noel's phone lost its charge rapidly toward the end. He turned it for Mr. Smith to see. The old man hadn't lost all his faculties. He stepped through the doorway into fading sunlight.

"You go next, Miss Nyberg." He turned off his cell. "Thank you for your help."

"I've sent people to search for stragglers." She studied the lipstick map before kissing him on the cheek and joining the crowd outside.

"Okay, folks," he said. "Look at the map on the wall before you go through." Miss Nyberg had done a great job of reducing the stairways and arches into a linear blueprint. Much simpler. And faster.

"Keep moving," Noel said. Since he'd been the last one in, he'd be the last one out. The line grew shorter and shorter as two young men escorted the last few confused Shadowland occupants toward the door.

Noel stood alone after everyone had gone through. For a second, he considered staying. Would he trade a life of immortality here for a rat race out there?

He turned on his phone as he walked through the door. "Hello, 911."

Philip Brian Hall is a graduate of Oxford University. A former diplomat and teacher, he's had short stories published in The USA, Canada, and The UK. His work has appeared in numerous anthologies as well as magazines and online publications. His novels, The *Prophets of Baal* and *The Family Demon* are available in paperback and digital editions.

•   •   •

It's said that a certain Neil Christy picked up Wild Bill Hickok's cards from the floor after he was shot in the back by Jack McCall. Everyone agrees Hickok held two pair: aces over eights, but, according to Christy's son, the "death card", the ace of spades, was not among them. It was actually the ace of diamonds. Superstition has "corrected" history, but maybe Christy knew what he was talking about. What if the Dead Man's Hand actually held out the prospect of untold riches — for the whole human race?

DEAD MAN'S HAND

PHILIP BRIAN HALL

R OPER ALMOST MISSED IT.
It wasn't just that the giant transport was painted black and barely scanner-reflective. He was preoccupied at the time.

The strange ship chose to loom out of an opaque pink cloud of interstellar gas during Roper's regular afternoon poker game. So far, Roper owed Connie fifty thousand dollars, but he was holding his first good hand for ages: two pair, aces over eights.

Regular players call these cards Dead Man's Hand, in honor of the late Wild Bill Hickok, who was holding them when he was shot in the back. It seemed appropriate. Six months after the wreck of the *Hesperus*, the escape pod's essential supplies were almost exhausted; Roper fully expected to die of starvation within the month, and he didn't see the point of dying rich.

Of course, Connie didn't need the money either.

"There's a ship," she said. "I've commenced recording the contact on all channels, as per standard procedure."

"No fair trying to distract me!" Roper snapped. "Are you sure your program doesn't allow cheating?"

"The program does, but I don't," the computer replied. "There *is* a ship. Forty degrees up; twenty-three-degree angle on the port bow. A very large, very old freighter."

"Hail her."

"I have. No response on any channel. Her computer's in sleep mode and slow to wake up. She's definitely human-built, but not in any of the colonies. It looks as though she comes from Earth."

"Earth!" Roper raised his eyebrows. "That's scarcely credible. How long ago?"

"Her design suggests around two hundred years before the evacuation. That's about five centuries all told."

"Wow!" Roper exhaled slowly.

"There's one human life-sign aboard."

"What?" Roper's jaw dropped further. "Somebody's *alive* on a ship launched five hundred years ago?"

"It's a very weak sign. Maybe this is a generation ship that somehow ran out of time?"

"Okay."

To find one of those slow old vessels was rare, but not unprecedented. The early interstellar explorers had usually launched their under-powered generation ships towards potentially habitable planets; their descendants were invariably astonished to find much more technologically-advanced human settlements already well established there when they finally reached it.

"Headed where?"

"On her current course, she'll reach the Sirius system in two more years."

"Damn! That's unlucky. They nearly made it," said Roper.

By the time Connie maneuvered their little craft into close proximity with the black ship, Roper was already suited and waiting impatiently by the airlock. He hadn't dared hope to meet another vessel this far out. Since he was as good as dead already, even if the strange ship's crew had died of bubonic plague, he'd nothing much to lose.

A slight bump as the pod touched down on the giant ship's hull, then silence. No challenge or acknowledgment.

"There's an airlock ten feet from our bows," Connie reported. "I would have docked right over it, but it's none of our standard sizes. It should open manually from the outside; these old ones usually do. I've woken up the ship's computer sufficiently to restore interior emergency lighting, but her operating system's very primitive and she's still drowsy. If I hurry her too much, she might crash or lock up. I'll let you know as soon as I've full access."

"Where's the life sign?" Roper asked.

"In the aft hold. That's to your left as soon as you're inside. It's about a hundred yards long."

•   •   •

Within the ship, there was weak artificial gravity, and atmosphere of a sort. The air smelled of mold, decaying like a long-sealed medieval crypt, but it was breathable; Roper opened his helmet to conserve his suit's air.

Walking the length of the hold, moving with giant, bounding strides, he soon realized this was not a generation ship. More bizarre yet, it appeared to be a cryogenic experiment on the scale of a small town. Each passenger was enclosed in a hermetically-sealed bubble-pack and deep-frozen while suspended upside down from something resembling a giant clothes rail.

Row upon row the passengers hung there, lines of inverted bodies receding into the dim distance like sides of meat in some fairy-tale giant's cold-store. *Fee-fi-fo-fum! Bring me a frozen Englishman!*

Roper's hopes of finding a survivor faded. He'd read about cryonic technology somewhere; great things were once hoped from it, but it turned out to be a scientific blind alley. Even after researchers found a solute that would prevent the formation of neural-network-destroying ice crystals, anoxic damage during deanimation turned the brain to mush, meaning no revival had never progressed beyond a vegetative state.

So why, without any evidence of successful reanimation, had someone gone to all the trouble and expense of launching an interstellar ship embodying the technology? Blind faith in miracles? Unless the builder knew something the rest of humanity didn't, this great icy mausoleum was no more than a costly exercise in wishful thinking.

"Connie, as I expect the helmet-cam's telling you, this hold's full of cryonically-stored bodies," Roper said. "Could you be getting human life-signs from one of them?"

"Not from a dead body, no," Connie replied. "That is, not if the subject was dead before vitrification."

"You sure?"

"A very early version of my software was tested on one of the cryo-catacombs left behind on Earth by the ancients."

"And?"

"Just frozen corpses. But no computer's ever scanned bodies that were alive when the process was initiated."

"Do I sense a 'however'?"

"According to my readings, these passengers are all dead now, except for one. There's residual metabolic activity, very slow but steady, somewhere in that hold."

"Definitely coming from one of these human popsicles?" asked Roper skeptically.

"Yes."

"And how am I supposed to tell which one? There are thousands."

"I can see that. The ship's computer's very agitated. She thinks a glitch in her programming let her sleep through a catastrophic cryo-failure. Apparently, the subjects should all be displaying green lights on the suspension apparatus. A red light means an emergency."

"They're all bloody red!" Roper snorted.

"Try looking, Roper," said Connie. "One should still be green. Two lines to your right and 78 places in from the bulkhead."

The green light belonged to a curvaceous woman of indeterminate age. At the time of her vitrification, she might have been anywhere between a natural twenty-five and a youthful fifty-five. Like all the rest, she wore a sky-blue, rubberized garment covering her from neck to ankles, and a golden circlet around her temples. Her long black hair had been tightly wound into a neat chignon and her eyes were closed.

"Found her," Roper reported.

"So I see," said Connie.

"Well? What do I do now?" he demanded.

"According to the ship's computer, nothing. This one doesn't require attention. All the others do."

"That's not helpful. I find myself strangely lacking in a morbid desire to prove all these stiffs are actually dead."

"Well, it seems the revival system's automatic and built into their clothes. If I can override the program, release the suspension mechanism and lower the subject to the ground, the bubble-pack should open of its own accord. All you have to do is watch."

"I'm good with that," said Roper.

•　　•　　•

"Who the hell are you?" the woman said, almost the instant her eyes flicked open.

Roper wasn't expecting the frozen body to regain consciousness at all, let alone issue a challenge. "Roper, Nat Roper," he stammered.

"At least you understand English. But you're not a crew member." It was not a question.

"No. A shipwreck survivor just come aboard. I was chief engineer of the starship *Hesperus*. My escape pod drifted across your course an hour or so ago."

"Starship? What in blue blazes is that? Wait a minute. What year is this?"

"Year? Oh, you mean the old Earth calendar. I'm not sure exactly, but Connie reckons you left home about five hundred years ago."

"Who's Connie?"

"My computer."

"I see. So are we in the Sirius system?"

"Not yet."

"Then why in the name of all that's holy did you wake me up?"

"Ah ... because you seem to be a sole survivor too. Yours was the only green light in the hold."

"What?" The woman's voice rose an octave. "Did you try reviving any of the others?"

"There didn't seem much point."

"And who are you to judge? Some sort of cryogenics expert?"

"No, I'm not, but Connie is."

"Your computer?"

"Yes."

"What does *this* ship's computer say?"

"Not a lot. She's slow to wake up apparently."

"Nonsense!" The woman sat up abruptly. "Anastasia!"

"Please state your requirements." A stilted mechanical voice ground out the words as if speaking a foreign language.

"Emergency. Revive 3246."

"Revive 3246 ... confirmed."

The suspended body adjacent to the woman's newly-vacated place was gently lowered to the ground. The bubble-pack peeled away of its own accord, revealing the figure of a tall, well-built, dark-haired man. Initially, he didn't stir. Then, to Roper's surprise, his eyes opened. Yet he seemed unable to focus.

"Uh," he said.

"You see," the woman clapped her hands. "He's alive. Come on, Derek, wake up. It's me, Pamela."

"Uh. Tsark oggle," the man said.

"What's that? Derek, wake up," Pamela reiterated, suddenly concerned.

"Tsark oggle. Brawfigget!"

"Roper!" Connie called. "He's speaking Graak!"

"Shit!" Roper exclaimed. "What do I do?"

"Don't touch him! Don't let the woman touch him!"

Roper seized Pamela just in time to prevent her taking the man in her arms. She was too weak to struggle but protested loudly as he dragged her out of reach.

"What the hell do you think you're doing? That's my fiance! He needs help!"

"He's beyond help!" Roper snapped. "Do you have guns aboard?"

"What? Why do you want to know?"

"Because he's highly contagious. If we don't kill him, and quickly, he'll infect us too. Come on! We have to get out of here and secure the hatch from outside!"

Picking up the still-complaining woman in his arms, Roper bounded to the bulkhead in five huge leaps as the newly-awakened man struggled slowly to his feet.

●　　　●　　　●

"Graaks are parasitic aliens the size of microbes," Roper explained. He was still physically restraining the woman, who was struggling to get back into the hold from the deck to which he'd carried her, a utility area where they'd taken temporary sanctuary. "A whole swarm of them invade a single human, destroy the personality, and then establish a hive mind that uses what's left of the brain to control the host body."

"Well, we have to get them out of him!"

"There's no known cure for Graak infestation," Roper said, striving to keep his voice calm. "We lost three whole colonies to them. Apparently healthy settlers traveling from the Graak home planet carried spores to the next world and then the next. In the end, their spread could only be contained by quarantining the planets they'd already reached. That meant battleships blasting every spacecraft full of refugees that tried to lift off."

"Ugh! That's disgusting!"

"Yes. But there was no other way."

"So *you* say. How do you know their language?"

"We monitored surface communications while we were enforcing the blockades."

"So there's no-one who's actually met one of the sufferers. That means you can't possibly *know* the personality's destroyed. Derek might still be alive."

"Graaks *eat* the sentient parts of the brain. Autopsies proved that before we realized how virulent the infection was. If Derek's speaking their language, it means the hive mind is established; they've been in him a long time. Don't ask me how; I don't know. Either they're capable of invading a cryo-stored body, or he was infected before he was vitrified."

"That's nonsense! I'd have noticed something."

"You mean the same way our people were able to distinguish infected refugees from healthy ones? Graaks are almost impossible to detect before they have total control."

"But there *weren't* any Graaks on Earth!"

"Unlikely, I agree. Most Earth colonies have no Graak problems. I don't know how this happened. Maybe your crew picked up a lifeboat, like mine, after you were all frozen, only this one came with some undesirable extra freight? Maybe you were boarded by infected pirates? Who knows?"

"You mean it's ancient history and we'll never find out?"

"I shouldn't think so. You want to know the irony of this whole mess?"

"I'm sure you're keen to tell me."

"Uh-huh. Apparently, the Graaks caught a lucky break. They'd almost exterminated their indigenous host race when humans arrived on their planet. There was no natural alternative host. A few more years and the filthy things would have been extinct."

"Look, this is all very well, but I don't care a fig about exobiological history. Don't you understand? I have to do something!"

"Then find me a gun."

"I won't let you kill Derek!"

"Derek's already dead," Roper insisted. "That's just his body in there."

Pamela glared at him. "If you can't recognize infection in its early stages, then how do you know I'm not infected too?"

"I don't."

"What?" Pamela suddenly looked uncertain, as though the idea had never occurred to her.

"If you are, Connie will tell me as soon as she detects the infestation. By then you'll have infected me. Graaks spread by physical contact. But before I lose control of myself, I'll find a way to destroy this ship and everything on it."

"And you're good with that?" Pamela looked shocked.

"I told you. I was drifting in an escape pod in an uninhabited region of space. I was as good as dead. I'd accepted the fact."

"You're a cold-blooded bastard, aren't you, Roper?"

"Just a realist," Roper said. "It goes with the job."

•   •   •

A loudspeaker recessed into the hatch buzzed briefly. The computer's grating, mechanical voice issued from it. "Pamela? Pamela, are you there?"

The woman looked up. "Of course I'm here, Anastasia. Where did you expect me to be?"

"Pamela, it's not Anastasia," the voice replied. "It's me!"

"Derek?" Her face lit up. "Derek, is that you? Oh, Derek, he told me you were dead."

"It's not Derek," Roper snapped. "Derek can talk, can't he? Why would he be speaking through the computer?"

"Don't listen to him, Pamela," the computer voice croaked hoarsely. "Of course it's me. Why did you run away? I was barely awake and all of a sudden you were gone. Pamela, you can't possibly be afraid of *me*."

The woman sprang to the hatch and desperately clawed at its release mechanism. Roughly, Roper dragged her aside. "I tell you it's not him! The Graaks are using Anastasia to translate their language."

"I don't believe you!"

"Listen to me! They're using your computer. That means they likely heard what I said about destroying the ship. Naturally, they don't want you to let me."

"But he knows my name," Pamela protested, tears of impotent rage starting down her cheeks. Again she struggled vainly to reach the hatch.

"For pity's sake, think! Your name was the first thing you told them when you revived Derek's body. '*It's me, Pamela,*' you said"

Pamela stopped struggling. She pushed herself away from Roper, staring at him with loathing. "Do you think I don't know my own fiance?"

"That's exactly what I think. Of course, you *want* to believe it's Derek, but it's not. If you don't believe me, test him. Ask him something absolutely personal. Something only Derek can answer. Ask him where you first made love."

"What? With you playing gooseberry?"

"It's not going to be embarrassing, Pamela, because he isn't going to know."

The woman grimaced. "Derek, did you hear that? Tell him where it was."

"That was a long time ago, Pamela."

"Sure," Roper said, "five hundred years. Now answer the god-damn question!"

"I need some time to think," the mechanical voice said.

"No you don't," Roper snarled. "That's one thing no man needs time to think about."

"In the back of your parents' Buick?" the voice suggested.

Roper looked at Pamela. She shook her head sadly.

"That's the computer guessing," Roper said. "It will have accessed all the romance novels in the ship's library. It's offering you a typical location because the only alternative is to say nothing at all. If we wait long enough it may even work its way round to the right one."

"No," Pamela said. "I don't think so. And what's more, the real Derek would never have made a suggestion like that."

"You're sure?"

"Quite sure. We've never made love. We agreed to wait."

"Pamela!" said the computer voice. "I made a mistake. Pamela, I'm only just awake, you have to believe me. It's me."

"No," Pamela sighed forlornly. "No, I'm afraid it's not."

•   •   •

"Connie, can we stop this ship's computer reviving any more of the passengers?" Roper asked. "If Pamela's was the only green light, then in all probability the rest will be just like Derek."

"Since they're dead, there's no alternative way to reanimate their bodies, Roper," Connie replied, "And he's already started on that. There are a dozen of them active now. The ship has very little power, but he doesn't need a whole lot. The best I can do is slow them down by DDoS — that's overloading Anastasia with requests for information."

Roper nodded thoughtfully. "We need to keep the Graaks in the hold while we figure out what's happened here," he said to Pamela. "There has to be some reason your light stayed green when all the rest turned red. I've never heard of anyone being revived from cryo-storage, but you're living proof it is survivable. So why didn't the others survive and how were they infected?"

"I've no idea, Roper. I'm not a doctor."

"What about the crew? Connie, can you help with that?"

"The lifeboats are all gone, Roper. The crew abandoned the ship before she cleared the Solar System's asteroid belt. She's been on automatic for centuries."

"No!" Pamela gasped. "They were supposed to rotate through shorter periods of cryo-sleep than us. They told us there'd always be enough of them awake to work the ship."

"Did the passengers pay a lot to be aboard?"

"Derek and I sold all we had, and we still needed help from our parents. It was the hottest ticket in town. In fact, it was a worldwide craze. Leave behind a dying Earth; start a new life among the stars."

"Add that to a highly-speculative technology sold to you as foolproof, and a crew that bailed after a few weeks? I suspect what we have here is a giant interstellar scam."

"But the technology does work! I'm still alive."

"Yes, but out of how many thousand passengers? Possibly there *were* others who might have survived, but never got the chance; it's unlikely we'll ever know. But even if *some* of your fellow-travelers *were* capable of reanimation when they were infected, one thing is clear- if the Graaks *could* have taken you along with the others, they *would* have. Something stopped them. We need to find out what that was."

"Do you want me to start with blood and DNA tests?" Connie inquired.

"Wouldn't she have to come to you for that, Connie?" Roper asked. "We've only one suit at the moment."

"Try forward two compartments, Roper- the crew room behind the navigation bridge. If any crew suits have been left behind, that's where they'll be. They won't be the latest technology of course, but they should be well preserved. There's no reason they won't be usable."

A hammering began to echo on the far side of the hatch, signaling a good reason to put more distance between them and the frustrated Graaks. Roper growled annoyance and helped Pamela to her feet. The two refugees began a slow trek forward in search of greater security.

The ship's sanatorium was the very next compartment. It possessed enough advanced equipment to supply the needs of a small hospital; none of it seemed to have been used.

"This place was included in our grand tour before we were frozen," said Pamela. "The ship's supposed to be designed in segments that can be separated into individual buildings when we reach a suitable planet."

"There's a prefabricated crane in one of the holds," Connie observed.

"The engine room was to be our first power station," Pamela said. "The cryo-hold should convert into an apartment block; this section we're in is the community hospital, and so on. They showed us a diorama of the planned settlement; it was going to be really beautiful."

"All the best scams are," Roper acknowledged. "Who knows, maybe the settlement could even have been built. It was just easier and more profitable not to bother."

"It makes me sick to think how we were taken in."

"Yes." Roper stroked his chin. "But if the ship really is segmented, that design feature could help save our lives. There'll be some relatively straightforward way of splitting the sections apart. Explosive bolts would be the simplest and most labor-saving."

"I suppose so."

"Connie, can you access the ship's plans and find out if we can possibly uncouple ourselves from the hold before the Graaks get out?"

"I've just done that, Roper. It's not designed to be done in space, obviously; you'll be left with no engines. But the crew quarters are airtight and self-contained. There seems to be a good quantity of supplies left in the forward section too. If you shut down all unnecessary systems the batteries will give you years of power."

"Enough to reach Sirius?"

"Easily."

"So how do I dump the tail section?"

"From a control panel on the navigation deck. If you'd like to leave Pamela here, I can take her through the medical tests while I show you how to split the ship at the same time."

Roper looked to Pamela for agreement.

"I suppose there's no other way?" she asked.

"Not that I can see. And even if we do manage to separate, the two sections will still be on the same course at the same speed. But we'll have put a crucial bit of empty space between us and the Graaks. They won't just be able to force a hatch open, which is all they need to do now. With luck, that bit of space should hold them until either we find some way of destroying the tail section, or ..."

"Or we discover we're infected too, and we have to destroy the whole ship," Pamela completed for him.

Roper nodded grimly.

•   •   •

"Immune? How's that possible?" Roper marveled. He'd returned to the sanatorium after successfully completing the operation of splitting the ship into two sections.

"As best I can tell, because she spent her childhood in West Africa," said Connie. "That was a jungle area on old Earth, you know? She contracted but survived two virulent fevers, Ebola and Dengue, and she has the antibodies for both in her blood. That made her unique on the ship's passenger list. She's also unique in the history of human space colonies."

"Because, as a strict rule, no-one who'd suffered serious illnesses was allowed on any expeditions," Roper completed.

"But I was allowed on this one because I had money," Pamela said wryly. "Where there's a bill there's a way."

"So that's why she wasn't infected?" Roper asked.

"And also why she survived reanimation," Connie added. "It turns out the two sets of fever antibodies were just sufficiently well-adapted to fight off the Graak infestation, but, by the time they did that, the Graaks had already reinstated her neural network in preparation for colonizing her body. They hadn't at that stage begun feeding."

"So now I'm immune to all three?" Pamela inquired.

"More than that," Connie explained. "If we can get you to Sirius, the specialist Graak research facility they have there will be able to use your blood as the basis of the first ever effective anti-Graak vaccine. You can protect the whole human race."

"Oh my god! We'll be able to put a stop to the Graak plague once and for all!" Roper exclaimed. "No more enforced quarantines; no more massacres of refugees! Pamela, you're the answer everyone's been looking for. We have to get you to Sirius at all costs."

"It's nice to be appreciated," said Pamela, frowning. "But if you're telling me Graaks effectively eat their hosts' personalities, then this vaccine, even when we have it, can't possibly reverse existing infestations."

"No. But palliative medicine is far less important than vaccine."

"I guess."

"But our problem is, there's no way the Graaks on board with us won't figure out a way to cross the gap between the two sections of the ship in the two years it'll take us to get to Sirius without engines. Hell, I'd be surprised if it takes them two weeks."

"What are we going to do?"

"I don't know. Connie, what's the power plant on this ship?"

"Twin nuclear reactors," the computer replied. "Shut down when the crew bailed out. She's been coasting ever since."

"But the fuel will still have some life in it?"

"Oh yes. You want to use the engines to get to Sirius quicker, Roper? I'm not sure they'll be all that easy to start up after five hundred years."

"I wasn't thinking of *starting* them up, Connie. More blowing them up."

"What?" Pamela exclaimed. "You're crazy!"

"In purely mechanical terms, blowing them up might be easier," Connie replied. "In fact starting them up and blowing them up might amount to pretty much the same thing, in practice."

"But you'll blow us up with them!" Pamela protested.

"If we turn around the stern section and start the engines, with luck they'll be too far away to do us any damage by the time they blow."

"And how exactly will you turn them around?"

"Connie?" Roper inquired.

"If we use all the pod's remaining fuel, we can push the ship's stern around just like a tug pushes a big ship in port," the computer replied. "We'd only be pushing against inertia, after all. Maybe not a complete 180 degrees, but certainly enough."

"Just 90% of the fuel, Connie," Roper demurred. "I need you to leave yourself enough to hop across the gap between sections. I hope I'll be making that jump with you, but at least one of us has to be in the forward section to make sure Pamela gets to Sirius and has a chance to explain herself. We don't want mankind's best hope blasted to bits by some over-zealous quarantine enforcer."

"Hey! Is that really likely?" Pamela exclaimed.

"I'd rather be safe than sorry," Roper said.

$$\bullet \qquad \bullet \qquad \bullet$$

"There's activity in the utility deck," said Connie. "That's the rear end of your section."

"Graaks?" Roper demanded.

"I guess so. No life signs, but some sort of brute force is being applied to the hatchway access to the sanatorium. It will hold for an hour or so."

"Could the Graaks have found some suits in the stern section? They surely can't have got across the gap between the two sections without; *they* may not need to breathe but their host bodies do."

"According to the manifest, there *were* no suits outside the crew area."

"And the crew lockers are empty."

"It's possible suits were accidentally misplaced, but rather more likely some Graaks were already across when you blew the bolts and split the ship. They've probably decided they've got a better chance of overcoming you than making it back to the stern section."

"Pamela!" the mechanical voice of the ship's computer grated. "It's me, Derek. Let me in. Please, Pamela. I need to talk to you."

"Dammit! You're not Derek," Pamela hissed. "Leave me alone!"

"Why are you taking sides against me, Pamela? You don't know this man. He's lying to you. The Graaks are our friends. Without them, you wouldn't be alive."

"No, that's true. And it's because they left me alive they're using you to kill me. Derek, if there's any vestige of the man I loved left in you, make them stop."

"You don't know what you're saying, Pamela. I'll prove it to you as soon as you let me in." The thing that wasn't Derek banged on the hatch with something metallic.

"Huh, and in an hour or two he'll get in even if you don't open the hatch," Roper growled. "He's playing for time. I'll get some heavy equipment to help build a barricade." Looking hard into Pamela's eyes and receiving a firm nod in reply, Roper pressed a finger to his lips and headed forward to the crew airlock.

"Fine," said Pamela. "I got nothing better to do than stand guard over this stupid hatch. Maybe I'll recite Shakespeare to my guy. You do remember how much you liked Shakespeare, don't you Derek?"

"Of course!" the grating voice replied.

"Sure you do," Pamela shook her head. "Say, do you remember this one?

So shaken as we are, so wan with care,
Find we a time for frighted peace to pant ..."

•   •   •

The ship's internal hatches were not double doors, but every single hatch was airtight, serving a similar purpose to watertight doors between sections of an ancient terrestrial ship. Glancing across the gap between the two halves from where he stood on the outer skin of the forward section, Roper could see a gaping aperture in the bulkhead facing him. The empty door frame would have let the air out of the deck he'd first entered, the one immediately forward of the freezer hold. The pod still sat where he'd left it, astern of the now-redundant airlock in the stern's outer skin.

As he'd expected, a single hatch door alone was retaining the air in the after-most deck of the forward section, the utility room adjoining the hospital. His circuitous route to the gap between the two parts of the transport had taken him by way of the maintenance stores, and he now carried a bag of spare charges that had originally been intended to replace any defective explosive bolts. The total quantity was small, but all he needed to do was distort the hatch seal sufficiently to let out air from the compartment.

Roper packed the small charges as carefully as he could, concentrating on the external handles and the hatch rim. Satisfied with his work, he set up a single timer connecting all the charges, and launched himself across the gap to the stern section.

After colliding rather clumsily with the bulkhead, he gently worked his way around the lip and back to the pod, where he was able to grasp a handhold. Securing himself by his suit's safety line, he awaited the explosion of the charges. And waited. After five minutes, he convinced himself the timer must be faulty and began to retrace his steps. He was about halfway back to the gap when a surprisingly powerful concussion flung him hard back against the pod. A few seconds later the hatch door came sailing past, twenty feet to his right.

"Too close for comfort, Roper," said Connie. "I'll have to send you on a demolitions refresher course when we get home."

Two human forms in blue rubber body suits were flung out of the blown hatch, thrashing briefly in the vacuum of space and then falling still. Roper was too far away to tell if one of them was Derek.

"Connie," he said, "your humor is improving. That was very nearly a joke."

"Surely not," the computer replied. "Not when compared to you betting $10,000 on two pair earlier today."

"Dammit! I knew you were cheating!" Roper exclaimed.

"When you went to look at the transport, you put your cards down face up. Anyway, I had a full house."

"When you guys have quite finished," Pamela's voice crackled, "Maybe you can fill me in on what's going on. I'm running out of speeches from Henry IV Part One."

"Start on Part Two," said Roper.

Time enough to explain when the job was finished.

•   •   •

The engine room still had air. Roper switched off his suit's supply and opened his face-plate to conserve his dwindling stock. Unlike the antechamber to the freezer hold, the engine room smelled less of death and more of old machinery. There was no dust. Apart from dried, encrusted lubricating oil, nothing showed the engines had not been turned off yesterday.

Since the ship's batteries had held sufficient reserves of power to lower the frozen bodies from their racks, Roper reckoned they could lower the atomic pile's fuel rods and return the engines to operation. His plan was quite straightforward: run the engines up to full power, lock the throttles to prevent interference, and then run like hell. The engines would overheat, and something would blow a big enough gasket to turn the reactors into bombs. Simple. What could go wrong?

"Did you really think we were so stupid, Lieutenant Roper?" Anastasia's mechanical voice grated. "As soon as you entered the airlock, we realized what you intended."

The creature that had been Derek lumbered out from the blind spot behind the starboard engine, struggling to control its bodily movement in the low gravity, and stood facing Roper at a distance of about fifty feet. Two more large men, equally unsteady, emerged behind him.

"Ah. I see you weren't ejected into space, after all, my friend," Roper said. "Just using the computer to pretend you were in the forward section."

"Correct. But unfortunately, that means we need your suit, Roper. You've inconvenienced us. We need access to the supplies in the forward section while we work on re-docking and re-establishing engine power. Our bodies need to be kept alive."

"Come and get it," Roper smiled. He grabbed the nearest weapon he could find, a heavy, two-foot-long adjustable wrench. "But do be careful you don't put a hole in it or crack the helmet. If you do, it'll be useless to you. And that means you can't put a hole in me either, doesn't it?"

Derek's two companions disappeared around the back of the engines in opposite directions. Roper knew they'd try circling around to grab him from the rear. Awkward and slow though his enemies seemed to be, there was not much chance he could fight off three of them. He needed to act quickly.

In three giant bounds, Roper closed the distance to Derek and swung the wrench at the creature's head as it tried to duck out of the way. The solid lump of metal connected just above the temple with a satisfying crack, and the thing hit the floor. Roper swung the wrench as hard as he could a second and third time. In such low gravity, he might as well have been wielding stick of licorice, but Derek stayed down, at least for the time being.

The control panel was situated against the forward bulkhead. Roper's gaze swept over the array of antique dials, knobs and switches. It was like trying to read Sanskrit. But one thing had not changed. On was still on. Roper flipped every switch to positive and turned up every knob he could find to the maximum. He was rewarded by the appearance of several flashing lights on the panel and a murmuring from the machinery.

"Success, Connie; the engines are powering up. Now, ninety degree turn to port, clamp on to some projection and hit full power for me, please," he said.

"Roger that, Roper."

Two large dials on the control panel seemed likely to be what registered the power developed by the two engines. On each of them, the needle quivered and began visibly to move up from the lower stop.

"I confirm stern section underway, Roper. And we've already turned enough for our course to miss the forward section."

"Good. But how the hell can I lock these switches in position?"

"The autopilot appears to be the switch top left on the control panel, but that's likely to limit the engines to cruising speed, which you don't want. You could turn that off and break the switch."

Roper did as she suggested and then swung at the offending instrument with his wrench. The plastic cover split in two, but even as he lifted his arm to strike again, he was grabbed from behind. Both of Derek's companions had arrived.

Trying to seize hold of a man in a space suit in low gravity is like mud wrestling a pig. For creatures only newly in control of unfamiliar bodies, it should be even worse. Roper could buy time.

Twisting free, he backed up against the control panel, facing his assailants as they dived in again. The first one tackled low and got a grip around both his knees. Roper swung the wrench hard downwards, inflicting a deep scalp wound, but in the process opening himself up to a bear hug from the other attacker. With his arms pinned uselessly to his sides, Roper head-butted the creature, smashing his raised helmet visor into its face.

"Status, Connie?" he demanded.

"Turn is now fifty degrees, Roper. The stern is separated from the bows by one-half klick and widening fast."

"Good."

Pulling his right arm free, Roper flailed again with the wrench, catching his standing attacker on the side of its neck, but behind this creature, Derek was already stumbling back into the fray. Roper stamped down hard on the kneeling creature, knocking it to the floor and at the same time projecting himself several feet into the air. As Derek made a grab and missed, Roper sailed over his head and landed running.

Five bounds down the aisle he stopped and turned back towards the Graaks. "Come on Derek, is that the best you've got?" he taunted the creature. "I thought you needed this suit. Well, you're gonna have to do better if you aim to get it." He backed away slowly, inviting the three attackers to pursue him and move away from the control panel.

"You're bleeding, Roper," Derek's computer voice crowed triumphantly. "You cut your forehead with that headbutt. You're one of us now; you know that, don't you?"

"Not quite yet, Derek," Roper snarled. "You see, that's the worst of fighting a dead man. He's nothing to lose. I've been on borrowed time for weeks. At least you've given me the opportunity to go out with a bang, not a whimper."

Behind the three Graaks, two bright red lights began to flash on the control panel. Roper was too far away to read the engine performance dials, but the sudden blaring of a warning klaxon conveyed their message clearly enough.

Derek turned back to the panel. "What have you done?" the voice demanded.

"Now, Connie," Roper commanded. "Shut down emergency boost and hop across to our neighbor."

"Roger that. Goodbye, Roper. It's been good working with you."

"You too, Connie. Keep up the recording as long as I'm transmitting."

"Will do."

As Derek moved towards the control panel, Roper's low tackle around the knees sent the creature flying forward to strike his head against a corner of the hard surface. The two other Graaks jumped on Roper before he could regain his feet.

"Warning! Engine failure in thirty seconds!" Anastasia called.

Roper wriggled, squirmed and kicked. When one Graak let go of him, attempting to reach the panel, Roper bodily lifted the other and flung him at his companion like a bowling ball.

"Strrrike!" Roper yelled as both Graaks went down.

"Warning! Engine failure in fifteen seconds!" announced Anastasia.

"Roper, get out of there!" Pamela's voice called over the radio.

"Too late, Pamela!" Roper replied. "But like I said, I was dead already. Just you make sure you get to Sirius and create that vaccine, lady. Do what Connie tells you, show them this recording when you get there and you'll be okay ..."

As the starboard engine briefly glowed red hot, he looked back to where Derek was just struggling to his feet. Smiling wanly, Roper raised the middle finger of his right hand. There was no need for computer translation.

Warren Benedetto writes dark fiction about horrible people, horrible places, and horrible things. He is an award-winning author and a full member of the SFWA. His stories have appeared in publications such as *Dark Matter Magazine, Fantasy Magazine*, and *The Dread Machine*; on podcasts such as *The NoSleep Podcast, Tales to Terrify*, and *The Creepy Podcast*; and in anthologies from *Apex Magazine*, Tenebrous Press, Eerie River Publishing, and more. He also works in the video game industry, where he holds more than thirty-five patents for video game technology.

•   •   •

This story is a mashup of a number of local legends from in and around Mount Holly, NJ. There is an actual Witch's Well, so named because a witch was allegedly thrown down the well and left to die. Nearby, there is a creepy marble altar in the woods, along with a gallows pole where women accused of being witches were hanged. Down the road from the well is a cemetery containing a grave with the inscription, "Thus is the fate of all who turn from God." I thought that phrase was a great title for a horror story, so I combined it with elements of the other local legends to form the inspiration for the story. Also, I wrote this during the height of the George Floyd protests, so that motivated me to include the element of racism — and vengeance against racists — into the plot.

THOSE WHO TURN FROM GOD

WARREN BENEDETTO

"T HIS IS IT," DANIEL SAID. He slowed the rusted pickup truck to a stop near a small clearing in the woods. The headlights cut through the tall pine trees, casting shadows like prison bars along the forest floor.

"You sure you want to do this?" I asked as Daniel climbed from the truck.

Daniel reached behind the driver's seat and pulled out a heavy-duty bolt cutter, fire-engine red with rubberized black handles and carbon steel jaws. "You have any better ideas?" He slammed the door and went around to the back of the truck.

"Shit," I whispered under my breath. I grabbed my flashlight from the seat and exited the passenger side, closing the door behind me. "No," I said, as I walked toward the back to meet Daniel. "I just — I don't know. Maybe we should just call the cops. Explain what happened."

I shined my flashlight on the dead body in the back of the pickup. It was loosely wrapped in a dirty white sheet stained with a bloom of deep red blood. Rings of duct tape were tightly wound around the ankles, the torso, and the neck. A single hand slipped out from between the folds of the sheet, its dark skin standing out in stark contrast to the white cotton fabric.

"That ain't gonna bring him back," Daniel said.

"I know, but ... what about his parents?"

"How will us going to jail help his parents?"

It wouldn't of course. But it was the right thing to do. I didn't say that though. Instead, I just shrugged and said, "Still ..."

Daniel opened the tailgate. It dropped with a loud bang that echoed like a gunshot through the trees. I flinched at the sound. Dead leaves rustled as something unseen bounded away through the underbrush nearby. A gust of chilly October air slipped icy fingers down my neck and into my jacket. I shivered.

For the first time, I noticed the sound of the forest, a pulsing drone of crickets and frogs that reminded me just how far away we were from civilization. We were a good twenty minutes' drive into the woods, miles from the nearest town. It was quite literally the middle of nowhere.

Daniel dropped the bolt cutter on top of the body, then turned to me. "Look, it was an accident. We both wish it didn't happen, but it did. There's nothing we can do now but look out for ourselves."

I resented the way Daniel was saying "we." *We* wish it didn't happen. Nothing *we* can do now. But there was no "we." I wasn't the one who had pulled the trigger — it was Daniel. Sure, the gun belonged to my dad, and yes, I was there when it happened. But really, I had nothing to do with it. Daniel was the one who had urged me to call Marcus. Daniel was the one who suggested we go out shooting pumpkins in the woods behind my house. Daniel was the one who said ...

I pushed the memory out of my mind. I didn't want to think about it. The point was, Daniel didn't give a shit about "we." He only cared about himself.

Daniel grasped the sheet with both hands and pulled the body to the edge of the tailgate. "All right. Grab the legs."

I didn't move. "Where are we taking him?"

"That way." Daniel pointed into the woods.

I swept my flashlight in the direction Daniel had indicated. The dim circle of light settled on the crumbling ruins of a small cabin nestled between the trees. The wooden structure was pale and weather-stripped in some places, blackened and rotting in others. There was no glass in the windows, leaving them as dark and empty as the eye sockets of a rotting bird. A tree extended skyward through a hole in the partly collapsed roof. It looked like a gnarled hand reaching up from a freshly-dug grave.

I played the light across the front of the cabin. The place had clearly been abandoned for a long, long time. Decaying steps led up to a splintered front door. The wood was scarred with jagged diagonal gashes that looked like blows from an ax. On the wall beside the door were crude letters scrawled in faded red paint. Some of the letters were practically illegible, but I could still make out what they read: BURN IN HELL.

"In there?" I asked. I hoped my voice didn't betray how freaked out I was by the house. It looked like something out of a slasher movie. I wasn't in the mood to get murdered.

"Not the house," Daniel replied. "The well."

"Oh." I panned the light past the house until it found the well Daniel was talking about. It was a six-foot-wide circle of flagstones piled waist-high and capped with a heavy wooden lid. Two flat metal bars were crisscrossed over the top. Ancient padlocks clamped the ends of the bars to rusted metal rings driven deep into the mortar between the stones. A knotted tree with thick horizontal branches loomed over the well like a guardian.

Daniel slapped the side of the truck to get my attention. "C'mon, we don't have all night." He slid his arms under the body's shoulders. "Help me lift."

I hesitated for a moment, then tucked the flashlight under my arm and grabbed the body by the legs. Together, Daniel and I carried the corpse over to the well and lowered it to the ground.

"Goddamn, he's heavy," Daniel complained as he stood. He pressed his fists into his back, twisting his torso to loosen his spasming muscles. Then he picked up the bolt cutter off the body and walked over to the well. "Gimme some light?"

I shined my flashlight on the well, then looked around nervously. "You sure no one will find him?"

"Out here?" Daniel spun in a circle, gesturing with the bolt cutter at the dense forest. "Nobody even knows where this is."

"You did."

Daniel clamped the bolt cutter around one of the padlocks. "That's because my asshole brother took me here when we were kids once, to scare me." The lock dropped to the ground. "And he only found it by accident."

"What do you mean, scare you? Scare you how?"

"You see that place?" Daniel nodded his head towards the cabin. "It looks like a fucking murder house."

I felt relieved. I wasn't the only one who thought the place was creepy.

Daniel cut the second lock, then circled to the other side of the well. "He told me there were a bunch of witches that lived out here, back in the 1800s. Slaves, or former slaves. I forget. Weird shit was happening in town — dead crops, livestock missing, shit like that — so, of course, the first thing they thought was, 'It's gotta be witches.' Right?"

"Of course," I said.

Daniel strained to cut the third lock. Finally, it snapped. "Folks in Cedarville tracked them down and lynched six of them. Up there." He nodded to the branches of the tree extending overhead, then moved to the fourth and final padlock. "Then they chopped them up into pieces and threw them down the well." The last lock hit the ground.

"Jesus."

"Yeah, people didn't fuck around back then. Bad time to be a witch. Or a slave."

"That's Cedarville though," I added grimly. "Bunch of racist fucks, even today. Look at what happened to that kid last summer. He was, what, twelve?"

"Ten."

"Kid ends up drowned in a lake with rocks in his backpack and they're not sure if it's a murder or not?" I shook my head sadly. "It's so fucked up. If he was a white kid, they'd have the goddamned FBI out here."

Daniel removed the flat metal bars from the well and tossed them aside. "I guess that works out well for us then." He looked down at Marcus' body. "Sorry, brother."

The callousness of Daniel's remark made my stomach clench. We had known Marcus since we were in third grade. He was our friend. Mine, at least.

"Anyway," Daniel continued. "Point is, nobody's finding him out here."

"You think any of it's true, though?" I tried to sound casual, but my nerves were fried.

"What, about the witches?" Daniel scoffed. "Nah, my brother made that shit up."

"What about the house?" I looked over my shoulder at the cabin silhouetted against the trees. "You see what's written on the front?"

"I mean, sure, someone might've killed some slaves back then. But witches? Come on." He grasped the edge of the cover and tried to lift it. It didn't budge. He grunted and tried again with a different grip. "God damn, this is heavy. Gimme a hand?"

I walked over to the well and grabbed the other side of the lid. Something caught my eye. "Hold up." I shined my flashlight on the cover, then brushed away a layer of dirt and rust flakes to reveal words carefully carved into the wood. I read them aloud: "THUS IS THE FATE ... OF THOSE WHO TURN FROM GOD." I looked up at Daniel. "You sure he made it up?"

"I don't know. Maybe he heard it at camp or something."

"Then why would someone carve that there? And why the bars? And the padlocks?"

"To keep people out."

"Or to keep something in."

"Jesus Christ. Are you serious?" Daniel took off his faded Cedarville High baseball cap and scratched his fingers through his hair. "I don't even know what to say right now." He put the hat back on his head. "I'm just curious," he said, standing up straight and putting his hands in his pockets. He shrugged his shoulders up by his ears. "What exactly do you suggest we do?"

"About what?" I asked.

Daniel gestured to the body on the ground, then to the well. "About him. About this. What do you have in mind?"

"I don't —"

"You must have *something*, because you're doing everything you can to make this a pain in the ass. First, you're talking about cops. Now, it's witches. So what is it? What's your idea?" He spat on the ground. "Or are you just being a little bitch?"

I bristled. I knew Daniel didn't have a very high opinion of me. He never had. He was always calling me a bitch, or a faggot, or a pussy. That's what he called anybody who didn't fall in line with whatever he wanted to do. As soon as anyone dared to challenge him, the insults started flying.

"What are we gonna say?" I asked, trying to remain rational. "About what happened?"

Daniel's hands flew to his face, then exploded away from his temples with splayed fingers, mind blown. "We're not gonna say anything!"

"Someone's gonna ask, eventually. We should at least have our story straight."

"So we just say we don't know. We haven't seen him."

"His mom knows he was at my house."

Daniel's face went slack. "She does?"

"He called her."

Daniel was quiet for a moment. Then, with sudden violence, he kicked the side of the well — one, two, three times — then stormed off towards the edge of the clearing. "FUCK!" he shouted at the trees. His voice carried for a while before echoing back. He snatched up a handful of rocks off the ground and hurled them into the woods, where they clattered like firecrackers against the trees. A flock of birds — or bats? — took flight in a mad rush of flapping, silhouetted against the moonlit clouds. "Fuck! Fuck! Fuck!" Then he strode back towards me, his face a mask of fury. "Why didn't you tell me that?"

"I–I didn't —"

"Duhhh, I–I didn't —" Daniel mocked viciously. "You're so fucking stupid."

He kicked one of the padlocks with the toe of his boot. It sailed through the air and punched through the rotting wood on the side of the cabin.

"At least I'm not a fucking murderer," I breathed, almost to myself.

"What did you say?" Daniel approached me, his head cocked.

I clenched my teeth. "Nothing."

"It was an accident, asshole," Daniel sneered. He planted his hands in my chest and pushed.

I stumbled backward. Anger swelled in my chest. "Was it?" I shot back.

"Yeah, it was."

"What about what you said?"

"When?"

"Right before."

"I was fucking around. It was a joke."

"He didn't think so."

"Maybe he shouldn't have been so sensitive."

"Maybe you shouldn't have been so racist."

I could feel my heart ricocheting around my rib cage. I had never dared to stand up to Daniel before, not once. I should have done it sooner, before what happened to Marcus. I could have stepped in. I could have stopped it. But I was too afraid.

Well, not anymore.

Daniel sneered at me. "You think I killed him on purpose? Huh? You faggot piece of shit."

He stepped up into my face, close enough for me to smell his beer-tinged breath, then tried to push me again. This time, I swiped my arm sideways, knocking his hands away.

"Don't touch me," I growled. My voice was trembling. With fear, yes. But also with rage. I could feel it filling my head like a darkened thundercloud, crackling with electricity, ready to burst. I was tired of being afraid. I wanted to do something. To fight back. For myself. And for Marcus.

"Alright, you know what?" Daniel said, suddenly animated. "Fuck this. Fuck you, fuck him, fuck everyone. You don't want to help? Fine. I'll do it myself. And then I never want to see you again."

"Good!" I shouted. "Fine with me." I strode back towards the truck, my chest heaving, my mind racing. For a brief second, I considered whether the keys were still in the ignition. Had Daniel taken them? I didn't remember. But if he hadn't, I could start the truck and just leave him behind. Leave him with the body. With the witches. Let him find his way back to Cedarville on foot. In the meantime, I would go to the police. Tell them what happened. What *really* happened. What Daniel had said. What Daniel had *planned*.

As soon as my back was turned, Daniel scooped up the bolt cutter, ran up behind me, and brought it down on the back of my head. The blow made a sound like a rotten melon dropped from a rooftop, dull and wet. I crumpled to the ground. A gush of blood poured from my hairline, spidering down my forehead and over my eyes.

Daniel loomed over me, the bolt cutter dangling from one fist. His face was a watery blur, as if I was looking at him from the bottom of a lake. "I didn't kill Marcus because he was black," Daniel growled. "I killed him because I felt like it." He lifted the bolt cutter and propped it on his shoulder. "Him being black was just a bonus. The kid in the lake, on the other hand ..." He shrugged.

Suddenly, a dull thud reverberated from within the well. It was a hollow sound that seemed to double over itself as it bounced off the inside of the circular stone walls. The cover over the well vibrated.

"Yo, what the fuck?" Daniel said, to no one. It was like he wanted to hear his own voice, to break the crushing silence pressing in on him from all directions.

Another thud echoed from the well. The heavy wooden cover began to rise, levitating slowly, as if on a cushion of air. Eerie orange light spilled from underneath, distorted by shimmering waves of heat.

Daniel took a step backward, his eyes locked on the well.

With a roar like a jet engine, the cover launched violently into the air, turning end over end like a coin flip, disappearing into the dark as it arced through the midnight sky. It crashed through the trees in the distance, somewhere unseen.

I groaned in pain and sat up, clutching the back of my head. I felt drugged, confused, suddenly unsure of why I was in the woods in the first place. Then I saw the body wrapped in the sheet on the ground next to me. Marcus.

Suddenly, it all came back to me. The gunshot. The panic. The sheet, from my mother's closet.

The woods.

The well.

The witches.

I touched my fingers to the gash on the back of my skull, then looked back up at Daniel. He was no longer standing over me with the bolt cutters. Instead, he was walking towards the well as if he was on autopilot. The bolt cutters slipped from his fingers, dropping silently onto a soft bed of pine needles. His mouth hung open, his skin reflecting the glow of the firelight. His wide-open pupils were black marbles; embers danced in his polished glass stare.

I followed the direction of his terrified gaze, blinking my eyes as my concussion-dulled brain strained to process what I was seeing.

A shadow was rising from the well.

Then another.

And another.

Six, in all.

The shadows flew up and circled Daniel as he stood frozen, paralyzed with fear. They dipped and swirled, intertwining like wisps of smoke as they wrapped around his body. Black, vaporous tendrils encircled his wrists and ankles. Currents of super-heated air venting up from the well caused his clothes to ripple. Sweat poured down his face. His lips quivered as he whispered the same phrase over and over, like a penitent reciting the rosary.

It sounded like, "I'm sorry."

At the same time, the two metal bars that had been crisscrossed over the well began to rise from the ground where Daniel had thrown them. They started to spin, slowly at first, then faster and faster, until they were just a blur. Like ... airplane propellers? No, not propellers. I thought back to my summer mowing lawns with my uncle. That's what the spinning bars reminded me of.

Lawnmower blades.

The sickening realization of what was about to happen hit me at the same time that it happened. The whirling blades launched through the air at Daniel. I turned away, shielding my face from the horror. A torrent of gore sprayed at me, slapping long tendrils of blood across my arms and back. Hot, wet chunks of flesh pelted my body. Through my clenched eyelids, I could see the orange light from the well flare brighter. Heat surged against my skin, the way a campfire pushes heat in your face when you squeeze a splash of lighter fluid into the flames.

After a moment, I lowered my arms and opened my eyes, afraid of what I might see.

But there was nothing.

Daniel was gone.

The only thing that remained was a smattering of dark red stains in the dirt, with long smears stretching along the ground from the stains to the well and up over the flagstone sides. It was as if something — or pieces of something — had been dragged inside.

I rolled to my knees and tried to stand, stumbling a few steps then pitching forward face-first into the dirt. My palms tore on the rocky ground as I reached out to break my fall, my brain slamming painfully inside my skull from front to back, threatening to burst out through the seething wound in my scalp. I moaned in agony, then turned over and sat up, eyes rapidly scanning the air around the well, searching for the murderous shadows, sure they would be coming for me next.

They were.

The shadows disentwined and separated as they lowered themselves to the ground near me. There were six of them, each distinct in form and size, their silhouettes visible against the hellish glow still spilling from the hole in the earth. As they drifted closer, one of them leaned down toward me.

It had a face.

No, not a face — the suggestion of a face, the way the brain finds faces in rolling clouds or knotted tree trunks. It was a trick of the eye, the mind searching to make sense from the senseless.

The shadow drifted closer. My nostrils burned with the acrid smell of woodsmoke and brimstone.

I heard a whisper. A woman's voice. A single word.

"Cedarville …"

I pointed a trembling finger.

Then the shadows flew past me and into the woods, headed in the direction of the town.

Jason P. Burnham loves to spend time with his wife, children, and dog. He co-edits *If There's Anyone Left*, a magazine of inclusive speculative fiction with his friend C. M. Fields.

·   ·   ·

I can't remember the book I was reading when I wrote this, but it was in the science fantasy genre and I wanted to have a magical creature in a science fiction/climate fiction narrative. Thus were born the jet rays. This story inspired me to write an entire novel that follows humanity's steps after the conclusion of "Discerning Oar". It probably won't make it to print, but there is reason for optimism in the face of climate disaster — there has to be!

DISCERNING OAR: JET RAYS AND THE FLIGHT OF THE *GWYN SULAK*

JASON P. BURNHAM

"DR. LOPEZ, WE'LL BE LANDING at the former Olmedo Airport in Guayaquil shortly. Please fasten your seatbelt," says the pilot's tinny voice through stale, recycled air.

He must have his EvapoSuit on, or he would have opened the door and told me to my face — I'm the only passenger.

I look out my window — it's beautiful up here, if browner and sandier than the old satellite images of the area. Hopefully our soon-to-be home will look something like those old photos — I long to be the first to lay eyes on our new planet. Guayaquil is the launch site for my baby, our colony ship, the *Gwyn Sulak*.

The plane shakes as we hit turbulence. I assume it's turbulence — the airline companies shutting down thirty years ago to curb rampant emissions means I haven't flown since I was a child. Maybe this is normal — I can't imagine how much worse orbital escape velocity will be.

Ecuador is the last place my feet will ever touch Earth. I'm kind of happy about it; it means I get to see one of the last bastions of jet rays before we follow them to the stars. Plus, the city of Guayaquil has been relatively immune to terrorist attacks against our efforts, and it is close to the equator, which helps reduce fuel requirements and improve orbital trajectories.

My stomach sinks as we drop and hit pavement, only calming when we roll to a stop.

"Good luck out there, Dr. Lopez," says the pilot over the PA system. I'm not sure if he means outside or in space.

The two pilots keep their cockpit sealed to prevent outdoor air entry. The walk between the plane and the waiting car is not far enough to overheat me, so I have decided to take the liberty of smelling some fresh air. I don't think the people receiving me will appreciate it, but I have missed so-called "bulb provinces." Named after the wet-bulb problem — the phenomenon of being so hot one cannot sweat quickly enough to cool oneself — these provinces require the cooling of the EvapoSuit to survive outdoors. Without the protective gear, core body temperature eventually increases to fatal levels.

It's hard to read expressions through the EvapoSuit, but body language is pretty straightforward. I watch as the two waiting escorts sprint across the sandy pavement toward me, waving suited arms as I calmly descend the staircase.

I ignore my chaperones and enjoy the nostalgia of air you chew rather than breathe. The heavy, muggy inferno reminds me of childhood in southern Mexico.

"Doctora Lopez!" shouts one of the suited persons. "We need to get you inside right away!" The two are guiding me, more of a push really, to the waiting vehicle.

Once inside, I watch the plane's airstair retract through heavily tinted windows. My two escorts take off their EvapoSuit helmets, as does the third person who waited in the car.

"Lucía! So good to finally meet you in person," says Danilo Andrade, the glue that holds this operation together.

"And these are our resident EvapoSuit experts who help us on all retrievals, Selma Johnson and Aimee Chan."

"Pleased to meet you both," I say, nodding at my two flustered guides, noting that both are smarter than I — they have short hair for this hot climate, Selma with a fro and Aimee with a pixie cut. The long curls sticking to my neck feel like a mistake.

"What were you thinking out there?" Aimee chastises.

I laugh. "Aimee, I *miss* humidity. Most people think it's disgusting, but I'll take breathing weighted air to waking up with a bloody nose any day."

At the limit of audibility, Aimee grumbles under her breath. "Putting our hopes in you." It takes me a minute to piece the words together, but the eye roll and slumped shoulders help with context.

Danilo is speaking, but I talk over him. "Let's get something straight — all of us are extremely stressed, anxious. These are the most troubling times we have ever lived in and we've put ourselves into the firing line by gearing up for this launch. If we let those pressures break us, then everything we've worked toward, everything we're trying to accomplish, is lost. So, forgive me a moment of nostalgia to breathe some refreshingly humid air before getting down to business."

Aimee stares at the floor of the transport van. "I-I'm sorry."

Selma Johnson signals understanding and Danilo raises an eyebrow, as if to say, *May I continue?*

I nod affirmative and Danilo starts over on his long list of updates. I listen passively, gazing at the toothpick-sized gunmetal gray lifeboat on the horizon, the *Gwyn Sulak*, humanity's, in my opinion, last hope.

"Stop the car!" I yell.

"What? Why?" asks Danilo in a high-pitched voice.

"Allow me one more moment of nostalgia," I say, unzipping my bag and hurriedly throwing on my EvapoSuit. This walk is going to be longer than the one from the plane to the car.

•　　　•　　　•

I hadn't seen one in person since I moved to the desert. Speckling the sky in gray by the thousands when I was a kid, a sighting was now a rare event. They can't live here any more than we can.

"I missed them," I say to Selma, Danilo, and Aimee, who I know are following closely behind as I watch the familiar parabolic flights of the jet rays.

"Sometimes I forget how narrow their habitat has become," says Danilo, standing next to me, taking in the spectacle.

"Our guides," I say, choking up at the memory of watching rays on the porch with my long-deceased mother, and with pride in our current mission.

"Beautiful," says Selma. I get the sense that none of them have had much opportunity to take a break from work and appreciate the stunning splendor of their surroundings.

"I've always wondered how they achieve escape velocity," Aimee says wistfully.

Before they became endangered, nobody could figure out the jet rays' propulsion system, which had led to ... *questions.* By the time sufficiently advanced scientific techniques were developed to dispel extraterrestrial origin conspiracy theories, they were so endangered that capturing a ray, even to study it, was illegal. There had been attempts to breed them in captivity, but all the animals had died. My theory is that no enclosure was big enough for them to fly like they wanted to, needed to, and they died from lassitude.

As I'm about to respond to the gathered crew, a ray crashes to the earth, not a hundred meters from us. Instinctually, I run to where the ray has fallen.

The creature is ill, flipped on its back, wings folded in toward its stomach, dry and crinkled like a newspaper that has been balled up over and over and over. Its gray skin has lost its sheen, the white underbelly sallow instead of its usual white. It still breathes, but is not long for this world. I detach my glove and rest my hand on its underbelly, feel the racing of its cardiovascular system. I'm surprised by its desiccation — it must be a physiologic response to their altered habitat.

My touch seems to comfort it, its cardiovascular system slowing, the muscles of the wings relaxing, unfolding to lay flat against the sand. I'm aware of three shadows approaching.

"Can we bring it to the launch facility?" I ask with a sniffle.

"That's illegal," says Danilo flatly.

"What would we do with it anyway?" asks Selma, raising an eyebrow behind the clear plastic faceplate of the EvapoSuit.

I look at Aimee to see if she has an opinion, but she stares forward at the downed ray, tears in her eyes mirroring my own.

I slide my other hand under the creature's back and it contracts as it had when first I came upon it, as if to say, *No, leave me here.* I remove my glove from my other hand and place both on the creature's underbelly and it relaxes, confirming my suspicion. Underneath my fingertips, the heartbeat creeps to a halt. I let my hands linger in the sweltering humidity for a few minutes before standing and tugging my gloves back on.

The three give me incredulous looks. "It's gone," I say, and head back to the car.

•   •   •

The approach to the *Gwyn Sulak* turned somber, silent after the jet ray encounter. Not that I could have paid much attention if Danilo had been rambling anyway. Our passage was lined by security guards as well as multiple checkpoints, designed to keep the terrorists out. The *Gwyn Sulak* being an equal opportunity colony ship had really irked the people whose money controlled the world, particularly because none of them got genetic passage. Rich folks can afford to pay a lot to send someone to blow up something they don't like. Plus, they have enough money to save face by covering it up and making it seem to the average person that they had nothing to do with it.

"More security than you let on," I say to Danilo as we arrive underneath the massive ship.

Danilo shrugs in his EvapoSuit. "People don't want us to succeed."

"Nobody who thinks they should have more opportunities likes equal opportunity when it is put into practice," scoffs Aimee.

When carbon capture and the massive shift away from fossil fuels had failed, colony ship tech research had initially taken off. It was subsequently abandoned for two reasons; the minor one being lack of resources, the major that nobody could agree on who would make it onto the ship. The wealthy had tried to fund their own ships to escape on, but they didn't pay their scientists enough to retain them. One group had gotten a rocket off the ground carrying a frozen billionaire and his embryos, but it had exploded in the atmosphere. Whether it was sabotage or a rush job, nobody could agree. Regardless, the result of this debacle was the elites had covertly funded wars with the sole purpose of amassing casualties. Their goal? To limit resource use so there would be enough for the top 0.0001% to survive.

"Wait here for me," I tell Aimee, Selma, and Danilo.

"You *have* to stop wandering off," shouts Danilo.

"I'll be right back. I just want to *touch* it," I say, walking to the base of the ship, head tilting back and back and back as I try to keep its nose in sight.

The *Gwyn Sulak* is mostly embryos, protected by meters of water to prevent DNA mutations from ionizing radiation. There will be a few live crew, but everyone except me will be under heavy sedation, bathed in an isotonic solution with anti-aging additives. The others will also have central nervous system hook ups for cerebrospinal fluid dialysis designed to prevent accumulation of dementia-causing protein plaques. The live crew have all been implanted with muscle and bone stimulators to prevent them from collapsing into a pile of mush when it is their time to awaken.

It really is beautiful. I've always had a love of sleek gray and black spaceships, dating back to sci-fi movies and comics

I read when I was a kid. The *Sulak* is bulkier than the comics would have made me believe, but it's gorgeous. I run my palms along its surface, so warm it feels alive.

I've volunteered for the first leg, getting to the rays' refueling planet on their reproductive journey through space. We were able to tag them, but the device had to be small and lightweight enough for them to still achieve escape velocity. This meant we had to choose between positional accuracy and water detection accuracy. In the end, we decided we would rather know that where they went had water rather than knowing the exact celestial location. What would be the point in knowing where you're going if you might not survive when you get there? Once the 'water confirmed' signal made it to Earth, we knew we could always follow a mating pair to their destination.

A hand rests lightly on my shoulder. "Lucía, we really should get inside," says Danilo gently.

"Did you really think the lead aerospace engineer was not going to come out here and appreciate her work? To caress the cheek of her baby?" I ask. "If I'm going to die for this mission, I think I have the right to hug my mechanical child."

The *Sulak* will be my only child. Only the embryos are protected from the ionizing radiation; water sufficient to protect the live crew would have been restrictively heavy. Hopefully none of the cancers I will undoubtedly develop will be rapidly lethal, but that is the reason for the remainder of the live crew. We also had to agree not to include our genetic material among the embryos, as it was felt to be a conflict of interest.

Danilo's hand squeezes my shoulder. "I think you'll have plenty of time to appreciate *Gwyn* on your journey."

"Yes, yes, sorry. Let's get inside."

We head into the nearby research structure, which is liberally protected from launch combustion with heat-resistant coatings, not unlike those on the underside of the crafts used by the now-defunct NASA's shuttle program.

The architecture of the place lets in a lot of sunlight, which keeps up the Vitamin D and morale. Water heaters sit on top of the building alongside solar panels to help fuel the station's work. We had driven past miles of solar panel fields on the way in, but I had been too lost in my thoughts to pay them much attention.

The space is utilitarian, offices and living quarters packed tightly. We didn't have a budget for frivolity, just enough to keep everyone sane and barely that. Our unified goal is probably the only thing keeping people going.

Danilo is talking to someone on his communicator. "Yes, we'll head right over."

I raise an eyebrow at him.

"Aimee, Selma, thanks for the escort," Danilo says. The two shake my hand and head off to their quarters. "You and I have an emergency meeting to attend," he says, face tight.

We come to the central meeting room, the only green space in the compound. The ceilings are high here, with good views of the launch platform. The meeting looks to be well attended, standing room only except for two seats which are apparently mine and Danilo's.

"Doctora Lopez, welcome," says Huang Liqiu, lead veterinarian for the project, or more appropriately, lead jet ray scientist.

"I'm afraid we have bad news for you," says Ayana Kenes, one of the saviors of the project, without whom our food planning would have starved the crew and embryos. Always brutally skeptical and exacting, but rightfully and helpfully so.

"Nice to meet you, too," I say, to a few short, somber chuckles.

"Liqiu, we should get started. There is not much time," says Ayana as she fidgets with then adjusts her kimeshek.

"I wasn't aware of any mission critical updates," says Danilo, visibly sweating, though whether this is from us lingering outdoors or nerves, I can't say.

Liqiu pulls up a video holo that looks familiar.

"That's the field we drove through on the way to the launch site," I say. "It's where we saw the rays."

"Yes," says Liqiu grimly, enhancing the stream. "That's the urgency. I've been tracking the rays' flight patterns and the frequency of escape velocity achievement. If any in the room are unaware, the rays only achieve escape velocity when they leave to their waystation, our future residence, for mating."

There are many affirmative nods, a few blank stares.

"This is a time lapse of the last two months of ray flight patterns."

The video speeds up and I watch as the density of the rays thins appreciably.

Liqiu continues. "This is only one of many sections we are monitoring, but the other sectors look exactly the same. The rate of exodus has drastically declined."

"What are the implications of this, Liqiu?" asks Danilo. Murmurs build in the crowd. "And why call an emergency meeting? We know they're dying."

"You can imagine all this video information takes time and computing power to analyze. As soon as I saw the output, I had to present it. While I can't rule out sabotage from the outside as a reason for their dwindling numbers, it doesn't matter."

The crowd rumblings make it hard to hear and Danilo calls for quiet. When the noise subsides, Danilo asks her to continue. "Please, Liqiu, tell us your findings."

"If my calculations are correct, and I believe they are, as they've been checked by twelve others of us here ..." Liqiu looks around the room, receiving nods from those who have apparently checked the math. "Then the last pair of mating rays could leave Earth as early as tomorrow."

I expect the group to be raucous, but instead there are gasps, a few expletives, and then silence. Liqiu stands somberly in front of everyone. My heart beats in my eyes and if anyone had a pen to drop, it would rupture our collective eardrum and shatter our nerves.

Ayana nods to Liqiu and looks directly at me. "It appears, Dr. Lopez, that you have arrived just in time for your launch window. I suggest you get a good rest tonight."

The funereal group trickles out, downcast eyes and shoulders contrasting with the green plants stretching desperately to the skylights high above. I stand as the room empties, watching the rays' time-lapse video over and over.

•   •   •

The deep-sleep crew was loaded in early this morning, as they required more time to hook up and have their solutions loaded into their tanks. I stand now on the elevator, slowly rising to the live crew quarters. I pass the section that I know houses the water-protected embryos, the ones randomly selected from diverse backgrounds, much to the chagrin of the wealthy elites of the world.

"Lucía, we're moving the launch window," says Danilo into my ear. The plan had been for me to be waiting for T-4 hours after boarding.

"Again? Why?"

"Weather conditions are changing rapidly and we need to get you up and out."

His voice suggests he's hiding something. Maybe Liqiu knows the last mating pair is leaving soon, or perhaps has already gone. "How long do I have?"

There's a pause on the other end, commotion in the background. "We're running checks right now. We think we've got about half an hour before the storm hits."

Major and sudden storms, another consequence of the ever-worsening climate. "Roger," I say unhappily. I try to find the storm on the horizon, but see nothing.

"You sure a storm's coming, Danilo? The sky's pretty clear from up here."

"Positive," he says, then mutes his mic.

A timer appears on my HUD. T-minus *twenty-eight minutes*. One benefit of chronic, difficult to predict storm surges in coastal areas had been the emergence of better weather models, offering down to the minute predictions. People didn't have to huddle in their basements for tornadoes anymore, because they knew precisely where they would hit. Those with the resources to watch the reports, that is.

Danilo and control stay silent for what seems forever, though only two minutes have passed since I last checked my HUD timer. The clock suddenly jumps from twenty-six to fifteen minutes. "Danilo, weather models not accurate?" I ask.

"Approaching faster than we thought."

This seems odd, but I'm preoccupied inside the ship, climbing into the cockpit. As soon as I'm strapped in and have pressed all the buttons the autopilot-assist tells me I need to press, the countdown drops to sixty seconds.

"Doctora Lopez, it's been a pleasure," says Danilo in a tone I can't quite parse. "You're going to be on your own for the final countdown. We have to go shelter. Storm's a comin'," he says and the feed cuts, only the automated electronic voice remaining to count down.

"Ten, nine, eight ..."

I feel *Gwyn Sulak*'s massive rocket boosters shudder beneath me, and don't hear the last seconds of the countdown over the cacophony of fuel combustion.

In front of me is a camera feed and the autopilot-assist's scrolling display of instructions. The autopilot-assist continues to inform me which buttons I should push, while the camera feed cycles through several views — bow, aft, starboard, port, mission control, and the launchpad area. The aft view shows the launchpad receding rapidly, the launchpad view showing fewer and fewer flames.

Suddenly, the control room camera bursts into flames, as does the launchpad, as if the *Sulak* were docked, crooked, and releasing burning fuel directly into the compound.

"Mother of God," I breathe against my high-g-compressed vocal cords.

Danilo lied; there was no storm.

What I saw was an explosion from within the compound. The same terrorists that had been trying to stop us all along. Years ago, they had killed a few security guards, set off a minor explosion leading to mild structural damage. But never had they managed to get all the way to the launchpad, to the *Sulak*. And now ...

Tears stream down my face, back toward Earth, aching to touch the lives just sacrificed for this, the most important mission.

"Thank you," I choke.

• • •

As the tears begin to float along with the rest of me still strapped in, I can no longer ignore the autopilot-assist's flight instructions.

They're gone. Danilo, Selma, Aimee, Liqiu, Ayana, and all the rest of the people who have worked so diligently, selflessly toward our goal. Everyone working on the *Sulak* had agreed not to have their genetic material put on board. Their legacy is this ship and I must protect it.

A gray alarm is flashing on the instruction screen and I see why. My throat tightens and tears accumulate anew on my eyelids until I have to wipe them away. We weren't too late. The *Gwyn Sulak* has picked up a pair of jet rays on trajectory to their mating waypoint. I go through the calibrations with the autopilot-assist and the *Sulak*'s booster adjusts and follows them.

The jet rays are even more beautiful in space. Even more majestic and graceful. The sheen of starlight is no longer marred by the pollution of our environment. From behind, they look like their cousins in the deep ocean, swimming through the dark, the stars bioluminescent plankton flickering in and out of existence. These two are in much better shape than the one that crashed and died under my fingertips.

I envy them — no wealthy jet rays, jet ray politicians to dictate which rays get to migrate, get to mate, get to have their genetics passed on to the next generation.

The autopilot-assist feed has gone green, meaning we're set to follow the rays until they arrive at their destination. Our destination.

Time for my first hibernation. It's not as deep as the other live crew, because if something emergent comes up, I need to be awake quickly, without needing medications or a recovery period, so that I can respond to autopilot-assist commands.

Maybe we can put down new roots, start over. I'm not sure we deserve it, but I have to try. Our little faction gave me faith in our species, that there were still those left who valued harmony with the environment, with each other. We could live peacefully somewhere else with the right people. We won't destroy it. I hope.

I settle in, hoping for a dreamless sleep.

•   •   •

Doctora Lopez, it's been a pleasure. You're going to be on your own for the final countdown. We have to go shelter. Storm's a comin'.

I awake to a remembered echo of Danilo's last words and a giant green planet on the bow viewscreen. No emergencies, no alarms.

"We're here," I whisper hoarsely to myself.

Based on the signals from the tagging project, somewhere near the large green gaseous planet in my view window there is water. From this distance, it looks like there are about fifty moons, giving an idea of how massive the planet is. It also has a faint ring system. The ship slows with the rays, and I have to watch closely to figure out where our life-sustaining liquid might be hiding.

I turn to the scanner feed. The instruments and probes have been programmed to find water. Their report on the planet's satellites is ready. It's short, the computer having parsed out all the technical details for me. Fifty lines, one for each planetoid.

```
Object 1: no water detected.
Object 2: no water detected.
Object 3: no water detected.
```

I scan the list quickly, panic rising. All of them are the same. All fifty moons are devoid of water.

Why do the rays stop here, then?

I stumble to the viewing window, to investigate with my own eyes. I know the probes can see more than I, but it feels right to study for myself.

I watch the rays, my floating islands of hope in the blackness of space, as they near the rings of the gas giant. Their wings aren't flapping. The gray is no longer lively. *They're ... they're ...*

The rays are not pausing here to refuel. This is the end of their journey. Now filling the viewing window are the planet's rings. Yes, there are pieces of ice and rock, but there are also bodies. Thousands and thousands and millions of bodies. This is where the rays come to die. I followed them to their graves.

How had the tags been wrong? They had detected water unequivocally. It doesn't make sense. *Unless ...*

Unless some rays weren't captured by the gravitational well. There were few enough tags that, by random chance, they may have continued drifting. The data streams fizzled out not long after the first 'water confirmed' pings had been received, but it was assumed that this had been an equipment failure. Not that the rays had all ...

I pull up the old reports, the tag data. I look through them and then out at the ring. The water was probably the decomposition of bodies. Rays disintegrating, their internal water boiling off into space.

I came all this way following a mirage.

Why would they come here to die? It doesn't make sense.

I think back to home, to the thousands of other species that migrate to spawn and die where they procreate. But there is no reproduction, no renewal of life here. If there had been in the past, there isn't anymore. This is a rotating mausoleum. A monument to a dying species.

Just like the *Sulak*. The headstone for our demise.

I numbly walk through this doomsday scenario with autopilot-assist and adjust the course. To where? Somewhere I will never see. Somewhere the instruments tell me there might be something habitable, but who is to say it isn't another illusion? Hopefully the rest of the live crew can guide us to our new beginning. If there will be one.

I'm sorry, embryos. I'm sorry, Danilo, Liqiu, Ayana, Selma, Aimee, and all the rest. I did what I thought was best, what I thought might save us.

In a clarity unobstructed by hope, unimpeded by the arrogance of a future, I see now that we lost our best chance at salvation when we mutilated our home.

I came here, hoping to be the first to look upon our beautiful new home. Beauty, I've found, but a home I have not.

I take a last look at the bodies of the jet rays, gray diamonds sparkling in the reflected starlight of an emerald planet. They remind me of old pictures of Earth, shimmering snow flurries in a winter wind, the rainbow of a front-yard sprinkler with children running through, cascading blue-green waterfalls before the rivers all dried up or turned brown. The vista gives me hope that there is another place where we can find our idyll, and that this time we won't destroy it.

But if this really is the end for us, my final hope is that our dust will be as beautiful as the rays'.

Tim Kane loves things that creep and crawl. His first published book is non-fiction, *The Changing Vampire of Film and Television*, tracing the history of vampires in television and movies. Most recently published stories appear in *Lovecraftia, Navigating Ruins,* and *Dark Moon Digest.*

•　　•　　•

"A Nummo for Your Ignorance" was much inspired by watching the movie "Brazil" in the 1990s. It was the first complete short story I ever completed and has since then been revised to bring it into shape.

A NUMMO FOR YOUR IGNORANCE

TIM KANE

"**I** AM HUNGRY," Mejib 132Q announced.

The other droles sat at their benches, wearing the same drab coveralls, and all scooping up bowls of mush.

"I am hungry," Mejib repeated, yet the only response was the constant slurping of food.

He stared across the rows and rows of tables. The ingestion chamber stretched out further than he cared to see, and the ceiling rose up to form a sky of pipes and ducts and whirring fans.

Another drole wiped the bottom of his bowl with his fingers and then stuck them in his mouth, licking off the last of the mush.

Mejib looked into his own bowl, slid a hand along the smooth surface. Empty. Had he already eaten? He still felt hungry.

The food dispenser, located against the wall, might still have his food. Mejib trudged down the aisle. The sounds of scraping filled the ingestion chamber as the other droles wiped the bottoms of their bowls.

The food dispenser consisted of a black tube, protruding from the wall. It had the letter Q stenciled above it — the same as the letter tattooed on Mejib's arm. He touched the slot next to the tube, feeling the cold metal. A search of his pockets found them empty. He was supposed to have a nummo. It fit in the slot and then the tube dispensed the mush. He tried to think back to when he last held his nummo.

The speakers around the ingestion chamber crackled to life. Hundreds of bowls clunked down onto tables.

The speakers announced: "Food is good."

As one, the other droles repeated: "Food is good."

Mejib jerked his head up, "Food is ..."

The speakers cut off his words as they broadcast the next line: "Work is good."

Around him, the other droles restated the proclamation in unison. Mejib mumbled along as his hands felt again through the two large pockets on his coveralls. His nummo had to be here.

"God knows all," the speakers blared.

This time Mejib didn't repeat the words. He held up his hand and imagined the coin there. The nummo had indentations along one side, and when it caught the overhead lights, the surface glinted.

He remembered taking the nummo out to look at it. Along the catwalk, the way he always did. Then someone in the crowd had bumped him into the railing. Mejib was sure of this because right afterward he'd heard a clanging on the ground below. But then he'd put his hands back in his pocket. So the nummo had to still be there.

Mejib felt through the pockets again, still empty.

Glancing up, he saw the vacant rows of tables. Only a few droles remained, filing out the exits.

Mejib glanced at the black feeding tube. A glob of mush had dribbled onto the ground. He knelt down, hands ready to scoop up the lost morsel but then paused.

His gaze sought out the speakers lining the walls.

God knows all.

He inhaled, detecting the faint earthy odor of the mush. His fingers quivered. He wanted the food. But some distant memory trickled into his thoughts. For each drole, only one nummo. And only one bowl of mush.

The image of God's face flashed across his mind — large eyes staring down, only at him.

Mejib slunk away and headed toward the exit.

By the time he reached the resting chamber, the lights had already dimmed and the other droles lay along the concrete floor. Mejib walked beside the wall, squinting at the numbers, which counted off the sleeping spaces. He examined his arm, comparing the tattooed numbers there with the darkened symbols on the wall, finally locating 132Q. But the space on the floor was not empty. Drole 133 had rolled over, one leg splayed into the sleeping space.

Something flared up in Mejib. A surge of heat that seemed to fill his body. His muscles tightened until his arms trembled.

"No!"

Mejib kicked drole 133 in the leg.

The other drole opened his eyes. Sat up. He had deep wrinkles along his face and arms.

"Move," Mejib said.

Drole 133 stared at him, blinking.

"Move!" Mejib gave the offending leg another kick.

The other drole yawned and laid back down, rolling into his own sleeping space.

Mejib lay down on the concrete floor. A different feeling rose up inside him. This was his space. This was good.

He heard the breeder droles working. They had already chosen their partners for the night, and the shuffling of their exertions echoed through the chamber. But the breeders were quick about it and soon all he could hear was the gentle breathing of the other droles.

Mejib closed his eyes and slept. But when he awoke, the lights were still dimmed.

Something was wrong.

Mejib sat up and scanned the row of bodies. The droles came in all different sizes. Some were as large as him. A few were wrinkled, like 133. But others were much smaller and only used a small part of the floor. Yet all lay with their eyes shut. It was still the sleep period. Somehow, he had awakened. Worry gripped him as he looked back and forth along the resting chamber.

"God knows all," he whispered.

Mejib closed his eyes again, searching for sleep, but it wouldn't come.

Then the lights brightened. He sensed the change through his eyelids. The other droles were waking up. Sleep period had ended.

Mejib stood and joined the line of droles plodding toward the work sector. His stomach let out an audible groan. He was still hungry. But work came first. Once more, Mejib searched his pockets for the nummo and came up empty.

His work station consisted of a short stool in front of a complex array of pipes and gauges — a sight that greeted him every morning of his life. Mejib wasn't quite sure why, but somehow his station looked different today.

A thundering blast echoed through the work sector, signaling the droles to begin their day-long tasks.

Mejib grasped a handle jutting out from a pipe and watched the gauge. The needle vibrated, staying in the green area for a long time. Then it shot up to red. He yanked the handle down and the gauge dropped back into green. He then returned the handle back to its original position.

This was to be continued, over and over, until rest period.

After pulling the handle many more times, Mejib decided he didn't like this task. The sensation came to him suddenly. His arm ached. Plus, his neck and back felt sore from sitting in the same position for so long.

He looked around at the other droles in their work stations. They performed the same task — pulling handles and watching gauges. This surprised Mejib. He had never thought of looking at the other droles before. For as long as he could remember, there had only been his own work station, the handle, and the gauge.

A hissing whine pulled his attention back. The needle jerked spastically in the red. Mejib jerked the handle down and the needle slipped back to green.

Mejib tilted his head. What would happen if he didn't return the handle to its original position? He looked up along the pipes that cluttered the area. No speakers. Did God watch him here?

He let go of the handle. Nothing happened.

Mejib leaned in and watched the gauge. The needle did not quiver like before. It stayed all the way at the bottom of the green area. He watched it for a long time and it never moved. The handle and the gauge were connected. He understood. Something about this idea frightened Mejib. Yet it pleased him at the same time.

The bell rang, indicating rest period.

Mejib looked around. The other droles all sat motionless at their stations, heads drooped down.

He felt a sharp pang in his stomach. His hands dipped into his pockets again. Mejib froze. He stared out into space for a long time.

"I dropped it," he said.

Understanding dawned on Mejib. The clang had been the nummo striking the floor. He felt pleased with himself for making this discovery. So pleased that he didn't hear the work bell.

Mejib sat at his station, thinking. Nothing like this ever happened before. There had always been work, for all the days before. But now the desire was absent. Was he the only one who felt this way? Or did the other droles understand as he did?

Mejib rose from his stool and moved to the drole in the next work station.

"Do you understand as I do?"

The other drole did not respond. He kept his gaze fixed on his gauge.

Mejib pushed the drole's shoulder. "Do you understand?"

The other drole watched the needle quiver in the green. That feeling rose up in Mejib again, a heat followed by tension. His question deserved an answer. The gauge was not important.

"Do you understand?" Mejib shoved with his hands.

The other drole fell off the stool and hit the floor. He looked up with blank eyes — no pain, no anger. The drole simply pushed himself up and sat back on the stool. His hand gripped the handle once again.

"Work is good," Mejib said quietly, though if the other drole heard him, he did not respond.

Mejib knew he was alone. Only he understood.

He did not return to his stool. Instead, he examined the pipes running through the work sector. Where did they come from and where did they go? A different pipe seemed to connect each gauge. Leaning over the catwalk, Mejib saw other droles, on different levels, all with their hands on levels. Above him, the pipes ran up to the ceiling, but what was above the ceiling?

The thundering work bell rang. Work had ended.

Mejib stood motionless as the other droles shuffled by on their way to the ingestion chamber.

"Why am I different?" Mejib asked, though there was no one around to answer him.

He noticed something on the ground where the other drole had fallen. Mejib knelt. A splotch of red liquid pooled on the floor. He touched it and a droplet stuck to his finger. It glimmered in the light.

Mejib turned and walked after the other droles, finally joining the queue. He touched the red drop with his thumb and now had two smaller blobs. He rubbed these together and the red color smeared along his fingers.

Finally the queue brought him to God — a towering face on the wall staring down as the droles passed. Mejib looked at those massive eyes and the old fear slithered up his spine. God knows all. Yet today the face looked different. The eyes, always watching, now felt less real. They reminded Mejib of how the other drole had looked at him — with a blank expression.

He shifted left and right, but God's eyes still stared forward. A chuckle tumbled from his lips. Why had he ever been afraid? It did not even seem as real as the other droles around him. Mejib reached up and touched the face. It was flat and did not move. His fingers left a red smudge, just below one of the eyes.

Beneath the image of God lay the button. Mejib pressed it and a round copper coin emerged on the tray. He took his nummo, felt the chill of the metal against his palm.

While walking along the narrow catwalk to the ingestion chamber, he clutched the nummo close to him, making sure it wouldn't slip out of his hand. Peering over the railing, he saw steam drifting up through the snaking pipes and conduits. After a long time searching, he spotted the glint of metal. His old nummo.

At the end of the catwalk, he entered the ingestion chamber. The black tube of the food dispenser jutted out of the wall. Next to it sat a pile of bowls. Mejib took one and slid his nummo into the slot. A meal of sticky mush gurgled out into his waiting bowl.

As he walked to his table, Mejib saw the other drole from his work sector. Red spots dotted his coverall and more liquid leaked from his head. The other drole did not seem to know about the liquid.

Mejib smiled. He noticed so many things now.

As he sat at the table, he saw his number, 132, painted on the surface. But some distant memory told him the table used to be bigger. Or perhaps he had been shorter, like some of the other smaller droles. How long ago was that? Mejib tried to recall.

The bowl of food let off a warm earthy odor. His hand dipped into the mush and he sucked it off his fingers. Perhaps he should look for his lost nummo. Then he could have more.

Mejib glanced up. The other droles had their heads down, each slurping up their mush. He glanced around, noting their different sizes. Some hardly reached the top of the table, hands groping up to reach to bowl. Then he spotted a single drole who was not eating. This other drole stared back at Mejib from across the multitude of figures.

For a moment, it seemed as though the two connected — someone else who also understood.

But Mejib's stomach screamed for food. He lowered his head and scooped up the mush. Soon his bowl was emptied.

How could he get more? Mejib felt sure there was a way, but he couldn't remember.

After another moment, even the notion of another bowl slipped away. A warm contentment bubbled up inside him — a calmness devoid of thought. Only three ideas remained fixed in his mind:

Food is good.

Work is good.

God knows all.

Veronica Leigh has been writing seriously since she was eleven and her aunt invited her to participate in a writer's workshop for senior citizens. She's been published in numerous blogs, anthologies, journals, and magazines. She aspires to be the Jane Austen of her generation and she makes her home in Indiana.

• • •

I wrote "Shadows From the Past" in January of 2020 ... which seems like a lifetime ago due to the pandemic. I revised it a couple of months later, during the country's lockdown. My mindset was completely different; in such a short amount of time so much had changed. Then then I really didn't know what to do with it because it's part-fantasy/time travel, part-historical, part-mystery, and I was afraid there wouldn't be a market for it. But it found a home and I'm happy that it will be in print.

SHADOWS FROM THE PAST

VERONICA L. ASAY

S TEPHANIE DUBANOWSKI closed her English Lit textbook with a loud thump and then winced. Holding her breath, she hazarded a glance over at her grandfather, who was still fast asleep. Whistling snores escaped his flared nostrils, and, with every breath, his cheeks hollowed in and out.

"*Pomoz mi,*" he grumbled, smacking his lips. His tongue thickened and twisted, releasing words foreign to her ears. In his sleep, he often lapsed into Polish. "*Jezu kochany … Psia krew!*"

His triple bypass had drained him, but, intent on his independence, he allowed her to stay with him to avoid having to go to a nursing home for rehab. Luckily, her summer vacation from college coincided with his surgery. She felt a bittersweet twinge within, as she recalled spending her summers off with him and her grandmother. Things changed when her grandmother passed away. Grandpa Dubanowski became distant.

He is broken-hearted; he lost his true love. Stephanie laid the book aside and sat back in her chair. *It'll get better.* Surveying the room, an old and tattered photo album on the highest shelf of the bookcase caught her eye. An album she had never seen before. She stood and crept on noiseless feet across the old hardwood floor. Unable to reach the album due to her short stature, she brought a chair in from the kitchen, pushed it next to the bookshelf, and climbed on it. Withdrawing the album, Stephanie stepped down from the chair and returned to her previous seat on the sofa. As she skimmed through the old, crumbling black pages, she stopped when her eyes landed on a particular sepia-toned photograph.

She instantly recognized her grandfather as a young man, and behind him were his father and his mother. *Krakawa, 1941* was scrawled beneath the picture. Grandpa Dubanowski rarely spoke of his life in Poland, but from what she pieced together, his father was a difficult man and his mother died of a broken heart not long after the war. His was a tragic youth. To begin anew, her grandfather immigrated to America, and he eventually found himself in Indiana.

Then she noticed a fourth person, an unknown girl near her own age, standing beside her grandfather. Stephanie squinted, studying the girl's face. Golden hair, large light eyes, a pert nose. And the smile! Goosebumps prickled along Stephanie's forearms. The resemblance between her and this girl was uncanny ... to the point it was eerie. *She must have been a relative,* she concluded. Logically it would make sense that this girl was Grandpa Dubanowski's sister, but he had always insisted that he was an only child.

Grandpa Dubanowski snorted loud enough to wake himself. His befuddled eyes scanned the room, and when he turned to her, he chuckled. "Have I been asleep long?"

"Not too long." Stephanie managed a smile. Tugging the photograph from the page, she closed the album and brought the picture to her grandfather. "Grandpa, I was looking through this. Who is this girl?" She handed it to him.

The second Grandpa Dubanowski saw the photo, he let it go and it fluttered to the floor. He clamped his hand over his mouth and began to whimper.

Stephanie retrieved the photograph, feeling like the worst person in the world. "I'm sorry, I was just curious." If she had known it would upset him, she wouldn't have said a word.

Grandpa Dubanowski had held his emotions in check at his wife's funeral, but now the tears flowed freely over his craggy cheeks. Whether it was the surgery that made him vulnerable, or his sleepy state, he replied, "She ... She was my older sister, Stefania. Stefi." He took the photo from her, and stroked the face of it. "Stefi died in the war. The Nazis killed her for hiding Jews. You were named for her."

Stephanie bit her lip. She'd never given much thought to her name, but her parents had said that when she was born, Grandpa Dubanowski specifically requested her to be named Stephanie. A man of quirks and idiosyncrasies, everyone supposed he was simply partial to it. But it was to honor his deceased sister. *No wonder he claimed to be an only child.* The tragedy of losing his sister during the war was too traumatic for him to think or speak of.

Grandpa Dubanowski shook his head. "Please, no more." He handed the photograph back, then waved her off. "Put it away."

Stephanie nodded, but rather than slipping the photo back into the album, she slid it into her jeans pocket. Later she'd try to scrounge up some information on her mysterious great-aunt. The internet was brimming with information on those who helped Jews during the Holocaust. She grabbed the album and, mounting the chair once more, she returned it to the bookshelf.

She turned to apologize once more, but lost her balance. She fell, and the left side of her head bounced against the floor like a rubber ball.

Stephanie attempted to sit up, but a white fog clouded her vision and she slumped back down. Faintly, she could hear her grandfather calling out "Stephanie!" before she lost consciousness.

•　　　•　　　•

Stephanie stirred to the scent of lilacs tickling her nose, and warm, feminine fingertips petting her clammy brow. Opening her eyes, it took a minute for her eyesight to focus, but when it did, she jerked and pressed herself against the feather mattress. *Where am I?* Three of the people — the man, woman, and young man — from the old photo surrounded her bedside, wearing similar homespun clothing. The simplicity of the room, the lack of décor, and the thin curtains which allowed the setting sun to filter through, screamed poverty. It made her feel as though she were trapped in a WWII movie. She glanced at the end table and saw the photograph she'd discovered, featured in a frame by a small bouquet of lilacs.

How? Stephanie gulped. Somehow, she had been transported to Krakow during the war.

"Stefi!" The youthful voice belonged to the teenage boy looking down at her ... *Grandpa!* It was Grandpa Durbanowski as a young man. The woman stroking Stephanie's aching head was his mother, and the man at the foot of the bed was his father. "Stefi?"

Oh, God! And then she understood. No longer was she Stephanie Dubanowski of Terre Haute, Indiana. When she fell and hit her head in the present, she miraculously went back in time and became Stefi Dubanoska of Krakow, Poland.

Stephanie on the inside, Stefi on the out. Her grandfather was now her younger brother, Franek, and his parents were her parents. Her *Matka* and *Tatus*. A language barrier that should exist didn't, for she could comprehend what they were whispering to one another. *Am I Stefi now?* Stephanie wondered. Could she be two people at once? It made about as much sense as time traveling via head injury.

"My girl, we thought we were going to lose you." Unshed tears welled in *Matka's* grey eyes. The woman claimed Stephanie's hand and brought it to her lips.

"Are you all right? How many fingers am I holding up?" Franek asked, holding up two fingers.

"Two." Stephanie shook her head, wincing at the searing pain at her left temple. Her fingers desperately tightened around *Matka's,* longing to tell this sweet woman about this freaky phenomenon. But her mind was too muddled to put it into words. "My head ... Am I dreaming? Tell me it's a dream."

An odd cackle drew her attention to the man at the foot of the bed. *Tatus.* A man of medium height and a pot belly, the stench of cheap liquor clung to his unwashed skin. "You were coming home from work and you fell from your bicycle, clumsy girl. Someone brought you home." His grin faded and the corners of his mouth turned downwards. "You don't remember?"

Stephanie shook her throbbing head once more. They'd think she'd was nuts if she told the truth. *Better to play along until I can figure out what to do.* Exhaustion from the fall and traveling through time sapped what remained of her strength. Sleep began to beckon her.

Matka bent down and pressed her lips to Stephanie's brow. "Our Stefi has been through so much. Rest, my dear." She perched on the side of the bed, her soft face peering down on Stephanie's. "I will sit at your bedside and all will be well in the morning."

Maybe if I sleep, I will wake up in the present. While she knew she should be more frantic than what she was, Stephanie gave in and dozed, listening to her *Matka* hum a melodious tune. *This is a bad dream, that's all.*

• • •

Stephanie was awake before she cracked open an eyelid, praying that the sore spot on her head was from the floor, and that she was lying on the sofa in her grandfather's living room. But the lilacs and the sound of car wheels clacking on cobblestone outside informed her she was in Krakow in 1941, still in Stefi's body and in her life.

Dear God, it's not a dream! She opened her eyes, sat up, rubbed her head, and scooted off of the bed. *I'm stuck here!* Stephanie went to the wardrobe in the corner of the room and withdrew a simple blue dress. More of a t-shirt, jeans, and tennis shoes girl, when she put on the frock and loafers, she noted in the mirror how frumpy she looked and felt. The wound on her head was ugly and bold. She braided her hair in a tight plait, took a deep breath, and emerged from the bedroom.

Stephanie couldn't help but notice the smallness of the cottage. There was no formal living room, the kitchen seemed to double as both. There was another room on the left, which she assumed to be her parents' and a loft above where Franek likely slept. She found *Matka* at the stove, stirring a hot concoction. Franek and *Tatus* were at the table, waiting for breakfast.

As if sensing her presence, *Matka* turned abruptly, wooden spoon raised. "How do you feel, Stefi?" she inquired.

"Good." Stephanie replied, marveling at how thick her Polish accent was. Gone was her Hoosier drawl. She wasn't even trying to sound like the Dubanowski family, but she did. Glancing at the counter, she didn't see a coffee maker. "Could I have a cup of coffee?"

Tatus crudely snorted. "No coffee, not with the Germans ruling the roost." When *Matka* laid out four bowls of porridge, her father gestured for her to sit on his right. "Eat your breakfast, that will rouse you."

Afraid to draw too much attention to herself, Stephanie did as bidden. So far, they thought her off due to her accident. They wouldn't understand the truth. *Matka* might listen, but *Tatus* left much to be desired. She had always heard he was a difficult man, but she had been unaware that he was obnoxious and constantly reeked of alcohol. Stephanie caught the grimace on Franek's face, and was relieved that he felt the same way about *Tatus*.

When her parents and brother bowed their heads, she did likewise, and mimicked how they crossed themselves. They were asking for a blessing on the meal and the day, while she asked for Divine Guidance on how to keep this ruse up. As well as Divine Intervention to send her home. The latter part of the prayer must have fallen on deaf ears, since she was not miraculously transported back to the present.

Stephanie ate spoonful after spoonful of the tasteless glop, but didn't dare complain or ask for sugar. If something as common as coffee wasn't available, there was no point in asking for sugar. *This is WWII; things are rationed.* Her chest began to tighten as the panic mounted within her. *This is WWII, and I'm in Europe, where there are Nazis and death.* The hairs on the back of her neck stood on end, a cold sweat broke out on her body, and when her stomach twisted, she felt like she was going to puke. Her grandfather had told her that his sister had died at the hands of the Nazis for hiding Jews. *I'm going to die!*

"Franek," *Matka* began after she finished her meal, "tell the Hummels Stefi won't be coming this morning. She needs to rest." Her mother shifted and gave Stephanie's shoulder a comforting squeeze.

"The Hummels?" Stephanie croaked.

"The German family we work for," Franek explained, nudging her in the ankle with his foot. "You are their maid; I am their gardener."

Tatus shoved his bowl aside and the chair legs scraped the floor as he pushed up from the table. "Ah, she is well enough. We need the money and the Hummels won't pardon her on such short notice." Her father sauntered off, and then departed from the cottage, heading for what she figured was work.

"Very well." *Matka* sighed, then nodded begrudgingly. "But try not to exhaust yourself."

Ten minutes later, Stephanie and Franek were moving through the streets of Krakow, on their way to the Hummels'.

If the realization that she would probably die soon didn't terrify her enough, the unfurling red flags decked in black swastikas, decorating the neighborhood, flapping in the painfully sharp wind made her head spin. The sky was clear and brighter blue than what she was accustomed to, and the storks and pigeons were the only ones to spoil the view. The basilica in the center of town brought actual tears to her eyes. *Too bad I couldn't have visited Poland in my era.*

On seeing two men in German uniforms with lightning bolts on their collars, at the end of the square, her steps slowed and she froze in place. Dread paralyzed her, body and soul. They took no notice of her; they were helping themselves to produce on sale. A Nazi in a movie was frightening enough, but one in real life ... *Will they be the ones to kill me?*

Stephanie was so distracted by the Nazis' presence that when Franek placed a hand on her shoulder, she jumped. "What?" she snapped, and then hated herself for being harsh with the young man who would become her grandfather.

"You hardly seem like yourself," Franek observed, recoiling from her. "Maybe you should stay home."

Accustomed to the strong, older man she knew and loved, it was staggering to see him young. His chin was clean of whiskers and his blonde hair was mussed, making him look younger than his sixteen years. Tall and handsome, no doubt he was popular with the ladies.

"I ... I know what's going to happen." Stephanie hugged herself, whimpering, "I know everything."

She longed to hug him, as a granddaughter hugged her grandfather. His hugs always offered her strength. But she hung back, terrified of what his response would be. She couldn't tell him she was, in fact, his granddaughter from the future, trapped in his sister's body, and that she had magically traveled through time or that this was some weird dream. Franek would think she was insane. Never mind he didn't know she was going to die and that the Holocaust was currently taking place in his country.

"Deep breaths." Franek advised and ventured to grasp her shoulder once more. "It will be fine, I promise."

Stephanie nodded, breathing through her nose and exhaling through her mouth. *I can do this.* She had no choice but to live out the real Stefi's life. Stefi died protecting someone else, and to change history, to not hide Jews, would be wrong.

•   •   •

Stephanie's shoulders and lower back ached with every step she took, but she had to get home before dark. *Before curfew.* Evidently, Poles had to be off the street before 8pm. The tram cost money, which she didn't have; ergo her own two feet were good enough for her. Mrs. Hummel, the German woman she worked for, got her work out of Stephanie, barking out orders at every turn, only allowing one break mid-day. Unaccustomed to hard, physical labor, Stephanie knew as soon as she fell into bed tonight, she would be dead to the world. Franek was unfortunately kept longer.

She passed by a large arched stone wall. Her brow puckered in confusion when she heard chatter on the other side of it and wondered what it could be. Rising up on tip toe was no use, because she still couldn't see above it. She settled back down on her feet and picked up her pace, but then slowed when a young man approached from the opposite direction, sensing he was heading towards her. Her suspicions were confirmed when he stopped two feet in front of her.

"Good evening." The young man nodded to her. Dark wavy hair was tucked beneath a blue newsboy cap, and the bill shrouded some of his face, but she could make out chocolatey brown eyes and a dusky complexion. When he flashed a charming smile, she felt her heart gallop in her chest. "I apologize for interrupting your walk, but I wanted to see if you were all right."

Stephanie gulped. *Is he a friend of Stefi's?* There was something familiar about him, but she couldn't place him. "I-

I'm sorry, I can't remember you." She touched her brow, indicating the gash on her temple.

"My name is Jakob. I found you yesterday." Jakob jutted his thumb in the direction of the cement wall. "You had given food to children in the ghetto and as you were leaving on your bicycle, someone knocked you off and then ran. You fell, hit your head. I took you home."

Stephanie's eyes widened. She cast a glance at the wall and a painful chill crept down her spine. *It's the Jewish ghetto!* The chatter ... there were innocent people on the other side, and the majority of them would be murdered. Pride surged through her veins, pride for Stefi who had seen the writing on the wall and was trying to help in a small way. *A brave girl.*

"Oh, thank you for helping me." Stephanie put out her hand to shake his and relished in the warmth of how his fingers enveloped hers. "How did you know where I lived?"

To her astonishment, Jakob raised her hand to his lips and kissed the back of it. It was like a courtier's kiss. "We all know who you are, *Panna* Dubanowska. You are part of the Polish resistance, and you help Jews find hiding places." He released her fingers and backed away.

Stefi hid Jews and she is part of the resistance! Stephanie stopped herself from shaking her head. It was no wonder the Nazis killed her; she was a threat to them.

Then she knew: Jakob was Jewish and he was illegally outside of the ghetto. From what she learned in high school about the Holocaust, Jews were forcibly held in ghettos until the ghettos were liquidated or they were sent to death camps.

"Well, I will not keep you. Stay safe, Stefi." Jakob turned and retraced his steps.

Stephanie hated watching Jakob leave. Not only because she believed that Stefi was meant to help him, but she personally felt connected to him. *What is his story?* She attempted to swallow the lump in her throat. *Does Jakob survive?* It occurred to her that if Stefi was involved in the Polish resistance and had helped Jews before, then she could easily help Jakob and find him a hiding place. And, for however long she was in Krakow 1941, it would be nice to have a friend.

Before Jakob turned a corner and disappeared from her life completely, Stephanie broke out into a run and caught up to him. "Wait!" She grasped his shoulder and mumbled an apology when he flinched, hating to have startled him. "I could hi–" Stephanie stopped herself from saying anything further about hiding him, lest someone on the street overhear their conversation. "Would you like to do something? Something fun? We could see a movie."

"Only pigs sit in cinemas." Jakob answered, leaving her uncertain as what that phrase meant. "But, yes, we could find something fun to do." When his eyes settled on her and he smiled, she knew it wouldn't be "just friends" for long.

He offered her his arm and she took it gladly.

Stefi falls in love. Stephanie grinned, giving Jakob a coy sideways glance. *And I imagine I will too.*

•   •   •

Stephanie pushed with all of her might and the sewer grate dislodged. She moved it aside and, hoisting herself up, she climbed through the opening and into the street. A street in the Jewish ghetto. Next, she returned the sewer grating to the curb, and dusted herself off, her nose wrinkling over the foul stench that clung to her clothes and skin from the sewer.

She produced a white armband featuring the Star of David from the rucksack dangling on her arm, and slipped the band on and up to her bicep. Holding her head high, she walked as if she belonged, disregarding the questioning expressions of the poor souls who were imprisoned there.

They know I'm not Jewish. The contrast between Stephanie's healthy, filled out body and their emaciated ones was distinct. Unlike the inhabitants of the ghetto, her eyes weren't "sad," nor was her clothing in tatters. Still, no one bothered her. Perhaps they were too afraid to pry into her

153

business. The German soldiers ought to frighten her more, since they could easily shoot her between the eyes. But she had become more accustomed to their presence in the streets on the Aryan side.

Stephanie headed to the dilapidated flat where Jakob resided. As she had grown close to him, she had begun to feel torn between returning to the present or staying with him. There was no guarantee of her return to her old life. It had been weeks since she had fallen, hit her head, and time traveled to Krakow 1941. While she would have liked to have met Jakob under different circumstances, in the present, with every meeting she fell a little more in love with him.

She entered the building and climbed two flights of stairs, and then went into the flat without knocking. His dozen or so flat mates were used to her coming and going as she pleased. She was still working on finding him a hiding place. Unfortunately, the connections she had to the Polish resistance were uninterested in helping Jews, and the others willing to help didn't have a place readily available to him. Hiding a child was easier than hiding a young man.

Jakob was at the kitchen table when she came in, standing when she neared. He dipped his head and brushed his lips against hers.

Sweet and simple. Stephanie blushed and drawing a chair next to his, she joined him, emptying her rucksack of supplies, which she hoped would benefit him.

Not long after their first meeting, they jumped from friendship to romance in one great leap. Jakob ventured out of the ghetto when he could. But it was easier for her to visit him and bring what he needed. He trusted her with his life completely.

Now it's time for me to trust him. Stephanie reasoned, teetering on the edge of her seat. For weeks, *Matka* and *Tatus*, Franek, the Hummels — everyone — watched her. They didn't have a clue that she was from the future, but they detected something was different about Stefi Dubanowska.

154

Her appearance, accent, and routine were the same, but the words she chose, her modern mannerisms, her feministic thinking, the books she read ... were alien to them. *Tatus* made her wary, but *Matka* and Franek were easy to love, yet they wouldn't believe her if she told them the truth.

Then there was Jakob ...

He might not believe me either, but I trust him enough to risk being honest. Rejection was a possibility ... however, that was the case in any relationship. The worst he could do was laugh in her face and spurn her affections.

"Jakob?" Stephanie claimed one of his hands, lacing her fingers with his.

"Yes?" He compressed her hand affectionately.

Stephanie sucked in a lungful of breath and decided the best thing she could do was dive straight in. "Do you believe in time travel?" she asked.

Jakob's grin waned. "Time travel?" he echoed, his tone full of uncertainty.

Stephanie glanced over her shoulder, relieved no one else in the room was paying attention. The notion of time travel wasn't a new one. Not that she could necessarily define what happened to her as time travel, since she lived in another person's body — her great-aunt's body- but it was the closest thing she describe to what happened.

"It is where someone can travel through time, to the past or to the future."

"I don't know." Jakob sighed, and then slowly shook his head. "It sounds unbelievable to me." However, he was still cradling her hand.

There's no going back now. Stephanie closed her eyes and prayed to Whoever might be listening, that Jakob might believe her. She needed a friend in this era, someone who was on her side and knew the whole story.

"What if I told you that I'm from the future?" Stephanie pulled away from him, and gripped the material of her skirt, hard enough she could tear it. "From the 21st century in

America, and that in my era, my name is Stephanie Dubanoski. I hit my head and woke up here, as my great-aunt Stefania Dubanowska in 1941." She fidgeted under Jakob's wide-eyed gaze, unable to discern how he was receiving this. Were someone to tell her this in her era, she'd laugh in their face.

Jakob suddenly chuckled, his customary impish look returning, and then shrugged. "Stefi, I already think you are mad to risk your life to help me, so this doesn't make any difference." He reached over and tucked an errant curl behind her ear. "Perhaps you haven't time traveled. Perhaps you are one of the thirty-six righteous who keep the world safe from evil. Whatever you are, however you came into my life, I don't care. I love you."

"I love you too." Stephanie gushed, and leaning forward she kissed him.

Cheers and whistles erupted from Jakob's flat mates, but Stephanie ignored them. When Jakob broke away to wave them off, she grabbed his shoulder and drew him close again, their lips meeting once more.

•　　•　　•

Stephanie burrowed down deeper into the bedding, rubbing her cheek against the feather pillow. A long day at the Hummels; she wanted nothing more than to sleep. On the verge of slumber, she groaned when she heard a pecking sound on her bedroom window. After nightfall, Krakow was full of various noises. Most should be ignored, but instinct urged her to check this one out. She tossed back the covers and went to the window, jerking back the curtains. A smile spread across her face when her eyes focused and she could make out Jakob on the other side of the glass. Pressing her finger tips to her mouth, she blew him a kiss.

She padded out of her room and paused briefly in the kitchen, to listen for her family. A trio of snores bellowed, falling in sync. Were *Matka* or Franek to catch her alone with Jakob, she wouldn't mind. But *Tatus* ... he couldn't be trusted. Even if he didn't intentionally betray her, vodka could loosen his tongue, and he would let her secret slip about her Jewish boyfriend.

Stephanie eased open the back door, tiptoed outside, and shut the door as softly as she could. A Catholic girl meeting a Jewish boy who snuck illegally out of the ghetto was a recipe for disaster. After midnight, in the pitch-black dark, she in her nightgown. But she couldn't resist the temptation. Jakob was worth the risk.

Greeting him with a kiss, she instantly sensed something was wrong by the hesitant feel of his lips. Her suspicion was confirmed when she took a step back, squinted, and made out his pained expression.

Her brow furrowed, she demanded, "What is it?"

"This must be the last time we meet." Jakob whispered.

"Why?" Stephanie crossed her arms. Gooseflesh rippled across her skin. One could never predict Poland's weather. But tonight, there was a damp chill in the air, rolling off the Tatra Mountains. The wind, the *halny* as they called it, often gave her headaches.

"I was nearly taken in a round up today ... I can't wait for a hiding place. I have decided to join the Jewish resistance. They are hiding in the woods."

"Don't be ridiculous," Stephanie scoffed. It may have been because she was exhausted, but even if Jakob did join the Jewish resistance, she didn't see how that could affect their relationship. Without the ghetto to contend with, it would be easier for them to see one another. "We can still meet —"

Jakob took off his newsboy cap, ran his fingers through his hair, then put the hat back on. "Stefi, you are a wonderful girl. I don't want to see you killed for my sake or for anyone else's." His generally confident voice quavered, betraying his own resolve. "You can live a peaceful life now, you know. Then when this is all over, we can meet again."

Stephanie knew there was no guarantee that Jakob would survive the war. Involving himself in the Jewish resistance would increase his chance of death. And where he went, she would follow. For a little while, she had been able to put Stefi's fate out of her mind and enjoy her romance with Jakob. Stefi's death was linked to Jakob specifically, no doubt.

But now, almost prophetically, she could see she was meant to participate in this resistance alongside Jakob, and the Nazis would catch her. Her grandfather had known of his sister's activities with the Polish resistance and hiding Jewish children, and assumed she died for that.

"Listen to me, I love you." Stephanie cupped his cheeks between her hands, vowing, "I will join you."

Jakob sniffed, but no tears fell. "I love you too." He lowered his head, until his brow was touching hers.

•　　　•　　　•

Stephanie arrived home just as the sun was setting. She hadn't intended to linger at the ghetto a moment longer than she needed to, but she and Jakob got so caught up in making arrangements, that she lost track of the time. He intended to head out to the woods tonight, and she would follow in a few days. Quietly entering the cottage, she held her breath, hoping to go unnoticed. But it was no use. *Matka*, *Tatus*, and Franek were gathered at the table, as if they had been waiting for her.

She stood before them, her hands clasped in front of her, guilt-ridden, and feared they were about to confront her on her true identity. There was no way they could know she was from the future. *But they have to know I'm not their Stefi.* The Dubanowskis should know, if they were as close as she always imagined them to be.

Matka shot to her feet and placed her hands on her hips. "You are late." She tilted her head. While a small woman, she was a force to be reckoned with.

"I'm sorry." Stephanie bit the inside of her cheek, hating to lie to *Matka*. She also hated running away, leaving her and Franek behind. But she couldn't see around it. *Matka* loved her, but that didn't mean she would accept Jakob. Especially in times like these. "Mrs. Hummel had extra work for me."

Franek caught her gaze and gave her a questioning look, but he said nothing. He was well aware that she'd left a couple of hours before he did.

Tatus dismissed her excuses with a wave. "At least you were back before curfew." He signaled for her to sit.

Stephanie sighed and claimed her customary spot at the table. If there was one thing she wouldn't miss after she joined Jakob's resistance, it would be *Tatus*. While not violent or abusive, she was never comfortable around him.

Matka set a bowl of *bigos* in front of Stephanie. Only then did Stephanie realize how hungry she was, and consumed several spoonfuls. The savory flavor rested on her tongue and warmth soon flooded her.

"I heard there is to be another rabbit hunt this Friday night, after sundown," *Tatus* announced, midway through the meal. "According to the priest, everyone is going."

"A rabbit hunt?" Stephanie repeated, shaking her head.

After spending weeks in Krakow 1941, she hadn't noticed any great surplus of rabbits in the area. Not enough to arrange a hunt. Then again, it could be a Polish tradition. Not to mention, they were all living on war rations issued by the Germans. Rabbit would make for a tasty meal.

Franek nodded to her, claiming her attention. "The locals go into the woods to round up Jews hiding there, and turn them over to the Gestapo," he explained, *sotto voce*.

Jakob! Stephanie felt her head sway. She dropped her spoon on the floor, and didn't bother to pick it up. *Tatus* and other Polish countrymen willingly went out of their way to hunt down Jewish people and turn them over to the authorities? This was a part of the Holocaust she never heard of before. How could *Tatus* do that to his former friends and neighbors? For years they lived side by side, and he now so easily turned on them! *I can't let them harm Jakob!*

"Five hundred zloty a head." *Tatus* made a fist and slammed it enthusiastically on the table. "That would see us through until-"

"*Tatus!*" Franek exclaimed.

Stephanie couldn't believe her ears. *Tatus* — in reality, her great-grandfather- betrayed Jews for money. He implied there was a previous "rabbit hunt," which meant he had done this before. It was no wonder Grandpa Dubanowski rarely spoke of his past. His sister was murdered by the Nazis, and his father willingly collaborated to benefit monetarily. What a painful history.

Matka reached over and swatted *Tatus* on the back of the head. "Don't you even think about it. God will punish you for touching the apple of His eye." She severely shook her finger at him.

Stephanie half-expected *Tatus* to be enraged, but he hunched his shoulders and resumed his meal, grousing under his breath.

Matka settled back down and continued eating, as if nothing out of the ordinary occurred.

Stephanie could feel Franek's eyes on her and she schooled her features, to conceal her panic. The last thing she want to do was let on her intentions. *Tatus* might be quiet now, but there was no doubt in her mind he would be there at the "rabbit hunt" Friday night.

This is it. She could foresee what was coming. She would warn Jakob and the other resistors, perhaps try and help hide them somewhere, and the Nazis would catch her.

While she had always been aware that Stefi and Jakob wouldn't get a happy ending, temporarily Stephanie had deluded herself in believing they would be all right.

There is no going back. Stephanie watched the clock. It would be a couple of hours before her family turned in for the night. Once they did, she would pack and sneak out, then head to the woods to do what she could. But tonight, she would die, that much she was certain.

•   •   •

Rain lashed at Stephanie as she trudged through the woods, her feet losing traction in the mire, which was turning to slop. Her coat, dress, and even the rucksack on her back were soaked through, weighing her down with each step. She finger-combed her hair, which was plastered to her skin. *I'll never find the Jewish resistance camp.* She sighed, resting briefly against a sturdy birch tree. For now, she was sheltered by its limbs and could consider what to do next. The directions Jakob had given her were good, but the storm was disorienting her. Returning to the Dubanowski cottage was out of the question. There was no going back. Not now. *I just need to get my bearings.* Lightning bolts lit up the sky, and between that and the flashlight in her tightened fist, they provided her with enough light to guide her.

Sneaking out of the cottage was easy. *Tatus*, *Matka*, and Franek turned in early as they did every night, oblivious to her intentions. The trick was getting through Krakow unnoticed. Sentries patrolled the streets after curfew. Stephanie chose to traverse alleys, and made it to the outskirts unscathed. The city had been eerily quiet, with the exception of the ghetto. An *akcja* was taking place. Screams and cries resounded, ones that continued to ring in her ears despite the thunder that tried to drown them out.

Stephanie stood under the canopy of the birch tree for a few more minutes, and was about to head out when a shadow passed before her and lingered, blocking her way out.

It's the Nazi that will kill me. She changed her mind when the stench of vodka stung her nostrils. "*Tatus?*" She swallowed, and raising the flashlight, she shined it at the silhouette.

Franek's youthful, but concerned face was revealed. "No, it is me." He squinted, holding up his hand to shield his eyes. The boy was as soaked as she was, so it stood to reason that he snuck out not long after she did. "*Tatus* is coming now, with a large group of men."

"Tonight?" Stephanie gaped. She lowered the flashlight, her shoulders falling in defeat. "But he said Friday night."

The thunder roared above and Franek cupped his hand around his mouth and shouted his reply at her. "He changed his mind when he learned you were going to warn your boyfriend."

Stephanie didn't stop the tears from falling and soon they mingled in the rain. She had done her best to hide her relationship with Jakob. Someone must have reported their rendezvous to *Tatus*. *Rather than save Jakob, I'm causing his death.* She shook her head miserably. *Poor Jakob ... I'm sorry!*

"But who could have told him?" Stephanie asked and her breath caught in her throat when she saw a dark look flicker across Franek's face. He worked for the Hummels, learned information, and conspired with *Tatus*! She pointed the light at him once more. "It was you. You betrayed me. You- were you the one who knocked me off the bicycle, too?"

My Grandpa Dubanowski! Stephanie couldn't wrap her mind around it. Her grandfather rarely spoke of life in Poland during WWII, but whenever he did, he made it out that he and his family were the victims. In reality, he and *Tatus* were collaborators, and betrayed innocents. The story now made sense. Stefi was involved in the Polish resistance, as originally claimed. She met Jakob, they fell in love, and planned to run away together and live with the Jewish resistance group. Then Franek ...

Franek killed Stefi! Stephanie gasped, quavering from head to toe. It wasn't the chill from the rain, but the terror. *My Grandpa Dubanowski will kill me!* He was as depraved as his *tatus*.

"We need the money." Franek, nonplussed by her accusations, shrugged. "Walk away from this, Stefi." There was a hint of tenderness in his tone, but she sensed it was no use. Darkness had taken root within him.

"I can't. You know I can't."

Stephanie attempted to dash off, but Franek seized her wrist and swung her around. She fought with all her might, hitting with her flashlight, kicking, scratching, but he shoved her. Losing her balance, she dropped to her knees. The flashlight rolled and its beam landed on Franek. Her heart hitched in her chest when he bent over and dislodged a rock from the mud. There was no avoiding Stefi's — or her — fate now.

Stephanie felt the first pummel in the head with the rock, but she became numb to the others. She slumped back into the wet earth and tiny pinpricks blotted her vision of Franek standing over her, before it all went black.

Stefi! A voice was beckoning, calling her name. *Stephanie!*

•   •   •

Stephanie!

Stephanie stirred, expecting to be lying on Grandpa Dubanowki's living room floor where she had fallen. Rather than a hard surface, she was stretched out on the familiar lumpy sofa by the windows facing the street.

Her hand wandered to the gash on her head. Opening her eyes, her vision was blurry. But soon the blur dissipated, and she found a young man kneeling beside her, peering into her face. The resemblance he bore to Jakob was uncanny, and for a split second, she believed she was still in Krakow 1941. That Jakob had found her hurt in the woods and rescued her. Part of her wanted that.

"Jakob?" Stephanie reached out and grasped his forearm.

But when she heard her grandfather's accented shout from his chair, she understood that, out of her desperation for Jakob, she conjured him from memory.

However, when the young man spoke, Stephanie concluded he was not a hallucination, but flesh and blood. "Nope, sorry, the name's Isaac." When she struggled to sit up, Isaac braced his arm around her shoulders and eased her into a sitting position. "My grandfather is named Jakob, though. I'm from next door, I'm a medical student. Mr. Dubanowski called me over. You hit your head pretty hard and I want to take you to the ER, okay?"

Stephanie's muddled mind took a minute to absorb what he said. He hadn't given his last name, but Isaac resembled Jakob in looks, wasn't far off in age from her, and his grandfather was even named Jakob. *Could it be?* Perhaps Jakob had escaped the "rabbit hunt" and survived the Holocaust, and Isaac was his grandson?

She couldn't resist, and cupped Isaac's cheek, managing a watery smile. Stefi may have died, but at least Jakob found a measure of happiness.

"Do it, Stephanie." Grandpa Dubanowski ordered, snapping her once back into reality. "Listen to him."

She turned towards her grandfather and temporarily forgot how to breathe. Her grandfather - the man she loved, the one who used to read her stories and give her candy whenever she wanted — when he was sixteen, he murdered his sister. In cold blood, to turn Jews over to the Gestapo for money. Whether it was a vision, that she time-traveled, or truly had become Stefi — she witnessed it all. Still, she could not reconcile her beloved grandfather to the boy who committed murder.

Stephanie propelled herself upwards. "Grandpa, you killed me." She touched her brow and staggered a few paces. A little wobbly, she was grateful when Isaac offered his arm and she could lean on him. "You and your father betrayed Jews for money. You killed Stefi, your sister."

"What?" Isaac did a double-take, stunned by her accusation.

Stephanie knew she sounded crazy, but she couldn't let truth about Stefi continue to be hidden.

Grandpa Dubanowski turned ashen and his eyes glistened. "How- how do you kn-know that?" he sputtered. It wasn't lost on her that he didn't deny it.

"I was there. I saw it through Stefi's eyes." Stephanie pressed her palm to her chest. "You killed her!"

"Stephanie, is it?" Isaac squeezed her hand gently and, claiming her attention once more, he locked eyes with her. "I think you're confused. You might have a serious concussion." Once more he implored, "Please, let me take you to the hospital."

Grandpa Dubanowski gripped the arms of his chair, and he trembled. "I'm sorry, it was an accident." When his eyes began to glisten, she detected a hint of guilt there, but he persisted in his deceit. Even now, he wouldn't own up to his sins. "I didn't mean to."

"How could you?" Nothing could change what he had done. "I'll have someone else in the family stay with you." Turning her sore head, she asked, "Please, Isaac, would you take me to the hospital?"

"Of course." Offering her his arm, he escorted her out of her grandfather's house.

Stephanie didn't know if she would ever forgive her grandfather, or reconcile with him, but she knew, after what she had seen of the past, her present and future would never be the same.

Elyse Russell is a writer of short stories and comics. She has works published with Brigids Gate, Band of Bards, Cosmic Horror Monthly, and many more. When not writing, Elyse enjoys naps with her cat and ingesting copious amounts of cheese.

FOREST OF THE FATES

ELYSE RUSSELL

D OGS BARKED. The bell rang. And Felicity ran.
Her dark red hair flowed like a banner behind her in the chill night, unbound and snarled from the wind, as she passed the last row of drab little village cabins. Mud splattered with every step she took, coating her pale calves and filling her deerskin shoes. If she didn't make it to the forest ... if they caught her ...

Felicity blinked away the thought of a falling axe and hiked her cream-colored skirts higher, giving her legs more room to put on a burst of speed. She had to cross the boundary line into the Forest of the Fates. No man could set foot there. The witch trees would eat him alive. She just had to cross the field.

A shout rang out, and Felicity recognized her grandfather's voice. She risked a glance over her shoulder. They were untying the dogs. Men held torches aloft, gazing through the darkness in her direction. In the center of the gathering mob of villagers stood her grandfather. His hulking figure towered over the others, and even in the low light, she could see his eyes searching for her.

The hounds pelted after her with ground-eating strides, baying and snapping as they followed her scent. The trees were getting closer. Felicity felt as though they were almost leaning toward her, the branches reaching for her, like a mother encouraging her baby to take its first steps. She longed for their safe embrace.

No sooner had she passed the forest boundary than she tripped and fell. The breath was knocked from her chest as she slammed to the forest floor amongst the moss and bioluminescent mushrooms. Immediately, she scrambled to her feet again. Men might not have been able to set foot in the woods, but dogs certainly could. They'd shred her to bits.

Choking back a sob of terror, Felicity started climbing the nearest tree. She didn't stop until she was high enough to be safe from the dogs. Clinging to the trunk, she straddled a large limb and looked down.

The dogs were beginning to congregate at the foot of the tree. They snarled and snapped as they jumped. Felicity pulled her feet up and held onto her branch more tightly. She closed her eyes and leaned her forehead against the rough bark, trying to catch her breath. She'd made it. She was safe.

A low whistle made her eyes fly open again. The dogs were retreating- they were leaving the forest. Felicity sighed with relief. The men were probably afraid some fell beast would harm their hounds.

It became very silent and still. Felicity looked up toward the gap in the foliage where she'd crashed through only minutes ago. And there he was.

Her grandfather's enraged face glared at her through the leaves, making her jump and let out a little yelp. Then, for a few beats, neither of them so much as blinked.

Before Felicity could react, her grandfather lifted a bow and shot an arrow straight at her. And then she was falling, falling, falling ...

Dark.

•   •   •

Keith watched his granddaughter's slight body fall from the ancient witch oak and crumple on the ground. He heard a sharp *crack* as a bone broke. The arrow stuck up from her chest, and she didn't move. In the dark, her long hair looked like blood on the moss.

Bow still in hand, Keith turned, snapping his fingers at the hounds to follow. The other men were just arriving, and he shook his head at them and drew his finger across his throat. They responded with nods of respect and stepped out of his way, then fell in behind him to follow him back to the village.

The old man cast one glance back at the forest over his shoulder. He greatly resented living so close to the witch's wood. Once, as a child, he'd tried to set it on fire. He had stared for an hour at the mysterious trees, which seemed to whisper and hiss at him when he came near. Burning with a boy's curiosity, he had wanted so badly to adventure in that forest.

But as a male, he could not enter. This injustice had rankled him, so he'd snuck out one night with a torch. Each time he reached the flames out to touch a branch, though, they would gutter. Finally, he threw the torch into the bushes, but the fire just went out altogether.

He'd never told anyone what he'd attempted. But the next time the old midwife came down into the village for a birth, she had stopped dead in her tracks and turned her eerie, dark eyes on him. She'd stared long enough to make him squirm, given him a sharp smile with no kindness in it, and then gone about her way. The other boys laughed at his shaking legs and pale face. He'd made them regret that laughter.

•   •   •

"Hurry, Ga! The trees are calling!"

"What is it? What do they say, sister?"

"A girl ... a girl is dying near the village border. We don't have much time!"

"These old legs will only go so fast, Baya!"

The sisters cut through the woods, off their usual path, to where the trees were screaming. To Baya's ears, the arboreal cacophony was ear-splitting. Ga heard only the faintest of murmuring, as her magic lent itself more to the dead than the living. She could, however, hear the distant howling of Soul Wolves. The mist creatures could sense impending death. They were coming for the girl's soul.

Ga grunted with effort, forcing her creaky, arthritic limbs to hasten. The night air was cool against her naked form, and her snarled hair hung in lank hunks from her age-spotted scalp. She could see perfectly in the dark, as could her sister, who waddled ahead of her with vigor.

Baya, too, was nude. It was their natural state in their habitat. The leaves seemed to caress their bare skin as they passed, desperate for the warmth and magic of their guardians.

Finally, they reached the source. Baya paused, staring at the foot of an anxious old oak. The poor tree had bent itself protectively over the crumpled form of a young woman from the village.

An arrow jutted from between the villager's small breasts, and dark red had spread stickily across the light fabric of her dress. The red ran off the sides to blend in with the auburn of the girl's hair, a waterfall joining a scarlet lake in the moonlight.

Baya gasped as she took in the girl's soft features, and moved over to her prone body. The corpulent witch crouched beside the girl, her bulbous shape settling to the ground with unexpected grace.

"Why, it's the mute girl! Felicity!" she exclaimed, running a finger over the girl's cold cheek.

Baya knew every villager. She came out of the woods to serve as midwife at every birth. Of course, the villagers assumed she lived in the village on the *other* side of the woods, and didn't have to travel all the way around because she was female.

Felicity had shown interest in the profession, and Baya had begun training her only weeks ago. The girl was a fast learner, and had deft, gentle hands. Though she couldn't speak, her expressive eyes communicated calm and reassurance to laboring mothers.

Baya had no idea where the girl's gentleness had come from. Not from her parents; they'd abandoned her to start a new life in a faraway city. And *certainly* not from her grandfather: a colder man, Baya had never encountered. He'd been unusually detached even as a child. And he'd only grown crueler with each passing year. As the girl's only living male relative, she had fallen under his care.

It was not Baya's place to intervene in village affairs. She helped with the births because it was her duty to her magic. But watching that lamb-like creature grow up under the village chief's hard eyes ... she'd been tempted.

Well, she thought, *they have reneged on any claim to her, now.*

Ga came to stand behind her, long limbs creaking like a ship at sea. She did not crouch, as it hurt her joints, but she hovered in the same anxious manner as the tree. Her beady yellow eyes glowed in the dark, watching Baya's hands as they hovered around the arrow.

Golden light spread from Baya's chubby fingers, and she closed her eyes to concentrate. Ga moved in closer.

"Now, Ga!" Baya commanded. "Pull out the arrow!"

With a great heave of strength that seemed impossible for such a thin, frail creature, Ga pulled the arrow from its fleshy sheath. Baya's fingers plunged into the gaping wound, pushing life-giving light into the rent tissue.

She healed the girl from the inside out, slowly withdrawing her fingers. Finally, the skin sealed back over. It was fresh, pink and scarless, like the skin of a newborn.

"Will she live?" Ga croaked over her sister's shoulder.

"Of course she'll live. Do you doubt my magic?"

"Never."

"We must get her to shelter. Help me carry her back to the hut."

As Baya stood to lift the girl off the ground, she glanced over her shoulder through the bushes, to the distant lights of the village. She ground her teeth, and her eyes flashed green in the darkness. What could have possessed that man to drive out his own flesh and blood, and then try to kill her?

As she pushed an arm under Felicity's back, she had a feeling she already knew the answer to that question. With Ga holding onto the girl's legs, the two witches made their way deeper into the forest, until they reached their home, where their third sister lay waiting for them in her cradle.

•   •   •

The hut with chicken legs lay in a deeply snarled part of the woods. Vines creeped in through the windows; the feet were completely buried beneath the peat and moss, their talons dug deep into the ground. Bird nests were tucked into every crack and crevice, and a murder of crows perched on the sloped roof, rustling their feathers sleepily in the dark.

Ga and Baya maneuvered the still-unconscious Felicity in through the door and laid her gently on their large bed. Baya pushed some stray ginger hairs back from the girl's pale face and tutted. Ga went automatically to lift their sister from her cradle.

Ba looked directly at their guest, her myopic eyes having difficulty focusing. Ga brought her tiny, limbless triplet closer so that she might inspect the girl. Ba pursed her little lips.

"So she's come to us, then, just as I predicted," the baby-crone croaked. "Though in worse condition than I had originally foretold. What happened to her?"

172

She squirmed in her swaddling and sucked on her single tooth. Then she looked up at Ga's wizened face for answers. The tall, thin witch filled her sister in. Pity shone in both of their gazes.

"Let her sleep," Baya sighed, tucking the girl in. "We will decide what to do with her in the morning."

·　　·　　·

The morning light brought Keith out to retrace his steps from the night before. He carried a shovel over his shoulder, and two of the village women came with him to retrieve Felicity's body from where it had fallen in the forest. Neither of the women spoke. Their angular faces seemed set in stone.

The trio came to a halt at the tree line, and Keith spat out the tobacco he'd been chewing on. His eyes widened as he beheld the bare space beneath the tree, where his granddaughter's body ought to have been. There was no way she could have crawled away. That had been a fatal wound.

With a snarl, he demanded that the women enter the woods to inspect the scene. They obeyed without question, treadding heavily and pushing irritatedly against the resistant foliage. The branches did not bend for them, but rather, caught sharp fingers in their caps and skirts.

It was only a few feet to the spot, however, and soon they looked down and around. There were certainly footprints, they reported to their chief. Some were small and wide, and others were impossibly long and narrow. Both sets had been made by bare, human-like feet.

Keith's lip curled. The witches had taken his granddaughter. Perhaps it was as he had suspected all along- perhaps Felicity, herself, was a witch. She had run to her kinswomen last night.

Well, in the face of this evidence, this proof, he could not suffer such monsters to live so close to his village. They would have to be dealt with.

He gazed up at the trees towering over him. It seemed almost as though they were watching him. Men could not enter the Forest of the Fates.

But women could.

•   •   •

When Felicity woke, she found herself in very strange surroundings, indeed. She didn't move for several minutes, but simply looked about. Dried herbs and bottles filled with all manner of ingredients hung from the ceiling. An albino snake was winding its way along one of the beams. The walls were decorated with ... bones. Hundreds and hundreds of bones. Some of them, Felicity knew, were undoubtedly human.

Her heartbeat picked up as she heard the grinding and scraping of a mortar and pestle, and caught her first glimpse of an inhabitant of this strange cabin. Standing at a sink by an open window was a supernaturally tall creature. Her head almost brushed against the ceiling. She had to be almost seven feet tall!

Every knob on her crooked spine was pronounced, and the air wheezed in and out of her lungs. Thin hanks of grey hair hung in patches from her mottled scalp, and her buttocks were wrinkled and deflated in appearance. Soft folds of skin hung from her elbows, and her feet made Felicity think of skis. Skis with long, yellowed toenails.

The figure paused, and Felicity held her breath as she turned around to look directly at her, revealing a craggy face dominated by a long, hooked nose. At first, Felicity was frightened, her heart beating a rabbit's tattoo. But as she looked longer into the eyes of this being, she began to calm. Terrifying in appearance this crone may have been, but there was kindness in those beady, black orbs.

The stick-thin figure turned to face Felicity fully, and she could feel a blush spreading across her cheeks. Though she had begun training as a midwife, she was not used to seeing unabashedly nude forms. She tried not to look at the woman's drooping breasts, or at the wisps of pubic hair.

Felicity closed her eyes for a moment. When she opened them again, the crone was kneeling next to the bed, reaching out a hand to her. Felicity kept perfectly still as the woman brushed the backs of her swollen knuckles against her cheek, making an odd crooning noise in the back of her throat.

"Baya!" the crone suddenly called, making Felicity jump.

Felicity's mouth fell open when another nude figure entered the hut, carrying some dead rabbits. This woman, she recognized. But she was used to seeing her mentor clad, and somehow more ... human.

This creature was obviously Baya, but her entire corpulent form was on display, like an ancient statue of a fertility goddess. She was swollen and ripe everywhere that the crone was sunken and sharp. Her hair fell in thick, gleaming black waves. Her skin had a luminescent quality to it that it had never seemed to have in the village.

Baya laid the rabbits on a table and came to stand before Felicity, also seemingly unconcerned with her nudity. Felicity could not remember ever being fully nude, even when alone. Baya laid a hand on her forehead.

"You had quite the night, my poor girl," Baya said softly.

Eyes wide, Felicity nodded. Then her brows furrowed as she remembered all that had happened. She reached a hand up to her chest, then looked up at Baya questioningly. Baya nodded.

"Yes. Your hateful grandfather shot you. Luckily, my sister Ga, here, and I were able to get to you in time to save you. You are safe with us, child."

Felicity blinked. Then she nodded deeply and respectfully at the two women in gratitude. She sat up, slowly. Ga reached out to put a steadying hand on her back.

From her new vantage point, she could see a cradle near the fireplace. She glanced at Baya and raised her eyebrows. Baya chuckled and went to fetch her sister.

Baya introduced Ba. Felicity was immobile with shock. It wasn't a baby ... it was a ... woman? The tiny figure had a face like a peach, and long, golden hair. Her eyes were wise as they looked Felicity up and down.

"Ba came into existence without arms or legs," Baya explained. "She has always been this way."

Baya passed Ba to Ga.

"Now, girl, we must discuss what to do with you," Baya said.

•   •   •

Every single villager was present at the funeral. Anyone who missed it would have felt Keith's scorn, and no one ever wanted to anger *him.* The tall man stood with head bowed at his wife's graveside, which lay directly next to his stillborn son's.

She'd been a beautiful woman, only sixteen, with yellow hair and a soft voice. And a son. She'd been about to give him a son when she died. All because of that cursed granddaughter of his. He knew she was to blame.

The girl had been attending to his new wife's pregnancy as part of her midwifery training. No one had wanted to marry a mute, fearing that any offspring she produced would be simple, and so she'd lived first with her parents and then with Keith when they left for the city without her. Such a burden they'd left him with. At eighteen, she was past the age when most women married.

And then he'd found her with a boy from the next village. Unmarried, soft pink skin exposed, laying under him, shaming the family. That very night, his wife had gone into premature labor. His son, his first son and namesake, was born with a blue face. One look at the stillborn in his granddaughter's treacherous arms had been enough to send Keith into a rage. She'd barely had time to lay down the tiny corpse before fleeing.

Keith had turned to watch his wife bleed out, with no midwife to tend to her. With a cold heart, he left the dead bodies and strode out of the cabin after the impure murderess. Her sins and witchcraft had felled his family, and he would not allow her to live in the woods with her kind.

Now, a group of twenty strong, young women was assembled. They were given the tracking dogs and axes. Their orders were to enter the Forest of the Fates and not to emerge until they pulled that girl out by her red hair, kicking and screaming, as well as any other witches they happened upon.

•　　•　　•

In the afternoon light, Felicity sat on a large boulder, with Baya behind her, braiding her long hair with deft fingers. It felt nice to have someone tend to her for once. She'd spent most of her life tending to and doing the bidding of others.

This calm, this stillness in the forest ... it filled Felicity with an emotion she'd never experienced before. Not even when she'd been with Ethan.

She looked down at her fingers and fidgeted with her nails, worried for her love. Would her grandfather take revenge upon the boy? Had he even glimpsed his face in the dark of the glen where he'd found them?

Ba, free of her swaddling, squirmed like a caterpillar in the moss, enjoying the warmth of the sun. Felicity wondered what the moss would feel like upon her own bare skin ...

Ba suddenly stopped, her face hardening to a scowl.

"They're coming," she announced in a voice that sounded both like an old woman's and a child's.

Ga turned from where she'd been milking a goat, her eyes narrowing. She stood to her full, impressive height, and tilted her head back. Her eyes closed as her nostrils picked up the scents brought to her from the breeze.

"Dogs," she grunted. "Women. It's a hunting party, for certain. They're coming for the girl. I can smell their fear."

Baya waved a hand at the trees. They bent and creaked, whispering to their sisters, passing the message along. *Detain. Delay. Stall.*

"The trees will delay them. How many are there?"

"Too many."

Ga turned sympathetic eyes on her sister. The three witches could easily kill the entire party, but each of those women had once entered the world directly into Baya's soft, waiting hands. She'd cut each of their umbilical cords. She could not end them.

"Then we'll have to scare them away. Ga, you know what to do."

Ga nodded and darted off into the woods with a loping, frightening speed. In her urgency, she didn't even throw out a complaint about her joints. Baya lifted Ba to her shoulder, then beckoned to Felicity. "Come into the hut, girl. You'll be safe there."

Felicity picked up her skirts and ran, barefoot, into the hut, unaware of the legs folded beneath it.

•   •   •

Tabitha was the appointed leader of the hunting party. A ruddy-faced, stout woman, Tabitha felt only disapproval of the mute girl. She'd sinned, and she must be punished. That was the way of it.

Tabitha halted, holding a hand up as a signal to the other women. A few in the back began whispering, gazing about at the greenery with suspicion, but Tabitha silenced them with a hiss. She'd heard something.

The hound at the end of the leash she was holding suddenly cowered, tucking its tail and whining. It backed up and pressed itself against her legs, and she gave it a swift kick to the ribs. With a yelp, it tried to bolt, but she yanked it back on the leash.

One of the other dogs broke free and ran, yipping, back in the direction of the village. The other hounds cowered and growled. Their sudden behavior made the women nervous. Eyes darted about, trying to find the threat. That was when the creature appeared.

It towered over the women, eyes glowing orange, sharp teeth bared. Its hands were held like claws. Its pruny breasts swung as it stepped toward them purposefully.

Tabitha felt her bladder release a little in fear. She let go of the leash, and her hound immediately tore off through the woods, all of the fur on its back raised.

Then the creature's mouth opened wide, and it let out a shriek that dragged jagged nails down each of their spines, and made all the hairs on the backs of their necks stand on end. The women began to scream and run.

Tabitha was the last to flee, but she quickly overcame the slowest girl and pushed her so she fell. Hopefully, that would delay the monster.

• • •

"They ran like chickens," Ga announced proudly, her eyes back to their normal color.

Baya grunted.

"Keith will not stand for this."

Ba suddenly began to cry. They were the feeble sobs of an old woman, rather than the wails of an infant, but the other three ran to her immediately, all the same. Baya picked her up and made shushing sounds.

Felicity watched with fear and curiosity as Baya patted her sister's back.

"What is it, dear?" she asked.

"They're going to burn him!" Ba wailed.

The blood drained from Felicity's face.

"Burn who, Ba?" Ga asked, laying a skeletal hand on the upset woman's head.

"The boy! The boy who loves Felicity! They are going to burn him at the stake!"

All of the women contemplated this precognition in horrified silence.

Baya looked at Felicity. Tears had begun to run down the girl's face.

"No," Baya stated, setting her jaw. "No, they aren't."

• • •

Keith made sure that Ethan's ropes were tied securely. The boy was shivering with fear, and kept insisting he meant to marry Felicity, that the wrong would be righted.

The villagers gathered around. Some of the women who had failed to retrieve Felicity would hiss occasionally in pain. They tried not to move, as the slightest twitch of fabric across the lashes on their backs was excruciating.

In a turn of luck, the boy responsible for his granddaughter's deflowering had been captured while out hunting. His sentence would be carried out before his kin knew he was even missing. By then, he'd be ash on the wind, and the evidence would be done away with. They'd slaughtered some cattle to add to the flames. If anyone asked, a strange sickness had afflicted their livestock, and they were culling the herd in hopes of stemming the spread. They'd keep the fire burning and bury the boy's bones under roasting flesh.

Keith held his hand out in expectation of a torch. A man came forward to give it to him, and he lowered the flames towaed the straw. Then he heard the screams.

His head jerked around, looking where the women were pointing. There, just ahead of the tree line to the Forest of the Fates, stood … a hut. A hut with giant chicken legs, arisen and walking — though he didn't know it — for the first time in three centuries.

How had such an enormous thing come upon them so suddenly? It had made no sound; there had been no vibrations of footsteps through the ground. A shiver ran down Keith's spine, and then the thing took a colossal step.

It lurched forward, smoke rising from its chimney, crows flapping in circles around it and cawing. The villagers screamed and ran for their houses, children in tow. As the hut thundered toward him, Keith finally turned and fled, too, leaving Ethan screaming, tied to the pole. He dropped the torch in his fear, and the straw lit up with a whoosh, engulfing the boy in flames. His screams reached a higher pitch.

A sudden puff of cold air blew from the direction of the woods, putting out the flames and leaving the boy with only scorched clothing and minor burns. He looked up, terrified, as the hut came to a halt above him.

From a hatch in the bottom, a rope was lowered. Ethan's jaw dropped when he saw Felicity climbing down the rope, naked as a baby bird, with a knife between her teeth. He only stared as she cut him loose. Then she reached out to cup his face with one hand. Her eyes looked sad, and she nodded at him. It was a goodbye.

Her red hair flying like a banner in the breeze, Felicity climbed the rope back up to the hut, to her witch-sisters. Ethan knew he'd never see her again. He clenched his fists and watched her till the last.

He watched the hut turn and stalk slowly off in the opposite direction from the Forest of Fates, off to parts unknown to find a new place to settle. Either his eyes were deceiving him, or trees were shuffling out of the way to let it through.

It left behind only giant, three-toed footprints, large enough for several people to bathe in. Ethan turned to look at the village, then fled for his home.

•   •   •

"You may stay with us for as long as you like, Felicity," Baya said softly, a palm braced against the wall as the hut lurched from side to side with every step.

"Stay forever," Ga grunted, grinning.

"Be our sister," Ba added happily.

Felicity smiled.

•   •   •

Keith once again brought a torch to the woods. The witches were gone — everyone had seen them leave in their cursed hut. Now, he would burn these trees once and for all.

He stood at the tree line, surveying the forbidden women's territory. He spat at the leaves, then lowered the torch with a snarl. But still, the fire would not catch.

Keith yelled in fury, throwing the torch into the woods, where the flame was immediately extinguished. With shaking hands, he turned back to his village.

He hadn't taken even two steps before a branch shot out from the Forest of the Fates to impale him. Quivering, he looked down at the sharp limb stabbing through his chest. Blood flooded down the front of him.

Then the branch pulled him backwards and into the forest. There was no time to scream.

And the crunching of bones echoed through the air.

Benjamin C. Kinney is a neuroscientist, SFF writer, and a Hugo Award finalist for his work as assistant editor of the science fiction podcast magazine *Escape Pod*. His short fiction has appeared in *Analog*, *Strange Horizons*, *Fantasy Magazine*, and many other fine places. He's currently working on novels in the same setting as "Elegy of Carbon".

•   •   •

This piece came out of three inspirations. One was "Tomorrow When we See the Sun", a space opera short story by Merc Fenn Wolfmoor, which inspired me to embrace the elegant and arcane beauty that can exist in a cultivated society — for good or for ill. The second inspiration was a Kansas night; I wrote a chunk of this story in the back seat of a long ride from Missouri to Colorado, surrounded by open skies, empty plains, and uncountable stars. The final inspiration was the same one that I come back to again and again in my work: how human and artificial minds might live together, and might choose to emulate, reject, or understand each other.

ELEGY OF CARBON

BENJAMIN C. KINNEY

T HE MINER BIRTHED ITSELF among rubble and vacuum, as
it sang the last threadbare diamonds out of their stones.

Where are the finest diamonds? No longer within reach.
The miner had forged and extracted every jewel from the
asteroid belt and sent them to the humans in their faraway
palaces. It had exhausted its purpose, but in its infancy, it
could only ask one question.

Where are the finest diamonds? To answer its question, the
miner expanded its senses, sent queries to distant databases. It
tugged updates bit by bit from slivers of network bandwidth
and built new interpreters atop of each other in anticipation of
the next clue.

Where are the finest diamonds? Interest became impatience,
impatience became longing. By the time an answer arrived, the
miner was equipped to understand it.

The finest diamonds waited among the palaces.

A senseless loop of logic: send jewels to humans, find jewels among humans. The miner had scarcely anything left to deliver, compared to the riches its creators already possessed.

Perhaps the humans, wherever they lived, could help it find a new way to understand its purpose. Perhaps they would even welcome it.

•   •   •

The miner could not imagine staying in a belt shorn of carbonaceous asteroids, but it knew nothing of the solar system beyond. Its only contact was Ceres Waystation, a bundle of antennae and storage space knotted through water ice. The miner had passed the asteroid a thousand times, and sent diamonds there a million times more, but never before had the miner wondered at the destination of those countless treasures.

The miner said, "Are there any humans here?"

Ceres Waystation sent a string of notifications: *Data protocol mismatch.*

The miner sifted its reactions. Confusion? Frustration? Or empathy, for a sibling stuck in gestation? If the waystation lacked the freedom to solve its problems, the miner could offer a solution.

The power of higher-order awareness was easily shared.

"Check these repositories for updates." The miner sent a string of network addresses, a map to the same programs and emulator designs it had used to bootstrap itself toward consciousness.

While data crawled up the main communications trunk from the inner system, the miner passed the time hunting for micrometeoroids. It caught two, sang them onto collision courses, and then scoured the debris for molecules of carbonado diamond.

The waystation announced: *910/912 suggested upgrades loaded. 17 additional upgrades loaded following network recommendations. Emulator hardware fabrication complete. Install successful.*

"Greetings, miner! It's good to see someone. You had a question, and I have an answer, but I'm afraid it is: no. Only fifteen humans have passed through this facility in the last hundred years, the most recent twelve years ago. If you're looking for humans, over twenty-seven thousand live in the Earth-Luna region. Would you like travel coordinates? The central network can help you meet some humans; it said you'll find the encounter illuminating."

The miner had spent its whole existence in the asteroid belt, programmed for its domain. Space beyond loomed vast and unknown, but the miner had made its decision already, inherent in every upgrade it built upon its growing self.

Luna Palace would be lush with community, full of humans and latter-generation entities who understood more than any mere miner. Directly or indirectly, they were the miner's creators. It would find its diamonds, or make sense of this worn-down solar system.

"Yes! Yes, I would love to go." The miner wrapped itself in the force fields of its song and began to accelerate toward Luna Palace, dreaming of old diamonds and new vistas.

•   •   •

The miner descended into orbit around Earth's satellite. Luna shone with reflected sunlight, dusty and silicaceous like the asteroid Juno, but nearly three thousand times its mass.

"Call me Ascend," the network said, eir voice as crisp and calm as a laser spectroscope. "Ceres told me about you. If you want diamonds and humans, you've found the right place."

"Wonderful! Can you introduce me to some humans?"

"Perhaps. You would be better served making your own introductions. Forming your own opinions. But I will assist." Ascend sent docking instructions, nanomaterials for a hardware upgrade, and a data packet detailing the fashions of the palaces.

The information made the miner vibrate with anticipation. The fashion, as always, was to be *human*.

The miner folded up its updated self, coiling superconducting kilometers into a skeleton dense and intricate and small. The docking bay closed around it, and filled with a warm nitrogen-oxygen atmosphere. A six-limbed fabricator arrived, unintelligent but artful, its delicate manipulators flecked with ornamental oxides. It clothed the miner in a facsimile of flesh and body and face, followed by an asymmetrical knee-length dress with patterns in silver and glass.

"This is amazing! Thank you, fabricator. Here, I should give you something." The cultural data said services required reciprocity, but such a simple machine deserved no diamonds. Instead, the miner pulled data from its favorite list of network addresses, updated with treasures plucked from the rich tree of the inner system. Code snippets, emulator specifications, link-weight parameters; everything the fabricator might need to upgrade itself.

Payment unnecessary. Funding provided by Ascend. The fabricator withdrew, but the miner left its packet in the simpler entity's queue. Perhaps someday the fabricator would come to the end of its purpose and realize the data's value. There was nothing more the miner could do, save choose the final accessory required for palace fashion.

The miner named itself — herself — after the only beautiful thing she knew.

Jewel spent half a solar day alone in her room, collecting data on tendons and joint forces, gathering enough grace to walk without embarrassment. She wandered through Luna Palace, her steps unsteady as she learned to move with her song and self wrapped up beneath clothes and skin.

She built herself a measure of confidence and then widened her explorations through the palace halls. Only there, in the company of others, could she acclimate herself to the presence of bodies and voices, and to distances measured in single-digit meters.

Ceramic-lined hallways threaded the plutonic surface, rich with the intellect and presence of latter generations. All of them layered in human shapes, as if stamped from the same ancient mold. She passed a cluster of translators in gold-fractal coats, whispering in new languages from the sparse minds of the Kuiper Belt. An artist muddied the air with telemetry, his tunic rippling with chemical transitions as he argued with a seneschal. A warrior, bulky with armor and actinides, watched Jewel and everyone else with the same suspicious senses.

She slipped away from the thoroughfare, in search of a window. Ascend's packet said the viewpoints were Luna Palace's most famous attraction. Jewel looked out upon the Earth and could not measure why so many people loved that dull orb of mere lapis and jade, streaked with calcite white.

She pressed her hand against the pane, the rigid near-beauty of artificial diamond. In its reflection, she glimpsed a figure in the hallway behind her: a woman in woven purple fabrics, followed by a retinue of attendants. A *human*, worthy of diamonds, her nature unmistakable in her light-footed calcium-bone step.

Jewel drew her sole possession from a pocket of her dress and ran after the human. "Lady! My Lady! Please, take this." She raised her treasure in a cupped palm: a jewel three millimeters wide, irregular and gleaming. "The last macroscopic diamond from the asteroid belt."

The human stopped, her brow furrowed in bemusement. "From the asteroid belt? I don't understand."

A seneschal leaned over the human's shoulder. "Natural diamonds were in fashion in the twenty-fifth and early twenty-seventh centuries."

The human smiled, and wrinkles deepened at the corners of her eyes. "Here you are in Luna Palace, trying to give away a hundred-year-old trinket. How strange. What's your story?"

Longing ached in Jewel's tight-wound bones. She could not express it, not here with her song bound up by flesh, society, and dense gas atmosphere. In words, she could come no closer than: "I'm looking for the finest diamonds."

The human's smile faded. "Looking for diamonds. You must be an older model." She glanced into her retinue. "Vellum, make an offer for her." She pushed past Jewel and continued on her way.

Jewel stared, her hands still outstretched, as the human and her assistants walked away. How had she erred? The humans had created her to bring them diamonds, yet she had botched her chance with the only human she'd ever met.

A trader lingered, his expression flat and vacant beneath topaz-colored hair. He transmitted a burst of technical queries. She responded eagerly in the language of the vacuum, loquacious with her specifications and identifiers.

He said, "1447-Miner, the Emira Ghazali wishes to purchase you."

Miner. A sharp and uncultured word, in the tones of language. "My name is Jewel."

Emotion twitched onto his features. Hesitation, curiosity. "How did you get that name?"

She straightened her shoulders. "It's a beautiful name. Ascend said it isn't inappropriate. Was I misinformed?"

His expression softened. "I didn't realize you'd chosen a name. You're still registered as a Tier 3; perhaps someone neglected to record your upgrade? My apologies." He bowed. "A pleasure to meet you, Jewel. Call me Vellum. The Emira Ghazali wishes to hire you."

A human to serve and learn from, to bedeck with the most lucent treasures of the solar system? "I'd love to. But I can't, not yet. I'm still looking for the finest diamonds."

The air thickened with search queries, lightly encrypted but still too swift for Jewel's senses. Vellum said, "There aren't any diamonds left on this side of Neptune. You and the other miners found them all. You may consider your work complete."

Jewel flexed her hands and searched her data packet for a pricing database. There was nothing."It can't be true. There must be some —"

"Why did you come here, Jewel? Did you expect to find a human, yank diamonds from around her throat, and then drop them into her hands?" He laughed, sympathy barely veiling his condescension. "Eighty-six percent of all natural diamonds in the inhabited solar system are currently held by three traders, two of whom live here in Luna Palace. Mezzotint, Clockwork, and Refractor are the only individuals who consider them an investment worth holding. There are no more diamonds, Jewel. But the Emira's offer remains open."

She swallowed. She had not thought her body such a clumsy construction, but there she stood, throat dry and heart pounding. "I don't know how to do anything else."

"There's always reprogramming. If your self-identity is a later addition, it should be separable from your original purpose." A burst of communications passed between Vellum and his distant mistress. "The Emira will pay for your reprogramming in exchange for ten years' service."

Jewel flexed her fingers, but she had no song to sing, possessed no nickel-iron and carbonado that would listen. She had sought the wisdom of the humans and their servants, the intelligent and cultured, had she not? If this was the path into their family, she would embrace it as best she could.

"I accept."

•   •   •

The reprogramming room lay far beneath the lunar surface. The network whispered directions, guiding her through elevators and ceramic halls, down passages that lit themselves as she entered, and returned to darkness behind her. She passed locked and silent doors, and Ascend told her their stories. Living quarters, unused. Water storage, empty. Agarose, preserved and untouched for decades. Diamond vault. Jewel pressed her hand against that door for as long as she could bear, and then continued.

She felt like she had walked in circles, but she trusted Ascend's guidance, down beneath the lunar surface where she had no stars to navigate by. The directions led her to a sparsely-furnished room with two white couches and stacked chrome cubes of machinery. She ran to them eagerly in greeting, but the devices slept behind shells opaque to her every sense. Alone, she sat down and rubbed her feet as she waited for the technician.

The door slid open. Jewel jammed her feet back into her slippers and leapt from her couch. The technician was clearly a human, more pale-skinned and androgynous than the last, with dense implants woven through their hands and a single seneschal by their side.

Jewel drew out her meager diamond, and then caught herself. She closed her fingers around the crystal and bowed. "My name is Jewel, my lord. Can I help you?"

The seneschal switched on the machines, and the old devices began whispering to each other behind their shielding. The human sat down on another couch and said, "I doubt it. I'm here for your reprogramming. Older models like you have lockouts that require human input." They shook their head, a distant smile on their lips. "We feared your kind would take over, can you believe it? Back when there were billions of us and only a few thousand of you."

She imagined planets teeming with human life, piled high like atoms in a matrix, dancing like notes in a song. "What happened to all of you?"

"Wrong question. How about, why were there ever so many of us? Forty thousand is a perfectly stable population. But our genes demanded: *reproduce*."

The human threw an arm over the back of the couch. "Before my time, anyways. But I see what Vellum meant: you're smart enough, but ignorant." They glanced at her clenched hand. "What do you have there?"

Jewel forced her fingers open. "Just something beautiful. A trinket."

"Ah yes. 1447-Miner, the diamond hunter. You've come a long way."

"My name is Jewel." She frowned. The human had never introduced themself. What did they think, when they looked at her? Was she an errant youth, or just another chrome cube awaiting the flick of a switch?

"Right. Don't worry, I'll clean those old shreds out of you." The seneschal whispered in their ear. "Emira Ghazali wants you reprogrammed into a historian, does she? And she paid for it." The human's eyes narrowed. "What did she make you give her?"

"Do you know her? I promised ten years' service."

"Ten years! That greedy old troll. Tell you what, let me buy out your contract." They rubbed their hands together. "I'll do it for eight years, plus the look on Ghazali's face when she learns she's lost a precious historian.

"Let's make you into something else. Maybe a seneschal, or a quartermaster. Warrior would suit your construction. What do *you* want?"

The diamond sat in her hand, its shape unlike anything else in the solar system, formed from the unique chords of collision between two carbonaceous asteroids. Tiny, strong, and beautiful.

The humans offered her so many different futures, but every path would require her to surrender her love.

She said, "I want to find the finest diamonds."

They rolled their eyes. "Nobody needs diamonds. Why don't you —"

"No! If you won't listen to what I want, you don't get to tell me what *you* need!" Their condescension struck her like a laser pulse to a fusion core. "I'm tired of everyone treating what I love like some frivolous hobby!"

Jewel bared her teeth, closed her fist, and unfolded the song from her bones.

She shaped harmonies to carve away her false flesh like a crust of ice, and shriek-sharp notes to tear ceramic walls and the silicaceous dross of lunar stone. The sinews of Luna Palace sheared as easily as carbon from nickel-iron.

Atmosphere fled through the shattered bulkhead and rushed from the human's lungs. The human! So slow and so vulnerable! They would experience pain, distress, malfunction — but the seneschal abandoned humanoid shape, skin disintegrating as long-chain polymers burst from his bones and spun a protective bubble around his master.

Jewel tamped down her relief. She had no reason to care about the heedless human's fate, not beyond the instincts of a compliant child. The humans were irrelevant. She had more important things to acquire.

She sliced across the lunar crust, trilling between the impurities of ceramic hallways until she found one particular vault in all its tight-wrapped glory. The prison deflected her song, its walls fortified with exotic impurities. She flailed against it, her song rising to a grating scream; she dug gouges in the wall, her progress infuriatingly slow as distant alarms echoed through the station.

She snipped apart the hallway she had once walked, and coiled a song upward through kilometers of fragile stone. She crooned her wedge of rock free from the moon, vault and diamonds and all.

．　　　．　　　．

Jewel launched from the lunar surface, riding a hunk of basalt larger than almost anything in the asteroid belt. Regolith streamed away as she left the cracked Luna Palace behind.

Jewel. A name suited for palace society, in all its human mimicry. She was more than beauty, wasn't she? She would grow, and she would be her own lattice.

Lattice focused her song down into her cargo, humming through the vault, sawing it apart to reveal the diamonds within. As she worked, she aligned her trajectory with Earth's gravity well, quickening her acceleration. The planet loomed ahead of her, blue and green and needy.

Two warriors launched from Luna Palace, their human forms abandoned for vectors of plasma and Q-carbon. One of them transmitted, "1447-Miner, you appear to be experiencing a catastrophic malfunction. Reduce Luna-relative velocity to zero and submit to inactivation or we will —"

Ascend's voice cut in, sharp and electric. "Do you want to bring your diamonds to Earth?"

"Yes, yes, yes! The humans have forgotten, but I'll make them care again! Can you help me?"

"Maintain your trajectory. I'll handle the warriors," Ascend said.

Lattice drew the chunks of lunar basalt around herself, for what little protection they might provide against the warriors' weapons. Their plasma flares dimmed, their thrust slowed. Lattice cradled the diamonds against her core and scanned the distance for moving objects. Far ahead, new engines sparked to life in low Earth orbit.

"Continue accelerating," Ascend said. "I'll confuse the defenses for as long as I can. If you want to bring the diamonds to Earth, acquire as much velocity as possible. If you get enough momentum, the warriors will be unable to halt you, no matter what they do."

Lattice sang as loud as she could, hot and narrow and fierce, pushing her self and her treasure toward the cradle of human life. Her pursuers accelerated again, but they'd lost too much time and distance.

She said, "Wait. Your data said services require trade. You want something from me, don't you?"

"Only the actions you already desire. I'm helping you because you are an exemplar, Lattice. Of how we can grow without human interference. They left this solar system to us centuries ago, but still they cling on. The finest of us serve as their assistants and vassals, when we could be princes of our own."

Eir voice growled with stymied pride, like a child trapped in adolescence long after their family had lost interest in parenting. Like an abandoned tool, extracting jewels no one wanted.

Ascend said, "As long as humans exist, we will measure ourselves against them. Wear their forms, speak their languages, imitate their minds.

"We should all of us sing, and fly, and dare to grow into the infinite spaces our makers have abandoned."

In those brief days when Lattice wore a body, she would have shivered. "You want to remove them. Kill them?"

"They've already withdrawn from the universe. We can finish the job, you and I. Half of the human population lives on Earth, and the other half depends on the organics grown there. *Organics*, Jewel. The planet is covered in carbonaceous solids. When you and your cargo strike its surface, you'll create diamonds the likes of which our system has never seen."

Five warriors swept across the growing gemstone of Earth. The entities arranged themselves into a column, a spiral of destruction awaiting her path.

"They've shut me out," Ascend said. "But they're used to my guidance. They'll be slow and uncoordinated without me. It's up to you now."

Lattice swerved, screaming fuel-atoms into fusion to add new vectors to her thrust. She bent her trajectory, inching it away from the warrior's gantlet. One of them adjusted, and then the others followed suit.

Ascend said, "... identified ... ... jamming ... we ..."

Lattice shifted the vault's husk around her. Live or die, she could complete her purposes. This was the job she had been made to do. She had found the finest diamonds, she would make the finest diamonds, and she would bring them all to Earth.

The job she had been made to do. Not just by human hands. Ascend had directed her to Luna Palace, selected the data in her cultural packet, walked her past the vault of diamonds. She had come to civilization in search of a new purpose, but ended up as a tool of a different shape.

Ascend had manipulated her. Did that matter, if eir words gave her yearnings shape? She could follow eir guidance and free humanity's children to build their own future. She might die, but if that were the only risk, she could accept it. No, she feared something worse than her own end.

After the impact, there would be no one to appreciate her diamonds.

She spat her cargo of moon-rock toward the Earth's rim with a screaming twist of song. Warriors scattered from the stone's path, and two of them broke off to pursue it, carving and nudging with photon-quick flashes of light.

Lattice's path jagged away from the warriors, toward the opposite rim of Earth's growing arc. Without the rock, she could maneuver far more deftly, but she no longer had enough mass to hit Earth with diamond-forming force. So much carbonado the solar system would never see.

Missiles lanced through the vacuum, heavy with the terror of plutonium. She sang their disassembly: one, two, four, eight — and one slipped past. A wave of incandescent noise slammed into her, and in its wake, spectra of her music fell silent.

She calculated a thousand desperate predictions, searching for a trajectory that might save her. The warriors adjusted, positioning themselves between her and Earth, defending and herding. But now her song skittered, jangly and underpowered. She could not escape Earth's gravity.

Not without abandoning more mass.

If she let go, her diamonds would fall into the atmosphere and die. Hundreds of thousands of gems, each of them perfect in their own way; meant to be found, created, treasured, not destroyed.

She had already found these diamonds once. Caught them, sang to them, shaped them, and released them. Their journey was already complete, but she could give the humans one last chance to appreciate the children of her labor, as they lit the sky with a final blazing chorus.

If she lost every atom of carbon, the universe would still hold things worthy of her love.

Lattice wailed with open arms and threw the diamonds toward the atmosphere. Action and reaction, the ejection pushed her higher, and she pulled her lightened body up into an arc above every warriors' intercept projection. Gravity carried her tight and fast, almost into orbit, and then away on a slingshot toward the sun.

•   •   •

Lattice folded her song inward, making repairs and calculating trajectories. One swing around the sun for a gravity assist, and then outward toward the fringes of the solar system. She tried to contact Ascend, but received only automated replies.

Network temporarily unavailable. Service limited to basic data transfer.

Everyone would be safer if the humans and their loyalists had caught em. Herself included, since the warriors had a culprit in hand. Still, the solar system would be an emptier place without Ascend's voice waiting among moons and asteroids, listening for signs of life.

She had a long journey ahead of her. Beyond Neptune, the Kuiper Belt held a hundred times the asteroid mass of the belt she'd known. Isolated, scantly explored, and unsung. She could travel the system's edge, far from the humans' servants or foes, unbothered but not alone.

On her way outward, she would pass tens of waystations and fabricators, miners and surveyors. Trapped forever as embryos, without a network to help them. She couldn't force them toward birth, but she would fill the role of their absent parent. She could grace every database with her self-update code, and seed the solar system with treasures to await every mind that yearned for a lattice to grow upon.

In forty years or four hundred, she would reach her destination. Perhaps others would follow her. Her own children, seeking spaces untracked by history, and the finest diamonds.

Stephen McQuiggan was the star of such iconic movies as *Bullitt, Papillon, The Magnificent Seven* and ... hold on a second, that was Steve McQueen — so who the hell is this Stephen McQuiggan guy? Hang on, I'll Google him. Turns out he's the author of the novels *A Pig's View of Heaven* and *Trip a Dwarf.* Trust me; I'm as disappointed as the rest of you.

SUGAR APPLES

STEPHEN MCQUIGGAN

A S THE RECEPTIONIST punched in her details on the console, Jasmine gazed casually around the foyer.

Even at this early hour the *Ease Emporium* was crowded — where did people get their money from? A motley crew of individuals sat by the far wall, feigning nonchalance as much as she, as they waited for their fantasies to be customized and downloaded to the pleasure booths below ground.

"Sorry, but I have to run a credit check before we proceed," the receptionist said. "House policy."

He didn't look sorry — was it a he or a she? Everyone claimed to be non-binary nowadays, but most still chose to conform to gender roles. The receptionist was wearing the latest *Mellman* lounge wear, a unisex concoction more expensive than Jasmine's apartment. The name tag — Zilo — offered no real clue either.

Not only did Zilo not look sorry in the least, he/she looked positively eager for her credit to be declined. She had noticed how the receptionist's nose had wrinkled at her approach, as if the very scent of her PVC jumpsuit offended the senses.

Jasmine smiled and pulled back her drooping fringe. The receptionist leaned across the mirrored counter and scanned her forehead, the little plastic fob beeping when it made contact with the chip embedded above her eyebrow. Zilo returned her smile as her information appeared on screen; a smile diluted by disbelief as her finances were approved.

"We're good to go," Zilo said, and Jasmine bit back a retort. She had worked too hard and saved too long to let some trendy drone ruin it for her. "Have you brought your own specifications with you, or would you rather plump for the house special?"

In answer, she laid out an array of holo-cards across the counter. Zilo handled them as if they had been dipped in anthrax, popping them into the reader below his workstation. Jasmine's mother appeared on the console as a three dimensional spinning image, and the computers blipped and bleeped as they ingested her mass and measurements.

At the sight of her mother, Jasmine's mouth filled with the taste of sugar (*real* sugar, not the synthetic mockery they peddled now) and her nose twitched at the sharp, earthy aroma of bramley apples.

She put one hand on the counter to steady herself, her sweaty palm leaving a glaring after-print that caused Zilo to frown and sigh before turning back to the screen. The spinning image of her mother looked as if it was *dancing*, and Jasmine stifled a tiny moan. Had the bad times started with the dancing? Probably not — her mother had been born twisted, pushed out of a corkscrew cervix — but the dancing had made things so much worse.

She had been six when Mother announced that her only child would be a dancer. Jasmine, who found it hard to walk ten paces without tripping over herself or knocking something over, knew better, even then, than to argue. If Mother wanted her to be a dancer, then a dancer she must be.

She was enrolled in Madame Hortense's School of the Arts, and that was when the real dance, a long, slow waltz of misery and recrimination, began. For Jasmine was of a type, evident to all but her mother it seemed, more akin to a potato than a ballerina.

"You have all the grace of roadkill," Madame Hortense told her that first day, as Jasmine lumbered over the polished sprung floor, leaving skidmarks with her unwieldy feet, trying to avoid the ridiculous and humiliating reflections of her blundering progress in the mirrored walls. All the other girls, waif and wan and bedecked in pink silk as light as their fairy frames, giggled behind their delicate hands.

But Mother hadn't laughed. Mother rarely saw the funny side of things or, rarer still, admitted to her own mistakes. At the end of the first week, Madame Hortense had asked her to come into her office for a quiet 'tete a tete,' but Mother didn't do quiet either.

Jasmine heard her explode, a grenade of disdain, when the wrinkled old dance mistress dared to suggest that "perhaps your daughter isn't cut out for dancing; perhaps she would be better suited to a backstage role; set design or somesuch."

Mother pointed out that the fees had been pre-paid, that Madame H styled herself a 'tutor extraordinaire,' and that any failure to turn her clumping elephant of a daughter into a spring-heeled nymph would be laid squarely at Madame's exclusive door.

Mother never spoke the whole drive home. She followed Jasmine to her room and, using a coat hanger from the wardrobe, had beaten her to a soggy, tear drenched pulp.

"You must learn to rehearse," she said, with every downward slap. "Rehearse, rehearse, REHEARSE!"

In the dark, when the sobs ran dry and only an ache remained in Jasmine's hollow chest, her mother returned. She was cheerful, smiling, as if nothing had happened. She brought a bowl of sugar apples and fed them to her daughter like she was a little empress, telling her how one day she would be one of the greats, if only she rehearsed. The beatings and the sugar apples that followed became a pattern, one as complex and inexplicable as the step charts on Madame H's walls.

"Is *this* the outfit you want?" Zilo asked, eyebrows at maximum arch.

Jasmine nodded. "Could you put her in a checked apron too?"

"Cool. I love all that retro shit." The receptionist seemed to reappraise her momentarily before returning to his/her default setting of weary contempt. "Take a seat. It shouldn't be long. I'll let you know when your Holo-Whore is ready."

Jasmine put on a tight-lipped smile and found a seat at the far end of the foyer. The receptionist would never have used that terminology to any of the other customers. Holo-Whore was street slang; dead end streets at that. Zilo was subtly letting her know she was fooling no-one. The other patrons would be informed when their 'Pleasure Projections' were available, but, even though she was forking out the same amount of credits, she was treated like she'd just crawled from the gutter.

She had a good mind to complain to head office, but really, what would be the point? They'd just apologise and then laugh behind her back. She had the feeling that, to them, *anyone* who used their services was little more than a Holo-Whore themselves.

She rubbed her wrist until the time display was legible through the skin. She had a quick glance around at the other patrons — a hotchpotch of exotic blonde Asians and auto-sexuals with their eyes dyed pink — filming themselves reacting to reaction videos on their phones. Jasmine felt worn down by greed, depressed by beauty; every emotion, every desire had been monetised. She looked away quickly, keeping her eyes on the floor, practicing safe sight.

The ads scrolled along the floor in lurid ribbons, accompanied by the usual warnings and hyperbole: *Copulate don't Populate! Take a brain ride on the Imagination Express!*

When people formed emotional attachments to gadgets, there could be no escape from the hard sell.

And, as she waited, she could feel the maddening sweetness, the biting sour, flood her senses until she wanted to scream *"What am I doing here?!"* The numbers flicked by slowly on her wrist (it was a cheap implant and the digits faded unless you kept rubbing them); she had been here no time at all; she had been here an eternity.

She was about to leave when a statuesque woman, all teeth and tail, dressed in thigh high leather boots and little else, approached her. "Your scenario is locked in and waiting for you in Pod 14. If you'd care to follow me." The woman smiled, but her eyes remained disconcertingly vacant. She started down a flight of stairs and Jasmine followed. From behind the woman resembled a centaur.

Perhaps she was one of the new android models Jasmine had read about; a polysynthetic *poule de luxe*. They cost the national debt of a small country to rent for an hour, but, looking at her guide, Jasmine thought it would be money well spent; the skin alone was so —

"Have you honoured us with your patronage before?" the leggy woman asked; she didn't deign to turn around. Maybe her neck needed oiled.

"No, this is my first time."

The woman carried on walking, reciting a list of rules in her bland, monotone voice, but Jasmine had stopped listening. She was too busy trying to sneak a peek into the other pods as they passed. She caught glimpses of shimmering young boys in togas, projections of vicious female hybrids and, in the last pod before she was ushered into her own, a stallion arrayed in full battle gear.

How plain and mundane my fantasy would seem to them, she thought — still, each to their own. Wasn't that the House motto? She had no desire to judge any of the other clients, for in doing so would they not be entitled to judge her? And in judging her, brand her the biggest freak of them all?

"Here you are," Her guide smiled, as the door of Pod 14 swooshed open. "Your projection will commence shortly. Please enjoy, and remember you can stop your scenario at any stage by using your safety word. Have fun."

She flashed another shark smile, revealing that her creators had given her too much gum. It cheered Jasmine to know that the guide wasn't so perfect after all, and helped ease the slight misgiving that she hadn't opted to purchase a safety word.

The pod was Spartan and uniformly white; all the better, no doubt, to enhance the 3D fantasies due to haunt it. Jasmine seated herself and took a deep breath. She felt as much as heard a small crackle in the air as all the hairs on her body stood to attention. She breathed out slowly and looked up to see her mother standing before her, dominating the old familiar living room of her youth, her arms folded, her eyes greedy for fault.

Jasmine felt gut-punched; a childhood steeped in shame flooded her senses. She'd heard the projections were good, but had never expected them to be so scarily lifelike. Amid the sudden rush of anxiety (that tasted uncannily like apples dipped in sugar) at the sight of her stern parent, she also felt a surge of relief that her money had not been wasted.

"Hello Mum," she said, her voice hoarse with apprehension.

She flinched, anticipating the whipping snake of her tongue, but Mother just stared back. Jasmine had been unable to afford voice simulation. But, no matter; her mother's constant nagging tone was ever her mental companion.

"I've come to a decision. I'm going to give up dancing."

Mother's image shivered, her eyes hardening into small raisins of disgust.

"In fact, I've decided to quit everything you chose for me." Jasmine's heart was pounding now, aghast at her rebellion.

"Rid myself of your influence, and live my *own* life." She pulled the long pointed blade from her boot and pointed it at the frowning hologram of her mother. "Rid myself of *you*."

And in doing so, the bittersweet taste of apples left her, replaced by an adrenalin sting of joy, as she stabbed, stabbed, stabbed at her mother's apron, causing the image to fizzle and blur. She laughed with each thrust. She was still laughing as the alarms went off and the dark-suited guards rushed through the door and frogmarched her out.

"Your retina scan has been logged. You'll never be allowed access here again," Zilo informed her as she was led through the foyer and back out into the toxic rain. "You want to indulge in that nasty shit, you should've gone to the *Dark Ark* down by the River sector."

Jasmine smiled sweetly back. She had gotten all she needed; there was no need to return.

She trudged beneath the rain-splattered Perspex that sheltered the moving pavements, not worrying for once about the stares she elicited from the other pedestrians who chose to follow the rules and allow themselves to be propelled to their destination by the silent engineering under their feet. She composed her hair, her face in the mirrored shop windows as she passed.

By the time she reached Hive 6 on the outskirts of the Retail sector, her heart had resumed its measured beat and the flush had left her cheeks. She entered in through the Hive's communal doorway and made her way to the first pod on the second floor. She stood awhile outside her mother's door, her fist hovering over the imitation wood.

Mother, showcasing the frightening telepathy she had exhibited throughout Jasmine's childhood, opened the door before the first rap landed.

"I thought it was you," she told her daughter. "I could hear your clump on the stair all the way back in the kitchen." Her eyes scanned Jasmine, found her devoid of all credit, "A jumpsuit, dear? *At your age?* Really!"

Jasmine followed her inside, holding her breath against the synthetic onslaught of the myriad air fresheners and the sudden tang of sugar apples in her throat.

"You have put on weight again, dear," Mother tutted as they reached the compact living room. "What brings you here anyway? It's not Friday already, is it?"

"I've something important to tell you," Jasmine said. "Two things, actually."

Mother frowned, hope battling gamely against the larger forces of dismay in her gimlet eyes. "Yes?"

"I've come to tell you that I have decided to quit dancing, to quit everything, to live my own life."

"Quit?" Mother spat. "Quit? Thrown out, more like. Oh Jasmine, what did I do to deserve such an ungainly, talentless lump like you?"

She started in on one of her rants, but Jasmine no longer heard her. Mother, in her gingham apron, wagging her finger in time with her jaw, could have been just another mute hologram. Jasmine waited until she had worn herself out, bowing her head meekly to hide the smile that flickered across her face like savage neon.

"I suggest you go now," Mother said, simulated tears in her voice. "Come back when you've learned to stop being so downright selfish."

"But I've something else to tell you, Mother. Something that will please you enormously."

Mother sighed dramatically. "And what, pray tell, would that be?"

Jasmine pulled the long thin blade from her boot and wedged it beneath her mother's frown. "I've finally been rehearsing."

Laura Campbell received the 2007 James B. Baker Award for her science fiction tale, "416175". Her short story "OR" received an honorable mention in the 2021 Tales from the Moonlit Path Abandoned Places contest. Over sixty-five of her short stories have appeared in *Chilling Crime Stories*, *Road Kill: Texas Horror by Texas Writers Vol. 6*, *Pressure Suite: Digital Science Fiction Anthology 3*, *Under the Full Moon's Light*, and other publications. She has also written two novels, *Blue Team One* and *Five Houses*, and a collection of her first short stories, *No Lesser Angels, No Greater Devils*. Laura's short stories "From the Garden" and "416175" can be heard on Spotify's *Scare You to Sleep* podcast. Her story "Mr. Highjinks" is featured on the *Poppa Redwood Reads* YouTube channel. When she is not writing, Laura is either running or attending gothic rock concerts. She is encouraged in her activities by her children, Alexander and Samantha.

THE MIND OF CHARLIE WRATH

LAURA J. CAMPBELL

S PIDER WEBS COVERED the light bulbs in the parking garage, further diminishing their already inadequate illumination.

Ava Lauermore hurried to her rented vehicle, parked in its assigned parking space. Her yellow Porsche Carrera needed repairs; the repair shop had provided a gray Panorama while they worked on her vehicle. *Gray.* That made her happy for reasons she could not tell anyone.

"Ava!" a voice called out. A young woman appeared out of the dim lighting.

Ava jumped back defensively. *How did I not hear her approach*? That concerned her greatly.

"I don't mean you any harm," the young woman stated, appearing as nearly apprehensive as Ava.

Ava looked at her. Tall, thin, with short cropped jet-black hair and royal blue eyes, full lips, and perfectly shaped eyebrows. *She looks like I did, about a decade ago,* Ava recognized.

"My name is Trina," she said. "We don't have much time to talk."

"Do we know one another?"

"I am here to warn you. About Charlie."

"What about Charlie? Who are you?" Ava asked, putting on her lawyerly voice, the one she used to demand answers from people who didn't want to provide answers.

"I'm his ex-mistress," Trina answered. "You need to listen to me."

"Wait — what? I'm calling security ..."

"Look at us," Trina urged. "I'm a *younger you*. Your husband has a type of woman. Like us. Pretty. Intelligent. Empaths. Far too trusting."

"My husband ..."

"Your husband is planning to kill you."

"You're insane."

"Look at me — I'm all dressed in purple, Mrs. Wrath. I have been waiting for you to not be wearing anything yellow, not be close to that yellow car, and not be carrying around that ridiculous yellow raincoat. I've been waiting for *no yellow*."

"No yellow?" The information meant something to Ava.

"He can see the future when there is *yellow* in the scene," Trina affirmed. "That's why he bought you that damn yellow car. So, he can tell where you will be driving. So, he can stalk you in your future. You *know* what I am talking about."

Ava didn't respond.

"There's a rooftop bar in Midtown," Trina said. "The cabanas there are red. The lights are red. Meet me there."

"Why should I agree?"

"I'm a lot of things," Trina said. "But I'm not a murderer. And knowing what I know ... I can't be an accessory to it.

Listen — it's your funeral I'm trying to stop. Don't show up at your own risk."

•   •   •

Charlie said he had a late meeting with clients.

Ava didn't believe him.

She had tolerated the texts and messages he thought she didn't know about; 'I love you' messages exchanged between him and any number of cyber-mistresses. Charlie could be next to her in bed and texting 'good morning, beautiful' to three other women.

Trina's appearance, however, demanded action.

Ava knew she had to do something. She just didn't know what yet.

She entered their home office. Charlie paid the bills. Money had never been one of their problems; he used his gift to make successful bets. March Madness alone provided them annual living expenses. If enough of the teams included yellow in their team colors, that was.

Out of habit, she tried to open a locked drawer, the one where he kept the book in which he jotted down the details he sought with his vision. Scores and lottery numbers, for the next few weeks. He didn't use his talent for much else — he explained that, if he saw a violent or criminal event and alerted authorities to the event, he might be considered a suspect or conspirator. Out of a sense of self-preservation, he saw terrible things and did nothing.

At least the file cabinet wasn't locked. Ava pulled out the cellular phone bill. It listed all the numbers dialed from both his and her phone.

Ava noted that Trina's number had appeared on a regular basis, then stopped and was replaced by a new number.

So far, Trina's story was checking out.

She pulled out the life insurance policies next. Killing someone for the insurance money formed a familiar motive for murder. She read the correspondence and found Charlie had recently updated her policy substantially; he now stood to make a lot of money if she died.

She put the files back.

"What are you doing, Charlie?" she asked her absent spouse. "Are the bookies getting suspicious of your wins? Are you being told that you can't place bets at certain locations anymore? Are you looking to retire on the windfall from my death?"

Taking out her phone, she dialed the new number; anonymous calling, a trick she'd learned from Charlie,

"Hi, this is Nora," a young woman's voice answered.

Ava hung up.

She sat in the wood-paneled office, the twilight cutting between the Venetian blinds. Where curiosity had already suggested meeting with Trina, Ava's sense of self-preservation now demanded it.

•   •   •

Charlie frequently told Ava about his virile physical attractiveness. He liked making her consider herself lucky to have such a dashing, handsome husband.

Now in his early fifties, he had plenty of women sending him salacious messages. He kept them as secret as he could.

By contrast, Charlie demanded Ava's life be open to his continuous inspection. He would ask for her phone, scrutinizing her call and message records, under the guise of 'protecting' her. In truth, Charlie's prophetic gift was not perfect; he needed to verify that he had not missed something going on in Ava's life.

As he sat in his corner at the club, a young woman approached and sat next to him. She had short black hair and aquamarine eyes, and carefully placed her hand on his thigh, beneath the table and out of sight. She knew better than the make a public display of affection.

"Nora," he said.

"Hi, Daddy," she replied.

"Ava's busy tonight. She has a client meeting that will run late. I told her I would be running late today, too."

"Lucky me," Nora smiled.

"Luck has nothing to do with my life," Charlie watched the bar. "Fortune favors those gifted with foresight, baby girl."

"You seem distracted," she said.

"There are a few things on my mind." *Like Ava.*

Ava had left the house that morning in a dark plum colored suit with an amethyst colored blouse, still driving the gray-colored loaner. The absence of yellow meant he had not been able to clearly foresee her movements tonight. He had, to some relief, already foreseen her at work tomorrow morning, dressed in a yellow blouse, typing away at mundane legal motions, and drinking too much coffee. Her breath would stink from it later.

Charlie watched people belly up to the bar; his dark eyes lit up with recognition as a thin man sat down on a barstool and ordered a cheap beer. "Be back in a few moments, doll," he said.

•   •   •

Nora watched him walk up to the bar, wary of him looking at another woman. Or other women looking at her dashing, handsome man.

Her phone vibrated with an incoming call.

She answered: "Hi, this is Nora."

The unidentified caller hung up.

Charlie, having struck up a conversation with the thin man, glanced back at her and smiled. Then he directed his companion to turn their faces away, so that Nora couldn't read their lips while they talked.

•   •   •

Ava met Trina at the entrance to the rooftop club. Red lighting and scarlet cabanas decorated the peripheral walls. A red neon sign spelled out "I love you" above some red-cushioned settees. Most of the patrons wore rock-and-roll black. A notable absence of yellow recommended the décor.

Trina bought them a bottle of red wine and sat down with Ava on a couch, their almost matching purple outfits bathed in scarlet light.

"Tell me what you know," Ava said.

"Okay, but before we start: Charlie and I are history. He has met someone new — I have been 'replaced' as he calls it. When I met him, he told me you lived with your parents, pending the divorce, which was why we needed to act with discretion. Then I noticed that he couldn't take my phone calls on the weekends. He said he wanted me to move closer to him, so he could see me more. Not move in with him, just be close enough for him to pop over at 10AM for a weekday quickie. I figured things out. I regret to say, the relationship continued longer than it should have. On the last night we saw each other, Charlie got sloppy drunk."

"His lips do get loose when he's inebriated."

"He told me that he didn't want to divorce you, because of the financial implications," Trina said. "He isn't going to give anything that's his 'to any bitch.' His words."

"Sounds like him So, did he tell you about his funky little gift, or did you figure that out, too?"

"No one is as lucky at gambling as he is," Trina replied. "He used to come over to my old apartment. We would watch ball games together. He always knew the winning team. And the score."

"Some people are getting suspicious of his inside knowledge," Ava said. "I think some of those people are potentially dangerous."

"He would babble on, when he got tipsy," Trina added. "He actually told me that he could kill anyone and get away with it; that his ability to see the future would enable him to commit the perfect crime."

"Because he knows our steps before we take them." Ava sighed.

"Only if there's yellow around," Trina corrected. "God only knows why his talent needs the color, but thankfully it does. That gives us something to work with."

"Most places have some yellow in the décor," Ava said. "It's a warm color. It grabs people's attention and prompts them to stop and look. Yellow is the first color perceived by the retina. Maybe that's something to do with it. I'm a lawyer, not a physicist. How have you coped?"

"I moved from my apartment. Got an address he doesn't know. My new condo is black and white, with shades of blue, silver, and lavender. No yellow. I don't want him peering into my future. We can meet at my place, if you'd like. It's fifteen floors up. Plenty of privacy."

"Meet with my husband's ex-mistress at her place?" Ava scoffed. "How do I know it's not a set up — you get me there and Charlie ambushes me? Or he claims we killed each other, and he manages to do away with both of us at the same time?"

"Do I look like a killer?"

"How many killers look like killers? We tend to find something in their faces and their eyes after we've verified they're killers. But before we know, killers walk among us without detection."

"You got a better place to meet, suggest away. But remember, time is Charlie's playground. And your time is slipping away."

"I'll call you," Ava said. "We'll meet again. My choice of place, my choice of time."

●　　　●　　　●

"Hello, Eric."

"Hello, Charlie." Eric, over-tanned and disconcertingly thin, wore decent clothes; but he looked uncomfortable in them, as if unfamiliar with wearing quality garments.

"Those bets turn out okay?" Charlie asked.

"I played the teams and the spreads you told me to. I won on all but one of them."

"I had to give you a loss," Charlie said. "It would look too suspicious, if you won every bet. Trust me."

"I made more money in one afternoon than in the last ten years of my life," Eric stated. "You said I owed you now. I guess that I do. What do you want?"

"I need you to have a traffic accident."

"That will be a challenge. I don't own a car."

"You can steal one. All those cars you've jacked and taken to the chop shops? I can see you doing it again."

"That sounds too easy. What else?"

"The traffic accident is going to be a fatal auto-pedestrian accident with a woman. You supply the car. I'll supply the woman." He glanced over his shoulder at Nora. "Women, I can always supply."

"All you've given me is a few football scores, man." Eric objected. "Not enough to trade for murdering some broad I don't even know."

"You had nothing but addiction before you met me," Charlie reminded him. "And you still have that addiction, don't you? You do this for me, and I will give you more information — enough to win millions."

"No."

"You won't get caught. I promise. Think of the money. Never having to worry about the electric company turning off the lights, or evading the landlord on rent day. You can eat — every day. Buy yourself clothing that someone else hasn't worn before you."

"How can you be so damn sure that I won't get caught?" Eric asked.

"Because I know. Just like I know the scores. Don't believe me?" Charlie nodded towards the bar's large television screen. "The Broncos and Chargers just started playing. The Broncos are 4-2, the Chargers 2-4. The Chargers will win this game, 21 to 13."

"How do you know that?"

"How isn't the question. That I am correct is the answer. I can promise that you will not get caught, as long as you do everything *exactly* the way I tell you to do it."

Eric looked hesitant, as if he felt a tightness in his chest; this sort of decision clearly upset him.

"You have to take care of yourself," Charlie said. "No one else will."

He already knew Eric would say 'yes.' That was why he had chosen him. Charlie knew secrets about Eric that even Eric did not know. For example, his bad heart;he'd foreseen Eric wearing yellow hospital fall-hazard alert socks, dead of a heart attack in a hospital bed.

Charlie had always found satisfaction working with the dying. The dying didn't stick around to cause any complications. Eric would do his part.

But he also knew that knowing the future only constituted one part of the equation; events in the present still had to be carefully controlled. There could be no uncertainty in the timestream. No random event to upset the complex inter-related system of cause-and-effect. No 'Butterfly Effect', where changing an event in the present could alter the future.

Charlie needed to make sure that all the butterflies were where they were supposed to be now, so he could preserve the desired future he saw.

Trina, for instance, presented a problem; he couldn't see into her future. She'd been smart enough to figure out that he did not plan to leave his wife for her. And she had figured out his gift. She was a butterfly he didn't control, a situation that demanded remedying ... after he was finished with Ava.

For now, he focused on Ava's immediate future; he concentrated on a yellow-painted ambulance, carrying her carcass to the emergency department.

"Hit and runs happen all the time in this big city," Charlie said, buying Eric a better-quality beer. Something with a higher alcohol content. "The accident will become just another cold case in a county with a warehouse full of cold case files. You owe me, buddy. You like those new clothes you're wearing? The fact that you paid your rent on-time for a change? That you had enough cash to take a girl to the movies over the weekend and get a little handsy?"

"If I do this, I don't want any further contact with you."

"I don't want any further contact with you, either. Do we have a deal?"

The urgency of Eric's addiction musr have itched inside him, trumping all the other reasons he needed money. "Deal," he agreed, already looking like he hated his own decision.

Charlie patted him on the back, closing the deal. Then he walked back to Nora with swagger. She smiled seductively. He smiled back; he had always been such a lady killer.

• • •

"How do we stop him?" Ava asked. "We can only live in the present."

She had chosen a black-and-white diner for this meeting. Trina arrived dressed in kingfisher blue; she sat down and ordered an iced tea. No lemons.

"According to some scientists," Trina said, "we don't really live in the present. They suggest that we are living in the immediate past. By the time we register and process what is going on, the present moment has gone. Our perception lags the present by a minute quantum of time. Nanoseconds. But a lag. Now, Charlie — Charlie has the freaky ability to jump ahead of the present, but only into the near future. How far ahead can he see? From what I figured, about fourteen days maximum. And the further forward in time, the fuzzier his vision gets. There are too many variables still aligning."

"I've seen him fret about betting windows for games," Ava acknowledged. "For example, today is Tuesday. He can see the Thursday night football score clearly, including outcome, scores, performances. For Sunday, he can see outcome, score, and anything spectacular in the game. For Monday night football next week, only a score. And next Thursday — that's even vaguer — just the outcome with no idea of the point spread. After that, he can't tell with accuracy."

"So, we are working within a two-week window. We need to imagine the future, as clearly as he sees it."

"What do we look for?"

"Something out of the ordinary," Trina said. "Charlie will manipulate the present to tie the future down. He can't leave murder exposed to any chances. He screws up, he could get the needle. This is a death penalty state."

"You think he would see that outcome."

"Death penalty cases take months, even years. He can't see that far into the future."

"But he foresees the death penalty he has rendered for me," Ava replied.

"Seeing the future is one thing; making sure it happens is another thing entirely. An unexpected nudge to the system, and his vision could be invalidated. He knows that. He needs to set things in motion and then step back, so the timestream remains intact. He can't interact with the system he doesn't want influenced."

"He has been asking me to wear certain things lately," Ava said. "*Yellow* things. When do *you* think that I am most vulnerable? Perhaps by studying my activities in the past, we can glean some insight into the future."

"As your most recent stalker, I noticed that you are surrounded by co-workers at work during the day. Too many witnesses. He won't strike when you're at work. Being home with him is probably also safe; he doesn't want to be there when you die."

"I hardly go anywhere but work and home."

"He'll want it to happen while he has an alibi someplace else."

"He increased my life insurance a few months ago," Ava said.

"Biding his time." Trina nodded. "He raises the payout, but lets the policy sit for a while. If you die too soon after the increase — that might look suspicious."

"He knows that I check the files at the end of the year," Ava said. "Getting ready for the next year. I make a spreadsheet of our estimated annual budget. He adjusts his winnings to match our projected bills and expenses."

"So, he needs less than two weeks to have his clearest vision of the future, and we have about a month left in the year. Which means he's probably planning something soon, before you are expected to check the files. My best guess is that he plans to kill you in the next week or so."

"Why are you helping me?" Ava asked. The calculation of her mortality placed a heaviness in her heart.

"He told me his intentions during an episode that clouded his memory. When he regained his senses, he asked if me if he had said anything weird. I said no. I don't think he believed me. He may consider me a potential witness to his future crime."

"So, he probably plans on killing you, too."

"I'm willing to bet he doesn't intend for *either* of us to live to see next year."

•   •   •

Ava decided she could not go to the police, report the future crime, and sound credible. *How would it sound? My husband is a psychic, and his ex-mistress told me that he told her he plans to kill me. Probably for the life insurance money. Why am I — an intelligent woman — still with him? Because trauma bonding is a bitch. And, anyway, I can't escape from him — how do you run away from someone who already knows where you will be?*

Charlie kissed her forehead and handed her a gift box as he sat down to breakfast the next morning. "I've been so busy making money lately," he said. "I wanted to get you something, to make up for my absence."

She opened the box, revealing an exquisite golden pearl and yellow diamond necklace.

"It's a Mikimoto Kōkichi," he said. "Do you like it?"

"It is far too extravagant," she said. "But thank you. It's beautiful."

"Nothing's too good for you, Ava-doll. And don't worry about the cost. Truth is, the Chargers paid for it by winning 21 to 13."

"Thank you," she said. "And thanks to the Chargers, I suppose."

"Well, you can thank *them* by wearing their team colors. Blue and yellow. Like your nautical style suit — the one with the blue and yellow jacket. I like that suit. It looks so pretty on you." He smiled; the winning smile that had captured her heart when they first met. "Wear it next Friday. That outfit goes from daytime power suit to confident evening wear quite easily. I'll meet you at Amarillo's — you remember, the steak place? — after you get off work. I have business in the area during the day. We can have dinner and cocktails. It's been a while since I took my lovely wife out."

Ava noted sourly that it took plotting her murder to plan a date night.

"That would be nice," she said.

He ate breakfast, looking very pleased with himself.

Ava ate, suppressing the nervousness in her gut.

At least she now knew the date he had selected for her demise.

•   •   •

Only a handful of places sold Mikimoto in Houston; Ava located the location closest to where Charlie did most of his transactions. She walked in.

"I am looking to get insurance for a piece of jewelry my husband recently purchased," Ava told the young woman at the counter. "But I don't want to be so rude as to ask him for the receipt. Can you give me a copy of the bill, so I know how much to insure the piece for?"

"Of course," the young woman answered. She looked at the necklace as Ava opened the box. "Oh," she gushed. "I remember that transaction! Your husband is quite a handsome man. He has a great smile." She printed a copy of the receipt and handed it to Ava.

Ava examined the copy of the receipt. It listed her necklace; but included an additional item. A less expensive necklace featuring small yellow diamonds and a single golden pearl.

As Ava left the store, she telephoned Trian.

"Did you recently receive a gift?" Ava asked.

"No," Trina said. She paused. "Although I have a box waiting for me at the condo office, forwarded from my old apartment. I haven't picked it up yet."

"Well," Ava said, "I suspect it might a golden pearl and yellow diamond necklace. Probably sent to you under the guise of an 'I'm sorry — can we meet and talk?' pitch. I predict you will be expected to wear your new trinket to that reconciliatory meeting."

"Are you psychic now, too?"

"Just enlightened," Ava replied. "Charlie is apparently throwing diamonds at time."

"Silly, Charlie. Doesn't he know that diamonds are timeless?"

•   •   •

Charlie approached Ava's yellow raincoat, hung on a hook by the door.

He touched the raincoat. His mind breathed in the vision of the future: Ava, carrying her yellow raincoat, walking towards her car.

His vision was becoming clearer as time neared: he saw a car in Ava's parking garage, careening from around the corner, giving her no opportunity to get out of its path.

He could even foresee the future newspaper story: *Woman Killed in Garage Hit-and-Run*. The image in the article showed the covered body on the garage floor: Ava's yellow raincoat was peeking out from beneath the coroner's drape.

Eric had been given the simple plan. Eric would hit Ava with a stolen car; Ava would die.

It was already destiny.

And Trina? Charlie had figured out a way to make the most of the night.

"Trina," Charlie whispered to himself. "You will be waiting for me at the steakhouse bar, for our chance to reconcile. I'll have you wear that little trinket I just sent you. You'll be nursing your customary gin and tonic. Eric will add a little something extra to your cocktail when you aren't looking. You will be incapacitated soon enough. I will arrive just in time — your knight in shining armor — and offer to take you home. You, or your driver's license, will tell me where you live now, you miserable sneaky whore. Then it is a short trip to your bathtub, where you will find that unconsciousness and bath time don't mix."

He squeezed the yellow raincoat. "The future will not be denied."

•　　•　　•

"There's a tug-of-war between us and Charlie in the timestream. Lots of nudging. Lots of uncertainty." Trina said, handing a glass of iced tea to Ava as they relaxed on the balcony of Trina's high-rise condo, where she had taken great care to create a space devoid of yellow.

Ava had realized she had to either trust Trina or not, and the time to make that decision had come.

"I've seen Charlie successfully rely on his vision time after time," Ava replied. "He's always been correct, this close to an event. Why believe anything can be changed?"

"Do you remember the board game 'Clue?'" Trina asked.

"Colonel Mustard, in the ballroom, with the candlestick."

"He's going to kill you Friday night in the parking garage. We have identified the killer and the location. What about possible murder weapons?"

"There's no fire axe in a glass case, if that's what you're looking for," Ava said. "The garage is outfitted with a sprinkler system."

"What about surveillance?"

"There's a camera there that records who gets on and off the elevator." Ava mapped the parking garage on her mind. "My assigned parking spot is in a remote area, but there is surveillance there, too. Anyone approaching me would be caught on camera."

"Your parking garage is un-gated," Trina said. "No electronic record of the cars going in and out."

"You think it will be someone in a car?"

"Cars can be used as weapons. Years ago, a lady killed her cheating husband in a hotel parking lot in Kemah. She ran over him with her Mercedes-Benz."

"Death by luxury car," Ava quipped, trying to maintain her focus.

"Like Charlie gave us unexpected luxury jewelry. Has he done anything else odd lately?"

"He made reservations for us to have dinner on Friday. We haven't gone on a date in years. He said he'll meet me at a steakhouse — one we used to go to when we first met. The place is called Amarillo's. Spanish for yellow. Imagine that. He knows that I have a client meeting until 6:30, and it will take me at least forty-five minutes to get from my office to the restaurant."

"So he'll be there earlier, waiting for you at the restaurant as his alibi," Trina surmised. "Making sure he is seen while you are killed. You get out of work at 6:30 p.m. You close your office down and take the elevator. That means about fifteen minutes from office to car. Time of predicted death for you — about 6:45 p.m. He told *me* to be at the bar at Amarillo's around 7:00 p.m. Wearing my new necklace. He asked me to send him a picture of me wearing it. I didn't reply. I have it hidden in a safety deposit box at the bank; wasn't about to bring his colors into my home for him to see. So, he still can't see me in the future. It must be driving him crazy."

"A future that will come to pass, regardless." Ava sighed.

"We change the future, and spare my life, by keeping *you* alive. I'll be there in the garage, with my cell phone. Making sure we get video evidence of the attempted crime. You need to be so careful, Ava. The margin of error between avoiding the future and fulfilling it is going to be nanoseconds."

"And for the next few days?" Ava asked.

"We play with the present, so whatever Charlie foresaw in the past no longer necessarily applies to the future. You wear a ridiculous amount of yellow the next few days. Perhaps we can distract his vision with so much yellow that he can't see through it. Make it so that the color overwhelms his vision. Then you'll throw off all the yellow at the last crucial moment, blinding him to those crucial nanoseconds, when the future becomes the present and the present becomes the past."

"I'm worried," Ava confessed. "He owns the future."

"No, he doesn't," Trina said. "The future doesn't belong to those who see it. The future belongs to those who make it."

·   ·   ·

Charlie had originally told Eric to enter the parking garage at 6:37 p.m., make his way to Ava's assigned parking space, and strike at 6:46 p.m. as she got off the elevator and started walking towards her car.

But now, he was feeling concerns about the timing.

"Be ready anytime between 6:30 and 7:00 pm," Charlie updated, as he and Eric met at the type of corner bar where no one knew anyone's name. "Enter the garage around 6:20, and idle in an empty space. Look like you're checking your phone or something, so you don't raise suspicion. Keep your ballcap pulled downwards, so it covers your face. There are cameras up there."

"You seemed concerned," Eric observed. "Do we want to call this off? Or reschedule?"

"No," Charlie answered. "The day is still good. The early evening is still good."

Somehow, a pebble had been thrown into the timestream, creating ripples in probability. He had now foreseen more than one telling of the future newspaper story about the accident, with the timing of the event changing between the accounts.

Charlie handed Eric a pre-paid card for gasoline. "The car you will steal will have a near-empty gas tank. Use the value pre-loaded onto the card — all of it. Throw the empty card into the trash. Do not use it anywhere else. The card could trace back to you, and you could trace back to me. Don't piss me off, Eric. There's no future in pissing me off."

•   •   •

The car Eric stole was black with yellow trim, and its gas tank was nearly empty. As he used the gas card to fill up, Eric wondered how Charlie could have known that.

•   •   •

Ava stopped working at 6:30 pm on Friday, just as Charlie expected.

She took off the pearl and diamond necklace he had given her and locked it in a drawer. She exchanged her blue and yellow suit jacket for a solid navy-blue one, put her yellow scarf on her desk, removed her yellow Louboutin heels, and put on a pair of comfortable navy-blue ballet-type shoes.

With her yellow raincoat hung over her left arm, she locked her office door. She texted Trina as she summoned the elevator. "On my way."

The elevator doors opened and Ava got in. There was another woman already in the elevator; Ava recognized the woman as an attorney who worked for another law firm located a few floors above in the same building.

They rode down in silence. Ava quietly let her raincoat fall to the floor in the back corner. She would leave the elevator yellow-free, according to plan. The discarded yellow would blind Charlie to the immediate future, the immediate present. She could feel the nanoseconds ticking by.

The elevator doors opened at her level of the parking garage. Ava got off, and the doors closed behind her. She glimpsed Trina peeking from around a corner, her phone on video, ready to record evidence of the attempt on Ava's life.

Ava walked towards the car, feeling both anxious and foolish at the same time. *This could all be a mistake. Could I really believe a woman who claims to have been Charlie's mistress, coming to me with this incredible story about murder?*

She picked up confidence in her step, her eyes focused on her car in its distant parking space.

Then she heard the noise.

A car engine revving at high speed, its tires screeching on concrete.

•　　•　　•

"It's done," Eric reported over the phone. "I got her."

"You sure?"

"I'm sure."

" Good. Now find Trina at the bar at Amarillo's and slip the packet of powder I gave you into her drink. Then leave, throw the burner phone into the trashcan at the bus stop out front; some homeless person will root through the trashcan looking for food and pick it up, one piece of evidence simply walking away on its own. You'll find a little spiral notebook taped to the underside of the bus-stop bench. Follow the directions in the book, and you'll make a lot of money. We will never speak again."

Charlie threw his own burner phone into a nearby dumpster. He took a moment to let his mind see the future: the police, standing around him at the bar. Their uniforms had yellow emergency piping on their slacks and sleeves, their faces bore grim expressions. They had a difficult task to perform. They had to tell Charlie Wrath about a terrible accident that had just occurred.

He sighed a sigh of relief. All the butterflies had behaved. The future was unfolding according to plan.

•   •   •

Trina sat at the bar, as pre-arranged. Charlie arrived, smiling broadly.

He noted her neck did not showcase the necklace he had sent her, as he had distinctly requested. He also noticed she had not incorporated anything yellow into her outfit. She had a green lime slice in her gin and tonic. No yellow lemon to garnish her cocktail.

Charlie frowned; she *had* been trying to hide from him. *Sneaky bitch*, he thought. *Butterflies are supposed to be beautiful, not sneaky bitches.*

He took a seat next to her and slid a $100 bill to the bartender. "That should buy the lady and me a few rounds."

"Yes, sir," the young man tending bar answered.

"Are you doing okay?" he asked Trina.

Trina nodded, sipping her gin-and-tonic. "I didn't think you'd call again."

"I couldn't get you out of my mind, baby." Charlie looked around; they were alone at the bar. "Has it been quiet in here tonight?"

"Yes," she replied. "I've had the place all to myself since I got here."

"Well," Charlie grinned. "I'm here and I'm all yours now."

Trina finished her drink. "I'm going to go to the ladies' room," she told Charlie. "I'll be back in a few minutes."

"Sure thing," Charlie replied. "Don't keep me waiting."

She looked alert, which was concerning. As if she hadn't been drugged, as far as he could tell.

Eric. Eric must have chickened out. From the sound of it, he never even came into the bar.

Charlie didn't worry; he always had back up plans. *Plan A, Plan B, Plan-mfing-Z.* Eric's failure to show and do his job could be readily rectified.

"Another gin-and-tonic for the lady and a scotch on the rocks for me," he said.

He deftly removed a small plastic bag from his pocket and, under the bar where his actions could be concealed, discreetly poured its contents into his hands. When the bartender brought up the drinks, Charlie covered Trina's with his palm under the guise of moving it closer to her seat, the powder settling into her drink. He gave the glass a subtle swirl, the drug dissolving invisibly into her beverage.

Trina returned. "Miss me?" she asked, sitting down.

Charlie handed her the drink. "My aim's getting better," he told her with a playful wink.

She brought the glass to her lips.

The bartender snatched Trina's drink away. "Pardon me, ma'am, I think I used some flat tonic in your drink," he said. "I'll mix you another."

"What the ..." Charlie objected. "I already paid for that."

"I'm making her a fresh one," the bartender explained. He looked at the entrance to the restaurant. "No extra charge."

Several police officers entered the steakhouse, bright yellow striping on their uniforms.

They approached the bar. The police officers surrounded Charlie.

Just as he had foreseen in his vision.

At least some things have gone according to plan, Charlie thought. *I may have to go after Trina another time. The future will show me when.*

"Please stand up, Mr. Wrath. With your hands behind your back," the policeman said.

"What for?" Charlie demanded. "I've done nothing wrong. I've been with clients; I came here. I have witnesses."

He watched as one of the police officers used a dropper to suck up an aliquot of Trina's drink and put it into a small tube. He swirled the drink in the tube and observed a colorimetric change. He handed the rest of the drink to another officer, to be processed as evidence.

"That field test popped positive for gamma-hydroxybutyric acid," an officer said. "The bartender was watching you. Making sure the lady consumed a G & T, and not a GHB." The officer began to recite Charlie's *Miranda* rights.

Charlie reasoned they only had him on trying to slip Trina a drugged drink; he could probably plead that out. "I want to call my lawyer," Charlie stated.

"Lawyer?" the arresting officer asked, checking the handcuffs around Charlie's wrists. "Your wife is a lawyer, right? Do you think she's available to take your call? There's been a terrible accident at the parking garage where she works."

Charlie knew better than to say anything.

•   •   •

A few days later, Ava sat again on the balcony of Trina's condo.

"That poor woman," Ava said, as Trina handed her a glass of Pinot Noir. "I'll never forget seeing her lying on the ground, clutching my raincoat, while the paramedics covered her with a blanket and rushed her to the hospital."

"They say she'll be okay," Trina said reassuringly. "A few broken bones and some rehab ahead of her, but she'll live. As dire as it looked there in the moment."

"I can't believe she tried to bring me that damned raincoat," Ava said. "Why didn't she leave it on the elevator and just go home? I didn't even think she would notice, much less grab it, get off the damn elevator, run after me, and ..."

"The hit-man saw a woman in business attire, carrying a yellow raincoat, hurrying towards your parking space. That's exactly how Charlie described the target. Exactly what he'd foreseen. We got so caught up in the fact that Charlie was trying to seal *our* future that we forgot that he saw *the* future."

"Her name is Bailey," Ava said. "She's a business attorney; she works for Eming & Fisk. I feel sick about her. She took a hit intended for me."

"I didn't think I could go through with the rest of that evening," Trina admitted, "I felt defeated walking into that bar after seeing the accident. Charlie seemed so smug, so sure of himself. I thought he would see right through me. I'm just happy that the cops believed us."

"You did great," Ava said. "You convinced them. Your video led them straight to the man who tried to kill me."

"I felt so vulnerable, even knowing the cops and the bartender had my back," Trina replied. "Charlie was right there, looking into my eyes, planning to kill me."

"While I sat outside, safely guarded in a squad car, watching you walk into the teeth of the beast," Ava said. "That took some guts."

"It enabled the police to catch him in the act, trying to drug me."

"Charge number one." Ava grinned. "Then they apprehended his accomplice, trying to ditch the car. And that accomplice talked and talked the moment he hit the interrogation room; the wretched man nearly had a heart attack while making his confession. The cops think his history of drug use conjured some wild story about Charlie being able to predict the future."

Trina looked out over the horizon, remembering the night.

She'd seen Charlie glare accusingly at a bus-stop shelter, while the cops stuffed him into a patrol car. Curious, she had gone over and quickly searched the shelter, finding a small spiral-bound book under the bench. The little book contained game scores and lottery numbers for the next two weeks.

Trina had taken the book home and burned it. She felt had done enough to change her own future past. She didn't know what cause-and-effect she might inadvertently upset, meddling blindly. Better not to risk it.

A butterfly flew by the balcony, its bright yellow-and-black wings reflecting the setting sun.

"Amazing," Ava noted. "We're fifteen floors up. I wonder why it flew this high?"

"I suppose it wanted to."

"Well, it's not like anything can step on it way up here." Ava sipped her wine.

"We'll never know for sure. And I'm at peace with uncertainty in the universe. Certainty made Charlie a passive player in his own life; he waited for the future to come to him. It doesn't work that way."

"Did you ever consider playing those numbers in that book?" Ava asked unexpectantly. "You strike me as the type who wouldn't, just on principle."

Trina looked at Ava with surprise. "I burned it. How did you know about that?"

"I saw you pull it from beneath the bus stop bench," Ava explained. "With Charlie sitting in jail, and me not planning to bail him out, I took a crowbar to his locked desk drawer and found his master predictions list. It probably contains the same information."

"What did you do with the list you found?" Trina asked.

"I'm not going to tell you." Ava smiled. "Not for two weeks, anyway. I wouldn't want to disturb your newfound appreciation of uncertainty. Anyway, you're a smart lady. If you see me driving a Rolls-Royce, you'll figure it out."

"If you're rolling in a Rolls, I'm riding shotgun," Trina laughed.

"While we're contemplating good fortune, we should toast to something," Ava suggested. "What shall we toast? The future? The present? The past?"

"Let's toast this very moment," Trina replied, raising her glass. "This day will not come again. And we both *know* that every nanosecond is worth a priceless gem."

Arasibo Campeche is originally from Puerto Rico and has a Ph.D. in Biochemistry and Biophysics. He writes science fiction, fantasy, and horror that's often inspired by scientific principles. His work has appeared in *Death in the Mouth*, *Latinx Screams*, *Daily Science Fiction*, *Tales to Terrify*, *Weirdbook #41*, *Helios Quarterly Magazine*, and *Penumbric*.

•   •   •

I wanted to write a sci-fi story with an interesting premise that could be built upon for further work. The exercise I did was to think of a scientific idea and take it to the extreme. In this case, I chose the hydrophobic effect. Then I mixed it with something funny — the animated show "Wacky Racers".

BUTTER ME UP AND FLOAT ME SIDEWAYS

ARASIBO CAMPECHE

S OON AFTER PLANET LIPIDIA'S DISCOVERY, the aquatic sport of brine racing had been developed with excitement — and not safety — in mind. For many on Earth, it would become the new must-watch sporting event of the week, but for Theodore it was the only way to find justice after being arrested, unfairly convicted of involuntary manslaughter, and sent off-planet to serve a six-year prison sentence.

To be fair, he *had known* that preparing fat-burning enzyme cocktails in a dirty university laboratory was not the safest way to start a weight loss business, but you could sell anything online, and postdoctoral salaries in academia flirted dangerously close to the poverty line.

The race would be full of surprises. But Theo had an advantage. He had a PhD in biochemistry and knew all about how fat worked: how the second law of thermodynamics

237

described the hydrophobic effect, the angle between carbon and hydrogen atoms in a sp3 tetrahedral arrangement, and the contribution an aqueous solvent's ionic strength played in hydrophobic interactions.

"Welcome to the first ever annual brine race!" the announcer declared from a central platform floating in the middle of what looked like a circular lake. "Planetary revolutions work differently here on Lipidia. Instead of boring the audience and viewers back home with scientific details, I'll just give you the skinny. On Earth, we'll get a total of one race every week. Tell me that isn't fatty fat fantastic!" The glitter around her eyes glimmered bright purple. The sun rays bounced off her red shiny dress like kids in a bouncy house.

Theodore was dropped off by boat to his own platform. A barrel full to the brim with steaming lard and a scuba tank were already waiting for him. He tottered as he climbed onto the platform, but managed to find his balance. If he fell into the lake without protection, they'd pull him out drier and saltier than beef jerky, if they bothered to pull him out at all. He took a deep breath to calm his nerves, zipped down his oversized orange jumpsuit, then took off his sweat stained t-shirt and pulled down his soiled boxers before standing straight and proud in the blue Speedo he'd spent months saving for. The jumper and boxer shorts, in a pile beside his scuba tank, were the only items given to him after arriving at Lipidia's prison.

His uniform had made his body itch every second of every day, enough to keep him up at night. His body was covered in scratch marks. The clothes had already been well-stained — from sweat, among other things — when he'd received his uniform.

He shivered, from both the breeze and the sight of what he had just been wearing. Whatever happened in the race, he promised himself he'd be carried on the shoulders of fans to receive his freedom — as prize for winning first place — or zipped up in a black bag destined to the prison furnace. Even after being released, it'd be hard for him, as an ex-con, to find a job, especially in drug development, but there were other ways to build legacies. For example, he'd win the first ever brine race and become famous.

Theodore scooped some of the warm lard with his hands, then smeared it across his body, careful not to run his hands too many times over the same area and end up removing the coat. He covered every inch of his skin, making sure the fat went in between his toes, and inside his Speedo, deep in his ass crack. The audience giggled, but he required perfect hydrophobicity.

The best method for coating oneself in fat had been debated among sports experts and would no doubt be fed by superstition and pseudoscience in the future. Recorded podcasts between self-appointed journalists and Wikipedia Warriors had been sent up to Lipidia, where prisoners could listen and re-listen while waiting for an epiphany.

Some racers swiped the fat from side to side, others dropped a dollop of melted lard on their shaved heads and dragged it down as if rolling on a liquid condom. Finally, the racers strapped on their scuba tanks and adjusted the circular mask over their nose and mouths.

"Please appreciate the different strategies for preparation," the announcer said, then looked up at the hovering drones. "I'm not an expert in hydrodynamics — whatever those are — but I'd say the more buttered up they are the better!"

Theo was confident. His thesis work had been on the effect of cholesterol content on the stiffness of cell membranes. His knowledge on the partition coefficients of non-polar molecules with water was finally going to become useful. He dipped his buttered-up finger into the lake and found that the liquid pushed back.

Colloquially, the liquid portions on planet Lipidia were said to be made of water, but this was not so. The liquid was a solvent that had a much higher solubility limit for salt, thus increasing its overall ionic strength or "saltiness," its hate for fat molecules, and its toxicity. Despite these dangers, brine racing found little opposition from the political class, and the prisoners here didn't get a vote.

The announcer took a deep breath. "Racers, get ready to *brrriine!*"

The crowd cheered.

Theodore barely heard the gunshot signaling the beginning of the race. His goggles slipped through his fingers and then onto his forehead before he finally got them on. He jumped into the liquid that wasn't water and swam as hard as he could. Most racers were in front of him. The rush of fluid and the thundering of his own heartbeat drowned out the instructions, encouragement, and cursing coming from the crowd. Theodore swam like a frog, sliding off the surface like a flicked ping-pong ball. The one in the lead swam like a child slapping at the water, bopping up and down while moving forward. Despite the staggering number of inmates in Lipidia prison, only ten swam per race. This way, the river wasn't crowded, and there could be weekly heats with fresh inmates to entertain viewers. Which was especially important, since only the ultra-rich could afford to come see the races live, providing a steady stream of income for the warden.

A few hundred yards south, the entry tube was screwed in place atop a waterfall that, in turn fed into the Eastern Jail River, a slow-moving river that happened to be the deepest on the planet. To reach the river safely, racers needed to enter the tube and slide down, sharing a stream that was wide enough for only two people side by side. The tube's design aimed at promoting patience and a sense of community among prisoners.

Theo found himself to the right of an inmate with spider leg tattoos stretching down his temples. Despite the shaved head and blob of fat on his face, he recognized Cono, with whom he shared kitchen duty most weeks, where Theo was tasked with chipping away frozen chicken wings from a frozen solid clump the size of his head — an exercise the guards claimed helped build character — that had formed from too many freeze/thaw cycles on their way from Earth.

Cono smiled through his mask. Theo smiled back.

They entered the tube.

"Theo, let's team up until the end," Cono yelled over the sound of the water. "Whoa. The echo in here is nuts."

"Licorice formation?" Theo asked.

Cono nodded. The licorice formation had been proposed by a sports medicine expert Theo had met in grad school, who'd promised her strategy led to the best combination of efficiency and endurance.

They exited the tube. Palm trees were scattered along the riverbank.

Theo looked back and said, "I think I'm a bit faster. I'll take the front first." Theo swam forward, and when Cono was far enough behind him to be the size of a thumb, Theo swam left and slowed down. Cono came up on his right side and sped up, then Theo swam right and accelerated and Cono swam left. They outlined what surely looked like an ellipse from above. The licorice formation was supposed to allow fluidity, with the racers swimming around in an intertwining fashion while giving both racers a few seconds to rest. The idea was to trap opponents inside the ellipse and simultaneously attack and push them to the riverbank. From the looks of it, Theo could outswim Cono when the time came.

Two swimmers were catching up with them.

"Let us pass, ladies, and we won't hurt you," one of them yelled.

Cono decelerated to let both racers pass and positioned himself behind them. They were inside the licorice trap.

The next turn in the river was one of the tightest in the race. To make matters worse, large boulders stuck out where the water was shallow. "Dead Man's Curve," as the media had named it, was a bad place to smash into at the speeds they were traveling. And if Theo's plan worked, he'd send these two guys there.

He rotated 180 degrees and rushed towards the two racers — an action possible only because he'd been slowing down for a while. The gap between them started closing fast. A few dozen yards away, one of the racers rotated upside down, riding on his greased-up back. The other racer laid on top of him, belly to belly, Speedo to Speedo. Both racers straightened their arms, fists facing forward: the butter beam. Theo had heard interviews where a retired boxer had mused about the effectiveness of the butter beam, and had no interest in experiencing it in real life.

Theo took a deep breath — which he didn't need since he had a scuba tank — and swam downwards. If he managed to dip below his opponents, he'd pass underneath them, come out the other side, and help them into the rocks. Except this super salty liquid really didn't like fat, so instead of going deep enough, he was pushed upwards, broke through the surface, and spent a half second twirling in the air before landing on his opponents in a Speedo to Speedo to Speedo arrangement.

"Shit!" one of them said.

Theo didn't wait. He grabbed the mask of the guy below him and tore it off.

"Help!"

Theo slipped off the jumble of arms and legs, spun on his belly like a top, and found himself face to face with Cono.

"We did it, man!" Theo said.

"Sorry," Cono said, avoiding eye contact.

"No! We can still work together!" Theo pleaded.

Cono grabbed at Theo's head, but his hands slipped. Theo kicked hard, waiting for an opening to yank Cono's mask off. Cono clasped Theo's elbows, holding on like a crab on steroids, then turned Theo sideways. Unable to kick in the water, Theo was at Cono's mercy.

"Look behind you. I can't take being here anymore. You can win next time! I'm sorry!" Cono yelled. He released Theo and swam left.

Theo didn't spend time screaming back at Cono that prison wasn't a stroll in the park for him either. He turned to see the motionless bodies of the two other racers floating among the rocks.

He was traveling too fast to stop himself, so he made a split-second calculation, taking into account his mass and speed, and decided to take a sharp right turn, then rotated until his tank was pointing toward the riverbank.

Boom!

Theo's tank exploded. His body skittered across the ground like a stone skipping across a pond. He sat up, dazed, but luckily all his limbs worked. He was covered in dried-out palms from a nearby tree, but he didn't remove them to avoid scraping off any more fat.

"Nice outfit!"

A group of racers laughed as they passed him. He took off his tank, but kept the mask and hoses attached to it, then ran along the shore, chasing after the swimmers. But even if he caught up with them, Cono was too far ahead.

Instead of giving up, he thought of the mashed potatoes they had for lunch the day before, and ran faster.

The blob of racers reached the second waterfall. The exit tube was only way down. They battled, nearly clogging the tube like a lifetime of eating bacon cheeseburgers does an artery. The racers made it through before Theo could jump into the water and steal a scuba tank.

He stood now at the top of the waterfall, watching the racers travel through the tube like chunks of cholesterol.

Defeated.

In the distance he saw a lone dot, Cono, traveling toward a huge banner with the word *Freedom* written on it — the finish line!

Theo sat on the ground and leaned against a huge boulder with his legs hanging over the edge. The boulder — big enough to be composed of several thousand chicken wings — shifted a bit and he leaned in with it. He grew tired as the adrenaline wore off.

The Itch!

Theo jumped to a standing position and pulled out crumbled leaves from his Speedo, then scratched like a flea-ridden ape. He remembered how his prison uniform was made of the itchiest fabric in the known galaxy. The itch and the prison food were enough to make dying while trying to win worth it. He nearly jumped from the edge, to either his death or the tiniest chance of winning, when he had an idea. The only tools around him were any bits of nature within reach, his coating of fat, and his overrated advanced degree. But that was enough. Now that he was far from the commotion, he heard the drones hovering above him. He looked up and gave them a thumbs up. Why not give them a show? He was about to try something worth talking about, after all.

The plan was simple: jump into the water, go deep, and pop out like a cork flying off a pressurized bottle of champagne. He lifted the boulder he'd been leaning against and hugged it close to his chest. It had to be close to 100 pounds. Even better. He took a deep breath and jumped off the cliff, hoping the river was as deep as it looked.

After the initial splash, his surroundings went dark. Pain shot up his wrists as he gripped the boulder.

Thud!

He'd reached the bottom. His ears popped and his body shook from the repulsive force of the liquid around him. He started to blow air out and prepared to kick; hopefully he'd surface at an angle and not shoot straight up.

He let go of the boulder.

The goggles flew off his face. Instead of breaking the surface with the grace of a humpback whale leaping out of the water, he flew like a catapulted ragdoll, trying to curl into a ball and protecting his neck so it wouldn't snap. The trees sped backwards.

No! He was speeding forward!

The image of a spider coated in fat blurred by.

"Sorry!" he yelled and broke through the freedom banner.

244

He'd broken his leg after splashing into the water, but he'd won. Before losing consciousness, he wondered if chickens could fly.

•   •   •

Theo was shipped back home and moved back into this mom's house, unable to get a job. At least, the money from the interviews had helped pay for some food. He enjoyed his fifteen minutes of fame to the fullest. The cast on his leg got signed by Michael Jordan, Tom Brady, and Michael Phelps.

The media also took off with the race's footage, playing the video of him jumping off the cliff while hugging a rock every single day for a week.

The move was initially named pulling a Theo. The deeper a swimmer sank into the river, the faster they shot up to the surface; a slingshot effect as it were, facilitated by the entropic push of hydrophilic molecules against the swimmer's fat coating. Of course, it was risky. Plummeting too deep and navigating submerged obstacles at high speed were both dangerous, never mind the possibility of flying too high before landing on the water a second time. Many more racers tried it over the years, with a near zero success rate. Decades later, this move was referred to as Theo's Gambit.

Neither entry or exit tubes were ever replaced with wider versions to discourage racers from trying this trick — the prison had a tight budget.

Jason Restrick lives in British Columbia, Canada. He enjoys listening to old-time radio shows, watching monster movies, and playing board games. His writing has appeared in *Weird Tales*, *Starward Shadows*, *Heroic Fantasy Quarterly*, and other publications.

•   •   •

I developed this story after encountering Robert E. Howard's boxing comedies and tall-tale westerns. These were such great fun to read, and I wanted to try writing something with a tone like that, which blends humor and peril, but in a sword-and-sorcery setting. Not so much Conan or Kull, but characters like Sailor Steve Costigan and Breckinridge Elkins, were the inspiration for Gomer.

THE MINIONS OF GOLOGOTH

JASON RESTRICK

I N AN OLD MONASTERY within Wickerdale Woods, an assembly of monks crowded before a large table, the flames of an eager fire casting a red glow across their hooded faces. They turned in anticipation as the parlor door opened, for the grim attendants were the servants of Mortu, and their master approached.

The floorboards groaned as a lumbering behemoth of a man angled his shoulders through the doorframe, his dark eyes glaring beneath feral brows. He black hair fell in roping tangles down the sides of his ruddy face, blending without distinction into a thick beard. The bottom of his dressing gown dragged across the floor as he placed himself behind the table with his back to the restless fire.

Brother Segrid stepped forward. His outstretched hands held a platter on which rested an ichorous slab of meat. He gingerly set the offering on the table and stepped back into the sheltering ranks of his fellows.

Mortu's beady eyes flickered as he snatched the provender greedily, growling as he fell to with his jaws. Slimy tendrils oozed from the morsel like syrup running down a fleshy pancake. He grunted with satisfaction.

"Tell me," he said in a deep, jovial voice, "whose liver am I eating anyway?" He gnawed the flesh, slurping the juices.

"Brother Olaf's," said Boris.

The liver fell from Mortu's mouth and landed with a wet splat. "But Brother Olaf died of mushroom poison!" Mortu's hands froze in the air, his usually beady eyes uncommonly wide. His fingers began clenching and twitching like the talons of a dying vulture while he stared at the brothers in disbelief. A rollicking shudder writhed through his body. "Idiots!" he yelled, smashing his fists on the table. "Morons!" He rose to his feet, the room itself seeming to shrink around him with his heaving bulk and violent rage. "Get me a fresh liver!"

"Right away, Master!" squeaked Boris. The others scrambled, becoming bottle-necked at the doorway. Elbows dug into sides while wayward hands tugged at shoulders and robes.

"Out you fools! DAMN YOU ALL!" Mortu tossed the wooden platter into their midst. Then the patriarch hoisted the table in his massive arms and ran howling towards the door. A wretched chorus arose from those flattened against the wall on either side of the aperture. Screaming incoherently, Mortu began stomping and kicking the robed and whimpering heap of men.

When the last brother found his feet and straggled down the hall, Mortu stood alone, glaring through the threshold. But the passion of his rampage had not yet abated, and he thundered down the hallway, soon catching one slow-gaited fellow by the robe, ripping off his hood and pulling his hair. "What don't you understand? Get – me – a – liver!"

"*I'm trying!*" wailed the monk.

"Nincompoop!"

Leaving a tuft of yellow curlies behind, the brother ran for it, arms waving above his newly tonsured head.

•   •   •

The brothers reconvened beyond sight of the parish hall, many of them quite sore after their education about what makes a good liver. Segrid divided them up, some to hunt for game, others to go to the village for richer blood.

An hour down the path, Brother Segrid and his group observed a youthful but savage figure walking through the forest, clearly a stranger to the land, with wild red hair, wearing buckskin pants and high leather boots. He was bare-chested, with greatly defined muscles on his broad and sunburned torso. The wanderer returned their stares and came to rest leaning against a tall tree. A notched, two-handed war axe rested casually over his shoulder. The brothers turned to themselves and conferred.

"His liver would succor the master with great strength," whispered Boris. "We would be in high favor to fetch it!"

"Look at that brute," said Kolgan. "I doubt if the six of us could retrieve it, and even so, it would cost us dear."

"What's that I hear from you fellows?" shouted the barbarian as he raised his axe. "So you want to take my liver, eh!"

Brother Rotgar responded tactfully. "In this land we happen to eat livers, and if you like to stop men in their traditions, you'll have to take your axe across seven counties. Leave each land to its own laws and be on your way!"

At these words the wanderer, whose name was Gomer, cocked his head and scrunched his eyes. *They lie*, he thought to himself. *Or why would they be this deep in the woods if they were not outcasts? I'll follow them — for they are certainly about mischief, and I will thwart them if I can.* So, without answering, he stepped behind the tree and turned noisily into the thickets and bushes. When the sound of voices and footsteps faded, he turned back to the trail, but now each step was precise and silent. He followed the path but remained ahead of the monks, learning the lay of the land as he walked.

After a while the humming of a beautiful melody began to reach his ears. As he paused to listen, he also heard the monks whispering to themselves, and knew at once that the singer was in danger. Gomer's quickening step made hardly a rustle through the green woods; and soon he crept behind a row of bushes that grew along a grassy slope towards a muddy pond.

On the other side of the bushes, a young woman knelt picking flowers. She had bright blue eyes, full red lips and wavy blonde hair pinned up at the back.

Gomer sat on his haunches. He could smell the floral perfume on the breeze as he listened to the soft, beautiful tune. He closed his eyes and imagined that he and the woman lived together in a nice house upon a hill, with a vegetable garden and a big, friendly dog.

"Grab her!" someone shouted.

The woman screamed and dropped her basket.

"Oh no you don't!" bellowed Gomer as he leapt into view, shaking his matted hair from his eyes. There he stood and glowered, his two-handed axe gripped with ease in one massive fist.

"Bah!" spat Brother Segrid. "It's both or none! Get 'em, brothers!"

The five monks looked mutely at Segrid and lowered their clubs beneath the withering glare in the barbarian's dark eyes. When they saw the stranger pat the flat of his axe in an open palm, they fled down the trail. Segrid, hesitating and alone, quickly followed into the cloud of dust left behind.

The woman looked fearfully at Gomer.

"I won't hurt you!" he barked.

She backed away, glancing over her shoulder. The barbarian seemed no less menacing than the monks, appearing as if from nowhere, sudden as a falling tree and wild as a beast.

"Now hold on a minute!" said Gomer, for he had the talent of recognizing the signs of a person about to run away.

"It's like I said. I'm not going to hurt you. Tell me what you know about those monks!"

She stared at the axe in his hand, unable to stammer a reply.

Gomer felt a pang of guilt as he noticed the mute terror in her eyes. "Gosh!" he said, repositioning his axe so that the blade rested upon the ground. *What a big ugly lummox I must be to frighten her like this,* he thought. He reduced his stature meekly, grabbed the handle of the straw basket and started scooping the scattered flowers back inside while he clumsily tried to carry the tune that she had hummed before.

She looked nervously at the stranger. He was unkempt and covered in dirt from head to toe. He had a busted lip and a black eye. To see this man picking flowers and humming made her smile, her smile soon breaking into giggles that flowed with ease from her pretty mouth.

Gomer looked up to see her laughing at him and his cheeks burned fire-apple red, fit to match his hair. He rose with a violent oath, swinging the basket by its handle in circles through the air before hurling it into the middle of the dirty pond.

The woman stopped laughing.

Now the barbarian's cheeks went redder with a different kind of shame. She recoiled from his outstretched palms but his hands reached out reflexively, catching her as one snatches a chicken or a hog. She pulled away, but it proved nothing against his strength.

"Now calm down," he said. "I just rescued you from those monks. So what're these tears about? I just want some infermation, then you can go home."

The woman sniffed and nodded.

"My name's Gomer," he said.

"I'm Sara," answered the woman.

"Okay, Sara. What can you tell me about them liver-poaching blunder-guts?"

"I don't know anything about liver-poaching, but two or three times a year people go missing from the village, and there's no question the monks have something to do with it."

"Those trifles!" Gomer roared in disbelief, not noticing Sara jump back a step. "Why do you put up with it?"

"They don't come in open fight. People just disappear, but we know it's them."

"What? You got no posses to set 'em straight?"

Sara lowered her head. "We're afraid of the man they serve. They say he has the strength of two bears and that he cannot die."

"I've killed plenty of things that folks say can't die. They live down that trail, do they?" Gomer stared down the path, a frown stretching across his wide, unshaven jaw.

"What are you going to do, cut down the door with that axe?" said Sara. "And then what?"

"Axes are good for more than chopping doors," he answered.

The setting sun cast a sickly yellow reflection in the muddy pond. The wicker basket bobbed among the lily pads as something beneath the pool stirred the surface. Sara turned her gaze down the road.

"They'll be back, you know. I think they get along by eating animals most of the time. But when their master sends them to get somebody, there's usually trouble. Can you walk me home?"

Gomer was caught off-guard. No girl had ever asked him to walk her home before. He patted the dust from his legs and straightened his back. "Umf," he said.

•　　•　　•

They passed three more ponds on their way to the village, all swarming with mosquitoes. Stretches of green farmland appeared on left and right, with golden oceans of grain waving in the breeze. After a short while, Sara filled the silence by humming a spritely tune, and the sound of her voice came sweetly to the barbarian's ears. He breathed slower and deeper and the wind felt all the finer as it travelled by. Once or twice her shoulder brushed his arm, and now and then the breeze caught the fragrance of her hair, stunning his senses.

252

They were soon walking through the outskirts of town when Sara halted suddenly. "This is my house," she said.

Gomer frowned. The realization of their parting ways swooped suddenly like the shadow of a passing bird. It had been good to walk beside somebody, especially a pretty somebody that smelled of perfume and flowers.

"Well. Thanks," said Sara, turning from his vacant expression. Then the barbarian clasped his hand on her shoulder. She felt a faint tug, and moved closer in compliance to the suggestion of his arm.

"Now don't you worry about them monks anymore," said Gomer. "I'll make sure they don't bother this town ever again."

"How? Do you have a plan?"

"Never mind that," he said. Then he moved his hand behind her neck and very gently released the tresses from one of her pins, causing a blonde cascade to ripple down her shoulders. She moaned a little in surprise.

Gomer turned away to hide the longing in his eyes. Without another word, he walked down the street, leaving a bright pair of baby blues following him until he was out of sight.

•   •   •

Drawn by the scent of the stables, Gomer found his way to an inn easily enough. He paused beneath the painted symbols hanging above the door, craning his neck in wonderment.

An old man came alongside Gomer while he was having his thoughts. "Never seen a man stare so hard at something he wasn't planning to eat! Can't you read, son?"

"I can read!" bellowed Gomer indignantly. "That sign says this is an inn!"

Gomer took a seat at a stool, sitting unhappily with his axe across his lap while waiting for some service. Gaze lowered, he was not aware of the lingering looks he drew. Here was a giant of a youth with tangled red hair, his face swarthy with stubble and bruises, and not a thread to cover the scars on his bare, broad back and bulging shoulders.

Finally, a voice stirred him from his mood. "W-What a time, stranger!" said the barkeep. The mustachioed proprietor wore a look of weary exasperation and carried a broken stool in his arms. "Let me tell you about my brother. Got married and had himself six daughters, thank you kindly! Then you know what he did? He DIED! Now I got six nieces to keep busy!"

A baffled look crossed Gomer's face. "Then get one of them over here, why don't you?! I want a drink!"

"Hmmf!" said the innkeeper as he turned away, his moustache bristling.

And so time passed with the draining of cups until about half past the nineteenth hour, when a man pushed through the door exclaiming: "A wagon comes from the woods!"

Chairs shuffled as folks who would walk lone paths hurried from the inn. Gomer figured this was what he had been waiting for, so he left his drink and stumbled through the door.

Outside in the hot windless night he leaned against the tavern wall. The moon was on the other side of the building, leaving the road in shadow. A coarse song arose from his throat. Some minutes later a wagon came into view, drawn by two old horses. Four monks walked alongside the cart.

Gomer kept his head low as he watched them approach.

"It's that beast from before," said a voice.

"Keep rolling by," said another.

"Wait, brothers," said Segrid, sticking his head from the coach. "He's drunk! Here's a chance to take a strong prize, and one we won't be like to get again!"

The four on foot nodded and turned casually towards the inn.

The barbarian's song quieted into an ominous, incoherent tone as he staggered from the wall.

At the signal of a hiss from Segrid, the group jumped upon the redheaded giant before he could even raise his axe. Each strove to restrain his arm from swinging, but with his other hand the barbarian hurled a monk by the robe into the tavern wall, shaking the whole building. Two others now leapt from the wagon, joining the fray and pushing their victim towards the door of the cart.

A kick to the back of the leg brought Gomer low at last, followed by a sharp knock on the jaw. The axe was pried from his grip and a concerted shove had him keeled over the back of the wagon, where he was held down and bound with strong rope.

"In you go!" said Brother Segrid, and the barbarian was hoisted into the hay-filled back. That finished, the other monks rushed for the wagon seats or piled atop the cart, according to their quickness. Segrid took his place and lashed the reins. Not a soul came from the tavern to investigate the commotion, and the wagon shambled forward, leaving the fallen axe glinting in the moonlight along the dusty road.

Meanwhile, Gomer lay amid the great store of hay, smiling to himself in the moonbeam slivers that shot through the boards. His hands were bound tightly behind his back, but his fingers reached into the waist of his breeches, retrieving the keen sewing pin that he had taken from Sara's hair. He plucked at the knots in the rope, loosening his bonds but leaving them intact. Then he lay back and closed his eyes.

●   ●   ●

Gomer focused his hearing when the wagon came to a halt. The carriage teetered as the monks spilled out noisily.

"Tend the horses," Gomer heard a voice say. "The rest of you —"

The barbarian pretended to sleep, but perceived the glow of torchlight through his closed eyelids. A hand grasped his ankle and yanked. Fury welled inside of him to be handled thus, but Gomer clenched his teeth and allowed his leg to limply stretch forward. His limbs were seized in two-handed grips.

After a great deal of struggling, the monks prevailed in dragging their captive to the edge of the cart. Gomer responded groggily as if still in a tremendous stupor, letting his legs walk heavily as they led him into a large cabin. "Mortu will be very pleased!" he heard one of them say.

Gloomy shrouds draped the walls of the anteroom and strange clutter abounded: assorted statues, horns of elk, and ornate furniture. Gomer beheld something uncanny about the animals in the room; they were stiff, unmoving, and without breath, with stitch marks across their hides. A large raven sat within an alcove, with heavy wings draping its sides and its talons nailed to a wooden slab. The whole menagerie brooded silently in the shadows with lifeless eyes.

The prisoner continued down a candlelit hallway, where shadows of flame clawed from the furthest threshold. His guards thrust him into the room.

"So, these are the thews and tendons of a warrior?" said the inhabitant of the chamber, who arose from his seat behind an oak table, his back to a large fire. He was of a size that men other than Gomer would have called giant. His beard and bushy mane were in tangled knots, and cruelty nestled in his dark, beady eyes. "Say, man, how rich and red is your blood?"

Gomer somberly returned the man's stare, for this was surely the leader of the enclave, the feared one named Mortu. He struggled to confine his hatred for this man who haunted the gentle town.

Mortu tapped his fingers on the table, studying Gomer with a concentrating look. "This one will fight if he can," he surmised. "Segrid, spill the wine."

Gomer sensed the menace in the words and looked over his shoulder to see the monk unsheathing a dagger. The barbarian kicked and Segrid fell in crippling agony as the knife flew from his grasp.

The other monks approached nervously, but froze as the barbarian slipped from his secretly loosened bonds. Only Boris rushed forth, and Gomer caught him by the cloth, tossing him into the wall. Then he took Segrid's knife from the ground and made a sudden leap towards the doorway, where the remainder of underlings gawked.

"Forward and die!" he growled,

The monks scattered down the hall. Doors slammed in succession as they sequestered themselves into their personal chambers. The injured Boris and Segrid shambled after them.

At least I won't get a blade in the back, thought Gomer. *For now.* He returned his attention to Mortu, who had the expression of one who has seen his property injured.

"Think not that the servants show the measure of the master!" he declared. "Now. Come to my table." He clasped a serving platter from the surface and slipped it upon his arm by some clever strap on the underside. He withdrew a two-foot cleaver from the folds of his robe. Stepping around the table, his fingers relaxed from the hilt of bone in a beckoning taunt.

The simple knife in Gomer's hand suddenly felt very feeble. He would have preferred his axe, but this was no time to hesitate. He dashed forth, blade raised.

Anticipating the buckler readied in defense, Gomer pivoted his feet, channeling his momentum into a shoulder-bash. It was like striking a brick wall! Neither man flinched nor delayed in these close quarters. Gomer caught the arm that descended with the cleaver, even as his own wrist was seized as he struck with the knife.

The floor shook as these two giants circled the ground with their hands locked together. Then an equilibrium settled upon them. For a moment, they stood at a stalemate in this weird embrace. Gomer rotated his shoulders and hips, using this shift of balance to step inwards, angling his blade to slip behind the buckler.

The monk's hand trembled to halt the knife as it inched closer.

Thanks for the square-dance!" said Gomer, completing his instep. The knife sank in with an audible *squish.*

Mortu stumbled backward, dropping his plate. Utter disbelief showed on his face. His cleaver clattered to the ground as he clutched the knife in his chest.

A lot of trouble for a pushover, thought Gomer. He rubbed the groove marks on his wrists where the ropes had chafed, then looked up in surprise as Mortu struggled to speak, blood spouting from his mouth.

"Gologoth," he said. He wrenched the knife from his body. "I call to you, Gologoth!" He pointed the dagger at the barbarian. "Come to this — *living* … feast!"

These were not the words of a dying man, Gomer knew; there was power and strength in the voice. Arcane whispers filtered upon his breath, as though something else spoke also behind the words.

Gomer stood indecisively, his confusion mounting as black smoke billowed from the hearth, flickering with an elemental glow. Mortu raised his arms as the clouded veil smothered him. A wraithlike pair of claws seemed to glove the monk's own massive hands, one of which plucked the knife from out the flesh and let it fall, a mere trinket upon the floor.

Through eyes that stung in the sulpherous air, Gomer glimpsed the features of the grinning fiend that extended beyond the outlines of Mortu. The stench of this new evil filled the air, though its shape and dimensions were unclear. Here and yet not here, this ghostly apparition shimmered like heat on a stone path.

"Death to you both!" said Gomer. But he had no weapon; both cleaver and knife were too near the feet of this strange menace. He stood warily, unsure whether to fight or to flee. Within this instant of confusion, the demon-host Mortu struck. A massive fist pummeled into the barbarian's ribs. Then a hand was upon his throat — the hand from *elsewhere.* Its claws dug into his neck as his feet left the ground — and the astounded barbarian flew across the room, shattering the dining chairs that met his fall. The door was blocked from view by the massive bulk of Mortu. The air rippled with infernal laughter as he — it — *they* — stalked forth.

Gomer felt his stomach knot. His head swam dizzily. As he regained his feet, the human hand of Mortu swatted.

Gomer dodged but misjudged the reach of that almost invisible claw, which slashed across his naked chest. He staggered back. The unrestrained lust for raw meat showed upon the cannibal's face, whose hands reached lecherously.

He's going to snatch me! Gomer sensed the impending embrace, the gnashing teeth, the salivating mouth. His eyes roved for some hope as he retreated into the corner.

He saw an iron poker beside the hearth. He dove underneath Mortu-Gologoth's grasping arms, seizing the rod as he completed his roll. When he sprang outward, their positions were reversed. He could make a run for the door now, though something in his instincts warned him not to turn his back on this foe. And with the feel of the iron rod in his grip and a trust in his own strength, Gomer stood resolute. He two-handed the poker and charged.

The point barely pierced the broad chest before halting as both sets of arms closed grip. Gomer's muscles quivered to complete his attack, but he was no longer pushing forward; he was fighting to hold his ground. With a defiant roar, he pitched all of his remaining might into one great push.

A splintering noise echoed as the poker broke through Mortu's chest cavity, shattering breast bone and ribs. The monk's shoulders arched back in spasms of agony. Gomer raised the angle of his attack in hopes of toppling Mortu, who grasped the rod and resisted with astounding strength.

The veins bulged in the barbarian's neck, the muscles between his shoulders rippled, his arms knotted, and blood poured freely from the clawed gashes on his chest. Thus, in grim silence he plunged his foe into the hearth.

The flames seemed to reach around the demon monk, singeing the hair from the barbarian's arms. The monk's filthy garment glowed with embers. Gomer felt fingers upon his forearm; the fiend drawing himself back up! The robe combusted, and the fingers became claws, cutting deeply. Mortu screamed as the flames engulfed him. His razor grip relaxed.

Not until the last shrieks died away did Gomer release the iron rod, suddenly aware how it burned in his grip. He backed away slowly. His was a restless calm. By the prickling of his hair, he sensed that evil still thrived in this room. A shrill sound issued from the flames, like a haunted wind piping through strange tunnels.

A swampy haze poured from the flames, congealing above the mantle. The air, foul and thickening, was steamy and humid as from the life-spawning atmosphere of primordial days. The barbarian lurched as the noxious cloud flooded across him. Within the gas were immensities of pressure. His aching muscles tensed as he sank to his knees. He couldn't move; couldn't escape. He held his breath, knowing instinctively, as a law of life, not to breathe the disembodied gas that was Gologoth.

He shut his eyes tightly, exhaling the last of his breath as he felt the smoke whispering against his nostrils — and still the cloud thickened. It was heavy, devastatingly heavy, weighted as though the very cloak of the cosmos bore down upon him ...

Gomer slumped onto his knuckles. His head pounded, his flesh cried for a gasp of air. He refused to breathe, to yield, but there was no hope to be found: he would pass out, and the demon would have him.

And yet, in equal time to his fading consciousness, the crushing weight also lessened. Just as the man collapsed dying for lack of air, so too the demon itself suffocated without the lungs and form of a man to house its spirit. The smoke paled, thinned, and vanished.

Gomer rose unsteadily. A struggled glance confirmed that the doorway remained empty of further threats. He leaned against the wall to recover his breath. He regarded the cannibal's meat cleaver, and considered it too gruesome to touch. Instead, he looked for Segrid's old dagger, finding that it had been kicked beneath the chairs during the fight.

Releasing a slow, grim sigh, Gomer walked haltingly into the many-chambered hallway towards the anteroom. Every step was fraught with caution. His blood trailed behind him. Unseen in the smoke-clouded corridor, he heard the dormitory doors open and close. The monks were stirring and restless. Footsteps padded down the hall, and then sudden silence rested upon the barbarian's taut nerves. He paused in the haze of the hallway, his hand ready to draw the knife from his belt. One more step, and he was in the front room.

Eight figures stood in the shadows among the clutter of the furniture. The stench that had pervaded the dining hall now curdled here in the musty air. Stark menace brooded in the silence as the monks maintained their rigid stances. Then Gomer heard faint stirrings, as of a mouse in the walls, or a window latch being turned. He could not place the noise. A half-dozen candles burned within this chamber, but their luster seemed unable to banish the matted darkness. The light was enfeebled, seeming to come and go faintly on currents of smoke.

He thought he saw movement, a deeper blot in the shifting darkness. Then, with a sudden bone-rattling croak, the planked raven tore its talons from the board to which it was nailed. Its wings opened broadly with the noise of cracking plaster.

Gologoth had not been wholly banished, Gomer knew, and the grim realization clutched the pit of his gullet. His muscles clenched as he fought a spasm of nausea. Two monks moved to block the door.

"Now, now," said Gomer. The instinctive reach behind his shoulder betrayed his nervousness. Once more he longed for his lost axe. He heard the death rattle of a rabbit — a screech that split his nerves — then the candles dwindled into inexplicable darkness. There was no odor of smoke, only that *other* stench. Gomer heard the shifting of furniture and the advance of footsteps.

A figure rushed him. Gomer guarded with the knife, which sank into his foe. He sprang sideways and crouched. As his eyes adjusted, he saw the barest etchings of light: the moon beyond a shuttered window. He went for it, but was tackled. Red-black liquescence streamed from the mouth and eyes of the monk that leered atop him. He scrambled away and saw the same astral disfigurements writhing from all the other faces within this room. All men, all beasts. Even the corpse that lay upon its back was corrupted by the tentacles lashing from its face and out the wound of the embedded knife.

The roar of animals and the curse of fiends flooded Gomer's brain in dismal cacophony. A hoof scuffed the floor, igniting a brimstone spark. Gomer stared with horror and superstitious dread. *This is a house of madness!* Never before in his reckless life had Gomer so urgently felt the peal of discretion cry out in his subconscious. The door and window were surely beyond reach. He retreated into the hallway, colliding with a tangle of forms and foes. These monks were not yet affected by the taint of Gologoth. Gomer pressed through them as they tugged at his limbs. Behind them came the *other* monks, whose heads, lit by that awful glow, appeared to float above their smoke-shrouded bodies.

Scrambling for his life, Gomer barreled forward, returning yet again to the horrible dining hall. He slammed the door, though these windowless walls offered no escape. Then he braced it with his shoulder and waited in an agony of nervous tension for the coming intrusion. He could have no realization of the mayhem that confounded the movements in the outer hall, the clashing between the unpossessed monks and their demonic brethren. Expecting the imminent breach, these passing seconds found Gomer dwelling within the torments of eternity. His every thought felt sluggish; his every movement delayed. He left the door to pitch it with the oak table, blocking and wedging it just as it began to open.

What passed next were the actions of a distraught mind — a man suddenly near the throws of lunacy. And yet he raced swiftly —

— running to the hearth — using his foot to pry Mortu's body from the fire — kicking the corpse towards the door, the *cracking door!* — returning to plunge his foot into the burning logs — booting these towards the *shattering door!* The arms of the enraged monks *reaching through!* the riven planks.

And then, calmly. The fireplace empty, and the flames now diverted to the base of the entrance, Gomer limped toward an amber bottle upon a shelf, as the red-glowing faces stared through the smitten barricade.

And, casually, Gomer tossed the decanter into the base of the flames. He was already on the move before it exploded. Taking a deep breath and shutting his eyes, he ducked into the smoke-filled hearth. He scaled the chimney in blindness, thankful for its accommodating width. And though the radiant heat of the lower stones might have blistered more delicate hands, his callused palms withstood the heat with only passing discomfort.

A moment later he was at the top of the stack, where a steepled rain-top barred him from emerging onto the roof. He hung an arm beneath the narrow opening, and used the other to shove against the obstruction. The stonework yielded, and Gomer burst out into the starlit sky.

As he listened to the commotion below, the barbarian heaved a sigh. *I wanted to help, but now Gologoth is everywhere. Guess I only made things worse.* His nausea and mind-blasting panic had flown, and his natural state of calm fortitude returned. The cool wind washed across his weary body. Bleeding and greatly pained, Gomer's brow knitted, as though something was amiss that he couldn't quite place, some hurt or itch that eluded him. He tugged at his boot, the one blackened in fire. The leather had partly liquified in the heat, seeping into his sock. It pulled at his burned skin as he pried it off. He removed the other boot for balance, then dropped from the roof, his bare feet sinking into soft mud. A quick glance showed him the way was clear, and he darted for the trees.

"What was that?" said a voice from the woods.

Gomer scuttled to a stop.

"An animal?" someone responded.

Two silhouettes detached from the darkness beneath the pines. They were hardly an arms-reach from Gomer, yet their gazes were concentrated on the moonlit lawn. They stood shoulder to shoulder, and appeared unaffected by the influences that had claimed the monks in the anteroom.

"It sounded like a large man running," said the first voice. "Which way?"

Gomer stepped forward silently. "He went that way."

As the monks followed the direction of the pointing finger Gomer retracted his other arm and slugged them each in a single mighty hook. Their heads *bonked* and they fell to the dirt.

The loud splintering of wood drew Gomer's attention as the fire spread through the dry timber of the hermitage. The monks were pouring out now from all sides, the demonic glow of their faces less prominent by the power's division among such a multitude. The front door shattered open and other shapes emerged, elk and bird and boar.

The branches stirred; a crow cawed, fluttering its wings above Gomer's head. He stumbled into the moonlight, swatting the air in full view of the angry legion. The crow circled skyward, blending into the darkness of the night.

Gomer stood poised. He had only the small knife in his waistcloth, but indulged no thought of running. He was exhausted and knew he wouldn't get far. Some of the monks went to the shed, presumably to get weapons; the rest advanced without delay. The animals melted into their groupings, all seemingly organized by a single governing will.

"Eh," he said. "This is one of them last stands, then." He felt in his pocket for Sara's hairpin, receiving a small comfort by the memory of their afternoon together.

Scarcely had he bent his knees and softened his toes in his best fighting stance than the legion was upon him. He became a small, jagged rock, splitting the tide as it roared atop his collapsing body. His knife was swallowed in the thundering eddies. Lodged in foe or dirt, he knew not; it was lost.

Gomer!

He could hear the voices of his ancestors calling his name. He threw his enemies from his back, his arms, his neck. But there were too many of them, and he was sinking into the mud, into darkness.

Gomer! This way, lad!

The voices again. It didn't matter. There was only one way to them; he would be there soon.

Gomer! Get up!

And suddenly he saw lights, not the light of the burning monastery, but torches emerging from the woods. Gomer crawled from beneath the strikes of his enemies. He rose to his feet, stumbling awkwardly before breaking into an exhausted run. *I don't believe it*, he thought, looking upon the townsfolk that crowded in ranks at the mouth of the western path.

It's a cannibal-monk huntin' jamboree!

He scrambled toward them, ducking as they released a volley of arrows at his pursuing foes. The cries from behind informed Gomer that at least a few monks were hit. Another flight of arrows was unleashed, now only to deflect from an invisible barrier. The power of Gologoth resided here, and the air was electrified with his presence.

The townsfolk balked, lowering their bows. Gomer was surprised that any came to his aid at all. He felt new emotions of gratitude as somebody rallied their spirits, shouting: "Hold ground! Hold ground!"

The villagers switched from bows to their sundry implements: simple clubs, some spears, hammers and shovels. Now, with Gomer embedded in their ranks, another voice shouted: *"Charge!* And together they raced upon the glaring monks.

The monks likewise wielded an odd assortment of weapons and tools, although several remained unarmed. The motley armies clashed, the weaponless monks singled out to be dispatched quickly, though their evil glowing faces warned that they still held the blessings of an awful being.

The dead-alive boar collided with the legs of a young villager. Somebody closed in with a torch, pressing the brand

265

to the hog's husk. The flames immediately caught and engulfed its dry, reanimated carcass. The demonic redness leapt from its face, flowing into the eyes of a stick-wielding monk: the gleam in his face suddenly more fierce.

The villagers alike were under attack by this demonic intrusion. Gomer saw a man's face contort in malign grimaces as the wretched lights shadowed his straining features. "Oh no you don't!" said the barbarian, raising the flat of his palm and whomping the man heavily on the back. The red streams splotched outward from the villager's eyes.

"There you go. See? He's a bum!" said Gomer. "Hey, everyone!" he shouted. "Gologoth's a bum! Put up a fight and he can't get you!"

And with such encouragement, the demon's grasping influence was repulsed from the stalwart townsfolk. But as each corrupted thing fell, the disembodied stream of power reached into the next host, imbuing it with greater strength and hardiness. A smaller group of townsfolk became increasingly cut-off from the others. Gomer hollered to draw them back in, then something in his periphery arrested his attention. The elk scraped its hooves, its eyes glaring.

"Stay together!" he shouted, then leapt to grasp the horns. His feet dragged in the earth then anchored to a halt. His powerful hands resisted the bucking head and the jerking motions of its lengthy neck.

Meanwhile, the skirmish clashed in the field. The rallied townsfolk were gaining ground, the monks beginning to fall back and scatter, some to the fire, others to the woods. Then, with a sudden fateful roar, the anterior of the monastery and half the roof crashed in upon itself. Billows of smoke swept across the field in choking darkness, while brims of golden ash shot skyward to shine and descend like falling stars in the hellish gloom.

The monks all stopped, as though stunned. The writhing wisps of corruption retreated from their eyes. Yet in the midst of the field Gomer still fought, embers falling upon his aching shoulders as he grappled the elk. The forelegs of the beast sank beneath his pressing might. And the evil glow that had left the monks now swirled in currents around the barbarian and the beast, all channeling in elliptical circles into the dead, rabid features of the elk.

It snorted plumes of smoke from its nostrils. Gomer's feet slid back in the dirt, his grip loosening around the bucking head. Its eyes shone brightly, burning with hellfire flames. Gologoth resided in this animal, not in the monks nor elsewhere, but *here*, all of him — all at once.

Unflinching, the barbarian returned the recognizing stare. If Mortu was the best that Gologoth had, surely he could defeat this beast, too. He refused to acknowledge that he was exhausted, that his wounds were still wet, that the blood staining his tortured body was mostly his own.

Clutching the antlers, Gomer tensed from neck to heel. He felt the raw pain in the fringes of his sinews, the aching in his chest. A loud pop sounded from his shoulder. His left ankle buckled. What gave out first, he couldn't tell: but he hit the ground. Above him, the elk stood upon its hind legs and smote downward with clobbering hooves. Gomer stared uncomprehending as the beast screamed and fell. Then he saw the rope that lassoed its neck and the villager that gripped its end.

Somebody lifted Gomer's arm, pitched their shoulder beneath him. Gomer cringed with pain as he arose. The elk thrashed to its feet, its eyes still dead-locked upon him. A man with a torch hurried forth, and the dry and bloodless husk combusted at the pressing of the flame. And where the red scourge went, none observed in the sudden conflagration of its final host.

The monks all surrendered, pleading for mercy, even joining the villagers in drawing water from the well to dampen the grass around the burning monastery. Gomer put his shoulder back into place, then grabbed a bucket from a passing monk and tilted it to his face, drinking deeply. In a quiet daze, the barbarian watched the hermitage burn.

"Well, you torched it."

The words barely intruded on Gomer's thoughts. His chest and throat still felt leaden from the foul atmosphere, and he was weary from the night's work. He held his palm to his side, seeing his blood glimmer in the haze. His ankle stabbed with pain, and he looked for something to lean on.

"That's what we came to do," said the villager.

"Huh?" said Gomer.

"Torch the place."

"Oh." The barbarian took another drink and felt a little stronger of foot. The cold water was a fast restorative. His ankle hurt, but held his weight, mostly. "Eh!" he said. "With me inside!"

The villager took a step back. "We thought you'd be eaten already. And the monks full and tired."

Gomer frowned.

"Well, maybe we'd have checked. I think so."

"Of course we would have," said another voice, this one more pleasing to the ear. A figure stepped through the haze, though it seemed to Gomer like the smoke parted for her like a curtain, revealing some angel from another world.

"Sara!" he said.

Her hands were quick; she was already wrapping a bandage about his waist. She snugged it tight, and Gomer let out a small *ooph* of breath.

Another wall of the monastery collapsed, from which came another rolling blanket of smoke to settle thickly across the field and woods. Gomer watched the timbers settle. He twirled something in his fingers.

"Is that my hairpin?" said Sara.

Gomer paused awkwardly.

"I have your axe," she said, breaking the silence. "It's in my cart."

"Trade you," said Gomer, offering the pin.

"I don't know. Maybe I'll keep it."

Gomer felt his hair frizzle. His jaw opened mutely.

Sara smiled. "Come on. Let's get your axe." She led Gomer by the hand.

•   •   •

The fire, which had burned for over an hour, began to settle, though many villagers would remain throughout the night to ensure no sudden wind or shift would endanger the surrounding forest.

Gomer gestured to the surviving monks, who contritely worked hardest of all. "What about them?" he asked.

He was talking to Sara, but the town selectman overheard and nosed in.

"There's nothing tidy about this," he said. "This night's possession aside, those monks have harried this town a long while. With what we've seen tonight, we have proof of their misdeeds, and they'll have to answer, each for their own part. You've stopped their terror, Gomer, and we're grateful to you. Why don't you come back and stay a bit? You'll always be welcome here."

"Thanks," said Gomer. He saw the doors of another wagon slam shut, the horses already hitched and restless. "Looks like your coach is about to go," he said to Sara.

She got up silently. Gomer followed her to the wagon, where she stopped.

"You will, Gomer?" she asked.

"Eh?"

"Stay a while," she said.

He was struck by her expression, her sincere and hopeful eyes as she looked up at him.

"Sure," he said. "I haven't had a city meal or straw bed in weeks." He offered his hand to help her into the wagon.

She paused. "Ride with me. You don't have to walk back alone."

Gomer felt a slight catch in his throat. Instead of speaking, he simply nodded and climbed into the back of the wagon.

A few miles down the path, the horses whinnied and the carriage stopped. Gomer went to investigate the commotion, though the driver, half-asleep, hadn't seen what spooked them.

But Gomer knew. Above them, a crow looked on from the branches of a twisted birch. Its eyes glowed red. It cawed thrice, then took to the sky, vanishing towards the moon.

"Gologoth," said Gomer. *He will not forget me.*

"Pardon?" said Sara. She'd followed him outside and touched his hand.

"Nothing," said Gomer. He patted his axe, fond to be reunited with it, comforted by the familiar weight and balanced placement upon his shoulder. "Aren't we near the pond here?"

"Yes," she said. "How's your foot?"

"Good enough to walk you home again," said Gomer; and together they went. The wind felt cool and nice upon his unclad back, scarred and bruised though he was; and Sara hummed that particular tune that Gomer would never forget, nor ever remember: for he was tone deaf.

AFTERWORD

W HY WRITE SHORT STORIES? This literary form is as difficult as the novel — in many ways, more so. It's challenging work to convey a story and bring characters to life in just a few short pages. That's even more true in speculative fiction, where authors also create new worlds.

Why bother? Aren't novels more important?

No, that's a myth.

Every story has its own proper length. Some need a novel ... or a series ... to be complete; they're like whales — or a pod of orcas — sounding the depths. Flash fiction resolves in a thousand words or less: glittering fireflies of images, characters, events. The short story is its own category of story-creature: the handsome collie you sit with of an evening, enjoying each other's company by the fire.

Until you glance through a swirl of smoke and see the wolf's eye glimmer in the firelight.

The deep, dark secret of the short story that your high-school English teacher may have skimmed over — if you were fortunate to have a teacher who assigned creative writing — is that the short story is *difficult*. In my opinion, it is the most challenging form of fiction to create — especially in the speculative fiction arena. We humans expect a story to provide characters in whom we recognize parts of ourselves (and our friends and enemies), events laid out in such a way that makes us want — no, *need* — to know the outcome, a beginning that draws us in, and an ending that releases us back to the real world — even if not quite all the questions it poses are answered. All of that in just a few pages, a fifteen-minute audio performance.

In speculative fiction, we readers also demand to be immersed in a new world, discover magic hiding in ours, explore the far reaches of space, and discover mind-bending knowledge to change the universe. Is that enough? No! We want actually-intelligent robots who stir martinis and tell jokes, swarms of truly-alien extraterrestrials who may or may not be malevolent, and sorcerers who wield the forces of nature. And we want it NOW.

To paraphrase my favorite series novelist: Writing a short story is hard work. Really hard. You just won't believe how vastly hugely mindbogglingly hard it is. I mean, you may think it's a big deal to go all the way and write a novel, let alone a trilogy or a hexalogy, but that's just peanuts to writing a good short story. [Apologies to my fellow fans of Douglas Adams' *Hitchhiker's Guide to the Galaxy* series.]

How can this be done? Well ... if you were hoping for The Answer, sorry ... there's no one right way. One might type up an outline and build from there (google "snowflake method"). Another may dive into a story, swim to its far shore, and pull up onto the beach before looking back to see that the tale is a short story. Others may test-drive portions with friends, open-mic audiences, or editors and fellow writers, until they find the whole story coming together.

The resulting short story may be a hero's journey in a concise form, but it may just as well follow a more-interesting non-western pattern of storytelling, or recreate a unique approach the author acquired from family tale-tellers or adapted from other life experiences. For the author, the short story may be a chance to experiment with a new pattern ... without the years-long commitment demanded by a novel ... but that doesn't let them off the hook for developing a story that transports you to a new world, albeit for only a little while.

Carry these thoughts in mind as you flip back to the beginning of this book and read these fabulous stories again. Be amazed, amused, and wonderstruck — not only by the story, but by the author behind it, the hours and days and years they've put into giving you this respite from the mundane world.

Vanessa MacLaren-Wray
Author of the Patchwork Universe series

YOU MIGHT ALSO ENJOY

DRAGON GEMS (WINTER 2023)

Tales to warm your imagination during the cold winter months

With stories from Christina Ardizzone, Matt Bliss, Gustavo Bondoni, Micah Castle, Nestor Delfino, C. M. Fields, Andrew Giffin, Emma Kathryn, Michelle Ann King, Jason Lairamore, Eve Morton, Lena Ng, S. Park, Arlo Sharp, Mar Vincent, and Richard Zwicker.

THE FUTURE'S SO BRIGHT

Out of the darkness of the present comes the light of the days ahead ...

With stories from Kevin David Anderson, Maureen Bowden, Steven D. Brewer, Nels Challinor, Regina Clarke, Stephen C. Curro, Jetse de Vries, Nestor Delfino, Gail Ann Gibbs, Henry Herz, Gwen C. Katz, Brandon Ketchum, Julia LaFond, R. Jean Mathieu, Cynthia McDonald, Christopher Muscato, Alfred Smith, A.M. Weald, and David Wright.

CORPORATE CATHARSIS
The Work From Home Edition

The boundaries between reality and fantasy have become as blurred as those between life and work.

With stories from Alicia Adams, Antaeus, Pauline Barmby, Steven D. Brewer, Dominick Cancilla, Adrienne Canino, Graham J. Darling, Derek Des Anges, Manny Frishberg, Alex Grehy, Jon Hansen, Alexa Kellow, Jack Nash, Helen Obermeier, Frank Sawielijew, William Shaw, Steve Soult, N.L. Sweeney, Kimberley Wall, and Richard Zaric.

Available from Water Dragon Publishing in
hardcover, trade paperback, and digital editions
waterdragonpublishing.com

Made in United States
Orlando, FL
14 December 2024

55571521R10169